SHALIMAR

Marlyn's Norrie,
Enjoy!
Love Wendy
April 2013

Wendy Soliman

ROMANCE

BookStrand
www.BookStrand.com

A SIREN BOOKSTRAND TITLE
IMPRINT: Romance

SHALIMAR

ISBN-10: 1-61926-557-5
ISBN-13: 978-1-61926-557-8

First Printing: January 2012

Cover design by Jinger Heaston

Printed in the U.S.A.

PUBLISHER
www.BookStrand.com

DEDICATION

This one’s for Rachel, with my love and respect for all she’s achieved.

SHALIMAR

WENDY SOLIMAN

Chapter One

"Listen to me!" Mark grabbed Suzie's shoulders, stark emotion reflected in his expression. "It isn't what you think."

"Oh please!" She shook his hands away. "I know what I saw."

He ran a hand through his hair. "No, you just think you do."

"Don't try and turn this on me."

"It was all one massive—"

Suzie cut off him off with a wave of her hand, inchoate anger fuelling her determination not to be swayed. "Don't bother. I don't want to hear any more of your pathetic excuses. Whatever I saw, or didn't see, the fact remains that you lied to me. You were supposed to be on your way to the airport, not screwing Kate on her kitchen floor."

Mark let out an elongated breath. "She called me and said she wanted to talk to me. She said she was worried about you."

"Is that the best excuse you can come up with?" She turned away from him, afraid that the hurt now replacing her anger would show in her eyes.

"Suzie, don't do this to yourself. To us. I'm telling you the truth. Kate means nothing to me. We'll get over this, sweetheart, and I'll make it up to you, I promise." He reached for her, but she moved swiftly out of range. Allowing him to touch her would be a seriously bad move. "I love you," he added quietly.

"Perhaps you do, but obviously not enough." Suzie took a deep breath and looked him squarely in the eye "I'm leaving you, Mark," she said.

The expression that flitted across his face was one of abject disbelief. It obviously hadn't occurred to him that she wouldn't forgive his transgression, and he was too stunned to make an immediate response. Struggling to disguise the full extent of her devastation, Suzie wondered why she'd chosen to inflict this torture on herself. She could have taken the easy way out and simply left home whilst Mark was abroad. Confronting him to extract what satisfaction she could from being the aggrieved party was already testing her strung-out emotions.

"What! You don't mean that. You're upset, that's all."

She ruthlessly swallowed down her regret and met his gaze, refusing to permit his tortured expression to influence her. A debilitating pain ripped through her, the renewed agony of the double betrayal perpetrated by her husband and best friend supplying the impetus she needed to stand firm. Mark's meaningless string of assurances was exactly that—meaningless—and she wouldn't be played for a trusting fool ever again.

She listened to his attempts at justification, still confident in his ability to talk her round. He didn't believe she'd leave because he thought her incapable of living without him, but he was wrong. Dead wrong! She gathered up what was left of her dignity, ignored the abject misery that was already creeping into what was left of her heart, and prepared to walk out of his life forever.

Suzie had almost managed to convince even herself that she no longer cared for Mark. A special Oscar for a lifetime's role as best supporting actress ought to have her name on it. Struggling to keep the tears at bay, she acknowledged that was precisely what she'd been doing for the past ten years. Supporting Mark in his career, running his home, and waiting patiently for him to return from his endless business trips. She had long ago abandoned any ambitions for a career of her own and had become a nonperson—nothing more than an extension of Mark himself. As a couple, they were definitely Mark and Suzie, never the other way round.

As she turned away from Mark, her ankle gave out beneath her, and with a screech of pain, she crumpled to the floor. She landed flat on her face in an undignified mass of flailing limbs, both human and canine. Expensive shag pile carpet cushioned her fall but did little to restore her dignity. She cursed her stupidity in forgetting about the large amount of gin she'd fortified herself with before confronting Mark. About the three-inch, confidence-giving heels she'd donned in an effort to boost her flagging morale. They showcased her legs and were supposed to issue a reminder to Mark of what he'd so casually thrown away through his inability to keep his fly zipped. Most importantly though, she'd forgotten that Sparkle, her beloved gangly-limbed, shaggy-haired mongrel, was glued adoringly to her spiky heels. With the infallible intuition peculiar to his species, he'd seemed to know that a crisis loomed and stuck to her even more closely than usual in a gesture of doggy solidarity.

At her side in seconds, Mark loomed over her. The look in his gorgeous chocolate-brown eyes was so seriously concerned that just for a moment her resolve weakened. Then images of her friend's naked body entwined with his sprang to mind. It filled her with renewed abhorrence and reminded her just why she could no longer live with the man whom she loved more than life itself.

"God, Suzie, are you all right? Here, let me help you up. Can you move?"

She wriggled her arms and legs experimentally and winced. Her ankle hurt like hell.

"I'm fine," she snapped. "It's Sparkle I'm worried about."

"Of course you are." There was a note of inevitability in Mark's voice. "But he appears to be none the worse for wear, either."

Sparkle peered down at the still prostrate Suzie, devoted eyes regarding her quizzically from beneath his shaggy fringe. Not the type of dog to bear grudges, he demonstrated his forgiving nature by giving her face a thorough wash. She reached out to scratch his ears by way of apology, playing for time as she contemplated the awkwardness of her situation. A rumbling sound caused Suzie to gently push Sparkle aside as she attempted to identify its source. Mark was doubled over, almost helpless with laughter. She pulled herself into a sitting position and glowered up at him.

"What's so funny?"

"Oh, Suzie, if you could have seen your face." He fell about laughing some more, and it took a while for him to regain control of himself. "Christ, baby, you don't really think you're gonna walk out on me, do you?" He appeared lazily amused at the prospect. "You can't even manage a dramatic exit, so how would you ever cope on your own?" He smiled into her eyes and then winked at her. "Come on, sweetheart, let me help you up."

He held out a long, slender hand, and just for a moment, Suzie was mesmerised by the sight of it. She remembered all the occasions over the past ten years when those hands had caressed and tantalised her body so expertly. All the occasions when those long, skilled fingers had stroked and probed, sending her so wild with desire that she'd been reduced to literally begging him for release. And she was intent upon walking out on all that. Was she mad?

Fortunately, images of those same fingers doing the exact same things to her ex-best friend came to her aid. No, she wasn't mad. She was simply fed up with being played for a gullible fool. This was the first time she'd caught him out, but how many other occasions had there been that she didn't know about? All those nights away on business. All those weekend seminars from which she was firmly excluded. She could see it all now and wasn't enjoying the view one little bit.

"I don't need your help, Mark." She paused for a beat before delivering her *coup de grâce* with as much dignity as she could muster. "In fact I don't need anything from you ever again."

Swinging her knees sideways, Suzie attempted to stand up, only to howl with pain and fall straight back down again. Mark knelt beside her again in the blink of an eye.

"What is it?"

"My ankle."

"Let me see."

Mark ignored her protests and, as usual, took control. He supported her already swelling ankle with one hand and probed gently with the fingers of the other. Suzie used every vestige of self-control to ignore the aching wash of desire that simply the feel of his fingers on her ankle sent spiralling through her. God, but she was pathetic! Mark was history, she told herself firmly. She wanted nothing more to do with him and simply would not allow the sensuality of his touch to affect her. She deliberately looked away from him and forced herself to ignore his ministrations.

"Can you move it at all?"

Suzie had no idea. "Ouch!" She winced. "Yes, just a bit."

"Good girl. That means it's probably just a sprain. We need to cool it down first to reduce the swelling and then strap it up. Then I'll take you to the hospital to have it checked out."

"No hospital!" She had no intention of spending hours in the local emergency room. Mark would use the opportunity to erode her resolve and talk her into giving him another chance.

"Okay, we'll see about that. But you can't stay there on the floor."

Without giving her time to object, Mark swung her into his arms and deposited her gently on a sofa. Then, whilst she impotently seethed, he disappeared into the kitchen and returned clutching a packet of frozen peas wrapped in a tea towel. Well, let him take his best shot. She was immune to him now. She'd meant what she said. She had no intention of going to the hospital, or anywhere else, with Mark but wouldn't be able to get out of here unaided unless her ankle was strapped up. And so she feigned disinterest as he continued to attend to her injury, ignoring the way his fingers—intentionally, she was sure—kept creeping up her calf, caressing it with a sensuous, featherlike touch that stole her breath away. She blocked her ears to his persuasively mesmerising charm, determined not to heed the exotic cadence of his voice or observe the molten tenderness in his expression.

He thought she'd change her mind, just like that, after everything she'd found out about him. That knowledge rekindled her dwindling fury and strengthened her determination never to be cuckolded by him again. Her car was loaded up, ready to go. The two cats were already in it, secure in their baskets. So was Honey, her rather dopey, lop-eared rabbit who thought she was another cat and behaved as such. It just remained for her and Sparkle to climb aboard and drive away from her life with Mark Alexander forever.

Whilst Mark was supposed to be playing golf that morning, Suzie had thrown all the things that mattered to her in the car. She wondered what he'd really been doing. A gut-wrenching bout of jealousy twisted Suzie's insides as she tortured herself with such conjectures. The pain was excruciating. Far worse than the ache in her ankle, a circumstance that angered her. Even after all he'd done to her, all the hurt he'd caused, just the thought of him with another woman still tore her comprehensively apart.

Mark was more than capable of bringing her round with a few heartfelt endearments and the application of his magical hands to certain parts of her anatomy. She was well aware of that and so thought it best to have everything ready. She would tell him precisely what she thought of him and make a speedy, dignified exit. She couldn't quite suppress a wry grin at how that dignified exit had turned out. It was just typical of her. She had right on her side, to say nothing of the element of surprise. Mark's jaw had literally dropped when he realized she knew about him and Kate. Never before had she seen her handsome, lethally intelligent husband lost for words. Against all the odds, and in spite of her broken heart, Suzie had rather enjoyed his discomfiture. For the first time in ten years of marriage she'd well and truly wrong-footed him. But under the circumstances, perhaps "wrong-footed" was a rather unfortunate analogy?

Be that as it may, she should still be able to drive her Jeep since it was automatic. The question was how to get to her car, what with Mark hovering around her, determined not to let her get away from him. Unexpectedly, he provided the answer by asking if she needed any painkillers. She knew that she couldn't take any in view of the amount of gin she'd ingested. But Mark didn't know that, and conveniently, there were no suitable pills in the house. She'd already loaded them, in her infuriatingly organized manner, into the car.

Who else would think to pack headache pills when they planned to walk out on the husband they loved? She'd had plenty of time to think about her final interview with Mark and discovered that focusing her mind on how she would feel when she was free of him was fractionally less masochistic than confronting the unpalatable truth about his extramarital activities. Anticipating that she'd be consuming copious amounts of alcohol until the torture of separation from Mark eased, she'd taken the precaution of stripping the bathroom cabinets of every headache pill the Alexander household contained. Being organized over the past couple of days, whilst she waited for Mark to return from Barcelona, was the only thing that saved her sanity.

"Yeah, I guess I could do with something," she said, careful to keep her tone bordering on the hostile. "But you'll have to go out and get some. We've run out, but the cut-price shop in the village is open all day and they sell them."

Mark raised a brow. Suzie was an ace organizer, always making lists, and they never ran out of anything. Clearly appreciating that this was hardly the moment to comment about her rare omission, he made do with grinning at her instead.

"Don't go away, beautiful," he said, sounding disgustingly sure of himself as he kissed the top of her head and reached for his car keys. "As soon as I get back, I'm gonna carry you up to bed, and then we'll have to see if I can think of some way to entertain you that doesn't involve moving your ankle."

Winking at her, a gesture that sent a bolt of desire ripping through her entire body, Mark left the house. A couple of minutes later she heard the engine of his powerful Mercedes roar into life. Typical! His answer to everything was still a roll in the hay. And, blast him, just the very thought of it turned her insides to mulch. In spite of everything he'd done, she still wanted him. It was obscene. After all these years of marriage, her husband could still make her yearn for him with just a few well-chosen, implicitly suggestive words. And she could tell from his smug expression that he knew it, too. He actually thought he'd done all that was necessary to win her over.

Securely cloaked in her rekindled anger, Suzie struggled gingerly to her feet. Hopping on one leg into the hall, she pressed a sturdy golf umbrella into service as a stick, picked up her handbag, and whistled to Sparkle. When she reached the kitchen, she paused to remove her engagement and wedding rings for the first time ever. She struggled to get them over her knuckle and laid them squarely in the centre of the kitchen table in a more eloquent declaration of intent than words could ever convey. Gulping down her burning anguish, she hobbled to her car and drove away from her marital home forever, tears of regret already pouring down her face.

* * * *

Annabel Burton studied the Situations Vacant column in the trade press, ruling out most of the jobs on offer with a dismissive swipe of her pen. She was about to give up when a box ad on the second page caught her attention. She paused to read it twice. Greenberg's in Basingstoke required a junior partner. There was a generous salary on offer and good benefits to the right applicant.

"Hum." She tapped her pen against her teeth, thinking about it. "Now that's a definite possible."

Annabel drew a large ring round the ad and scanned the rest of the page, but there was nothing else worthy of her talents. Greenberg's it just might have to be then. She knew of the construction firm by reputation but hadn't had any personal dealings with them. She spent the next hour scouring the internet for all the information she could find. John Greenberg, owner and president of the company, featured large in a photo gallery dedicated to his greatest moments. Wearing a hard hat that looked like a boil on his large head, he was captured laying foundation stones, in Wellington boots traipsing round building sites, and featured at endless gala dinners wearing a tuxedo stretched to the limit across his broad girth, surrounded by the wealthy and glamorous. He was also preserved in celluloid shaking hands with Basingstoke's mayor, presenting cheques to local charities and acting as spokesman for a crime prevention committee. Greenberg the philanthropist. She could see exactly what he was doing and why. Greasing the palms that mattered and making a name for himself in the local community. If she had any doubts about that, then the dozens of interviews she found in which he talked about himself and his path to success soon dispelled them.

"This guy's ego is bigger than his waistline," Annabel mused. "And that's saying something." She flashed a mirthless smile. "Could be just what I'm looking for."

But Annabel never did anything without first having all the information she could garner at her fingertips. Knowledge was power. There would be fierce competition for this vacancy and if she wanted to stand out, then she needed an edge. She'd found out all there was to know about John Greenberg's public image. That was the side of him he wanted the world to know about, but there had to be more.

There was always more.

Annabel picked up her phone and called an investigator who'd done work for her on several previous occasions.

"Jim," she said as soon as he answered. "It's Annabel Burton."

She didn't bother with social niceties. Why would she? The guy was about to work for her, and his time was her money. Besides, she didn't give a toss about his health. Wasn't interested how his family was, didn't even know if he had one and cared even less. Instead, she told him what she needed from him.

"It might take some time," Jim said.

"I don't have time." Applications for the vacancy closed in three days. "Get the information to me within two days and I'll double your fee."

Just as she'd known it would, the promise of monetary reward did the trick.

"I'm on it, lady," Jim said, cutting the connection.

Just as Annabel hung up, her assistant stuck her head round her office door.

"Sorry to disturb you. Barry in marketing is leaving, and I wondered if you'd—"

Annabel scrabbled in her top drawer. She threw a few coins into the envelope that was being waved beneath her nose and scribbled something illegible in the gaudy card placed before her. She had no idea who Barry was and didn't much care. Her assistant left without closing the door and Annabel could hear her on the phone in the outer office, discussing Barry's leaving do with someone. Annabel wouldn't be invited. She'd made it clear from the get-go that she wasn't into socialising, and it was a long time since anyone had tried to change her mind. It was also one of the reasons why she'd never make the grade in this large conglomerate. They didn't tell you that when they talked about fantastic career opportunities. She did her job ten times better than her male counterparts, but because she wasn't prepared to match them pint for pint, or share her innermost secrets with the women, she was labelled a loner. A non-team player.

If wanting to make as much money as she could as quickly as possible and set up on her own made her odd, then she welcomed the label. But it was time to move on, and perhaps Greenberg's—a smaller organisation—would be the place to pursue her ambitions.

Chapter Two

"Damn it, get a grip, woman!"

Suzie pulled into a lay-by and impatiently dashed at her eyes with the back of her hand. Sparkle pushed his damp nose under her arm as though trying to comfort her, but it only made matters worse. Unable to face the bleak future that stretched ahead of her, Suzie buried her face in his shaggy coat and sobbed her heart out.

After several such stops, she finally reached the pretty village of Malton, set in the rolling Hampshire countryside just outside of Basingstoke, and pulled into the overgrown driveway of Shalimar, the Georgian cottage that had belonged to her grandparents. She glanced at the shabby façade with genuine affection, a feeling of tranquillity replacing her earlier distress. She couldn't remember a time when the house had been in a good state of repair and accepted its deteriorated condition almost without noticing it.

Sparkle disappeared into the bushes as soon she released him from the car. Suzie rummaged in her bag for her key and forced open the swollen front door. The cold, unlived-in feeling of neglect that greeted her threatened to revive her depression. Before it could take hold, she hobbled into the drawing room, struggled with the window locks, and threw the French doors wide to the overgrown garden. Sunshine flooded in, doing its best to negate the mustiness.

A pair of old slippers permanently twisted into the shape of her grandmother's arthritic feet sat beside the settee. Suzie gasped when she saw them, overwhelmed with a different kind of grief as fresh tears brimmed. She brushed them angrily aside. She really had to stop being so pathetic. Struggling back and forth to the car to unload the animals and the most essential of her supplies, especially the gin, helped concentrate her mind. It took some time given the condition of her ankle, but finally the cats were decanted and Honey established in the ramshackle utility room, temporarily out of harm's way. She didn't take kindly to being caged and liked to check out her surroundings for herself, never averse to chewing through the odd electric cable if it got in her way.

Exhausted, Suzie flopped onto a sagging sofa in the drawing room, nursing a large gin and tonic. The ancient fridge wasn't up to producing ice, but that hardly mattered. Sipping at her warm drink, Suzie waited for the calming influence of Shalimar to envelop her. She'd spent more of her childhood here in the care of her grandparents than with her own dour, rigidly strict parents. She'd loved every minute of it, too. Her grandfather had been all manner of interesting things during his long life. A missionary, a member of a parachute regiment during the war, a treasure hunter, an entrepreneur. Suzie had never tired of sitting at his knee, listening to the endless, shamelessly embellished stories of his adventures.

When her grandfather eventually decided to put an end to his gallivanting, he purchased Shalimar outright. No one quite knew where he found the money, and he became very vague when questioned on the subject. Eventually people stopped asking, and Gramps adapted to a life of rural respectability with the same determination and old-fashioned charm that governed everything he did.

Suzie looked round the scruffy drawing room, reliving all the happy days she'd spent there before her grandfather had died ten years previously, just after her marriage to Mark. Before her grandmother had succumbed to Alzheimer's two years ago and removed to a residential home. Suzie had visited her every week. Sometimes Granny recognized her, was delighted to see her and entirely lucid. At others, she stared through her as though she'd never seen her in her life before. It was heartbreaking to see the robust, feisty little woman, who had been more of a mother to her than her own ever had, literally withering before her eyes. It was finally with a mixture of sadness and relief that Suzie received news of her death three months ago.

Oh, how she would love to be able to make her stay here permanent! Just thinking how sympathetically the house could be restored to its former glory filled her with energy and ideas. She loved the spacious, modern home she and Mark had shared, but it wasn't a patch on Shalimar and offered Suzie little opportunity to test out her love of interior design. She hadn't even suggested the idea of buying Shalimar to Mark, knowing he would never agree. It was too far away from London for him to drive to work, and he'd never consider commuting. Besides, for once she was in agreement with her father. It would cost a fortune to revamp the house. Mark earned an enormous salary and was very generous with it, but Suzie reluctantly accepted that the restoration of Shalimar was likely to be beyond even him. Besides, it was now a moot point.

She could still sense her grandparents' presence firmly imprinted on every room in the house. She could feel Granny's arms engulf her in an affectionate hug and hear her grandfather's barking laugh as he related outrageously exaggerated stories about his past. Already Shalimar was working its magic, and she felt a little better. Sparkle, curled up on the rug beside her, lifted his head as though reading her thoughts and flapped his tail.

"We're going to be okay," she said with determination, running her fingers through his shaggy coat.

Sparkle cocked his head to one side and then dashed to the open French windows, letting forth with a volley of barks.

"What is it?"

Suzie struggled to her feet and joined him on the circular terrace that led to the large gardens, her grandfather's pride and joy. They sloped gently down to three acres of paddocks belonging to the property and thence to the river. The view of the surrounding countryside was unimpeded, the only other building in Suzie's line of sight being The Grange. It was a rambling, dilapidated ruin set in the adjoining twenty acres, sold just before Granny was taken ill and now run as some sort of commune-come-animal sanctuary. The inhabitants of Malton had mixed opinions as to its suitability for such a purpose. Suzie was vaguely aware that petitions were regularly raised to rid the village of the eyesore that The Grange had become, but Suzie hadn't gotten involved. It was none of her business how other people lived their lives.

She gazed down to her grandmother's paddocks and did a double take. There appeared to be a donkey and a couple of goats in one of them. A Shetland pony, sheep, and what looked like a flock of geese in the other. That must have been what Sparkle, who'd dashed off to investigate, had seen. She hobbled further along the weed-strewn terrace, shading her eyes with her hand. No, she wasn't mistaken. Someone had filled Granny's paddocks with a hotchpotch selection of animals.

Hopping about on her good leg, undecided about what she should do, a figure appeared in one of the paddocks, halter in hand. She looked up, saw Suzie standing there, and waved. A short time later, a woman who looked to be in her fifties strode up to her. She was shorter than Suzie's five feet seven and slightly overweight, with long, greying hair and an open, friendly face that looked a tad weather-beaten.

"Hello there," she said in a strident voice, offering Suzie her hand. "You must be Suzie."

"Er, yes."

"I'm Jane Grant, owner of The Grange, for my sins." She gave a short laugh. "I was sorry to hear about Flora, but really, that was no way for her to live. It must have been a relief when she went."

Suzie was taken aback. Everyone else had muttered the usual platitudes when Granny died, but no one had been honest enough to say that she was better off out of it.

"Thanks. Did you know Granny well?"

"Unfortunately not. Not long after I came here she started to go…well, you know how it was, a bit doolally. Milk bottles in the oven, slippers on the doorstep, stuff like that."

Suzie wondered if she ought to be offended at Jane's outspoken remarks even as she found herself smiling. This forthright woman was a breath of fresh air and just what she needed to take her out of herself right now.

"Right," she agreed with a smile.

"But we did have a good few chats before senility struck. She talked about you a lot. Adored you, as a matter of fact. We got along well in the short time we knew one another, and she asked me to use her paddocks, in case you're wondering. She thought it was a good way to keep the grass down."

"Yes, quite," Suzie said when Jane paused long enough for her to get a word in.

Sparkle came hurtling out of the undergrowth, barking furiously at Jane, even as his tail spiralled with good-natured enthusiasm.

"Hello, who's this?" Jane turned to Sparkle, ignored the racket he was making, and scratched his ears.

"That's Sparkle. He was abandoned on Epsom Common a couple of years back when he was a puppy. Don't worry about the barking, it's all a front. He seems to think it's expected of him."

"So I hear." Jane chuckled. "Still, he's a good-looking chap and quite entitled to express himself. But what am I doing, making you stand out here when you're obviously lame? Come on, I'll help you get back inside."

Before she could decide if she wanted to be taken over, Suzie found herself being half carried into the drawing room by this charismatic woman. She deposited her on the sofa and glanced round the room with obvious appreciation.

"I love this room!" she said. "It has an air of faded elegance but still feels lived in and welcoming."

"Yes, it's always been my favourite, too. Did Granny give you a tour of the rest of the house?"

"No, I've only seen the kitchen."

"That doesn't surprise me. It was definitely the hub of the house when I was growing up here. When I've got the energy, I'll seek out some anthracite and fire up the Aga again."

"Yes, I can't remember it not being alight, no matter what time of the day I called in."

"Well, when I'm mobile again, I'll show you the rest of the house. I've never understood why it's referred to as a cottage to tell you the truth because it's a lot more than that."

"Yes, four bedrooms, I think Flora said."

"Yes, but the best bit is on the second floor. There's a dangerously worm-eaten staircase up to two gigantic attic rooms full to the brim with the assorted treasures of two long lives."

"I'm surprised you haven't had a good rummage through them before now."

Suzie hesitated. "I haven't been feeling emotionally strong enough."

"Is that why you haven't been back here since your grandmother died?"

"Yes, it was too painful. My grandparents were wonderful company, and whenever I come here, I… well, I know it sounds silly," Suzie said with a little shrug, "but it feels as though Gramps is still here, looking out for me. That being so, it would seem like an imposition to root through his things."

"I can imagine."

"I'm sorry. I don't know why I'm burdening you with all this. You must have better things to do."

"Nonsense. Are you going to live here now?"

"Unfortunately not. I'm just staying for a few days. The house is left to my father—"

"The Bible basher?"

Suzie giggled. She was starting to like this woman more and more. "Yes. And he'll probably flog it and donate the proceeds to his church."

Jane snorted. "Stupid bugger!"

"I first came to live here when I was five," Suzie said, still unsure why she felt compelled to explain herself to a stranger. "My brother Derek was ten. My parents had just answered their calling as missionaries, and so we spent months at a time here. They were wonderful days," she added dreamily.

Suzie's words trailed off and her eyes drifted to her favourite picture of her grandfather, looking larger than life in the silver frame that sat on the mantelpiece. Kind eyes twinkled from a weathered face to which bushy white eyebrows and a thatch of dishevelled silver hair lent a distinguished air. A pipe was clamped between lips that smiled with a hint of puerile mischief.

"He looks lovely," Jane said, following the direction of Suzie's gaze.

"Oh, he was." Suzie's eyes filled with tears. "And Granny was a sweetheart, too. You know, when she succumbed to Alzheimer's, my father was all for putting her in an NHS Home. He reckoned that since she didn't know where she was half the time, there was no point in paying the outrageous amount it would cost to keep her at a private home."

"There's gratitude for you."

"Quite. But Mark, to give him his due, was as angry as I was when he read my father's letter and stumped up the fees for her stay in the private home without ever once complaining."

"He's not all bad then?" It was Suzie's turn to snort. "Sorry, that was insensitive. Tell me more about your childhood here."

"My parents didn't approve much of the informality that was so much a part of my grandparents' existence but didn't have much choice if they wanted to go off and do good deeds. But I know now that the manner in which my grandparents brought us up was a constant source of friction between the two older generations. It all came to a head when my parents arrived here unexpectedly on a Sunday and found us on the riverbank, fishing with Gramps. I remember that we were laughing our heads off at one of his outrageous stories."

"What's wrong with that? Sound like a perfectly natural way for a grandfather to entertain his grandchildren."

"If you knew my parents then, you wouldn't have bothered to ask. Sundays are sacrosanct to them, you see." Suzie spread her hands. "Indulging in what they regarded as frivolous pastimes or laughing aloud on the Sabbath is inappropriate behaviour. Anyway, they were beside themselves, and we weren't allowed to stay here. Instead, we were dragged off to Africa for six months and had the Bible drummed into us for hours every day."

Jane pulled a face. "Sounds dire."

"It was the bleakest period in my life." Suzie paused for a moment, lost in reflection. "I was overjoyed when they eventually relented and I came back to school in England. Naturally they had more pressing things to attend to and didn't come with me so they had to agree to my living here."

"What happened to your brother?"

"Derek? He was always more impressionable than me and claimed to have seen the light." Jane elevated her brows. "He remained with our parents, and we see little of each other nowadays."

"Doesn't sound like much of a loss." Jane grinned. "You must excuse me if I seem a little blunt, asking so many personal questions, but I've always had a curious nature."

"Not at all."

"Right, what have you done to yourself?" Jane's gaze was fixed on Suzie's ankle.

"It's just a sprain."

"Hum." Jake prodded gently and removed the bandage. "Need to do this up again. It's come loose." She did so, swiftly and efficiently, applying just the right amount of pressure to lend maximum support.

"Are you a nurse?"

"Lord no, but I've bandaged more horses' fetlocks in my time than you've had hot dinners. Same principle. And talking of dinners, what are you going to eat?"

"Oh, I've got some supplies in the car, but by the time I'd unloaded the essentials I was worn out."

"The essentials being the animals and the gin, I see. Glad to see you've got your priorities right. Got another glass?"

Laughing, Suzie indicated the door to the kitchen. "But there's no ice, I'm afraid."

"No matter." Jane produced healthy measures of gin for them both but was sparing with the tonic. "Cheers!" She took a large sip and closed her eyes as she savoured it. "Ah, that's better. It's been a long day, what with one thing and another."

"Cheers."

"So," Jane said after a pause during which they both made healthy inroads into their drinks, "want to talk about the rest of it?"

"What do you mean?"

"About why you've appeared here, out of the blue like this in spite of your injured ankle, with animals in tow but *sin* dishy lawyer husband." Suzie gaped, causing Jane to chuckle. "Your grandmother might have been old, but she reckoned she could still recognize a hunk when she saw one."

The comment was so typical of Granny that Suzie found herself actually laughing.

"So you've had a row?"

"A bit more than that. I caught him with my best friend."

"Ah, I see." Jane wrinkled her entire face. "Some friend."

"Yes."

"Tricky one, that. What was his excuse?"

"Does it matter? I can't live with him anymore."

"Does he want you to stay?"

"He says so."

"Will you go back?"

"No!"

"He travels a lot, doesn't he?" When Suzie hesitated, Jane spoke again. "It helps to talk about these things to a stranger sometimes," she said with authority. "It'll make you feel better."

"I doubt that anything could do that at present." Suzie flashed a wan smile. "But yes, he's a corporate lawyer, specialising in European Law, and travels extensively for the pharmaceutical company that employs him. He's only thirty-five but has already reached board level," she explained, unable to prevent a note of pride from entering her voice.

"Impressive."

"Yes, he says it's his reward for having a firm grasp of the complexities governing the laws of the expanding European market. He thrives on the pressure and regularly puts in fourteen-hour days. That's part of the problem. Even when he is in England, I don't see much of him during the week."

"Can't you persuade him to do something else?"

Suzie shook her head. "He'd never listen. He knows his worth and is constantly being headhunted. His employers know it, too, and reward him with a humungous salary that ensures his loyalty."

"I take it he has a high sex drive, too."

Suzie was taken aback. She'd only known this woman for a half hour, which surely didn't give her the right to ask such personal questions? But something persuaded her to answer truthfully. "Yes. How did you know?"

Jane chuckled. "I've had my moments. And I happen to know that intellectual, ambitious men and high sex drive often go hand in hand. Has it occurred to you that sex and emotional involvement are entirely different beasts? Men like Mark would consider sexual gratification as akin to scratching an itch. Very different to what he feels for you, I should imagine."

"Hey, whose side are you on?"

Jane spread her hands and shrugged. "Just playing devil's advocate."

"Well, even if what you say is true, that hardly justifies him making out with my best friend when he had me available not five minutes away."

"You didn't say how that came about."

"Because I don't know. He tried to explain, but I didn't listen. I think he was trying to place the blame on Kate and cast himself as the innocent party." Suzie's voice projected a healthy dose of scorn. "Anyway, I think our marriage was all but over before this happened. We want different things, you see, and I obviously don't provide him with enough stimulation. And no," she added, waving a hand to prevent the interruption she could sense Jane formulating. "His intelligence is no excuse. I've often wondered what he gets up to when he travels but gave him the benefit of the doubt because I wanted to. Now I know he can't even be faithful on home ground, what hope is there for us?"

"Things are never that simple."

"They are for me. It feels like a double betrayal. Mark *and* Kate both sticking the knife in."

"I can imagine."

"Besides, I had an appointment with my oncologist that morning. Breast cancer," she added in response to Jane's quizzical look. "I've had the all clear. It was just a checkup. Mark knows I hate those appointments and kept saying he wished he could come with me but couldn't because he had to get to the airport." She let out a long breath and with it some of her tension. "Seems he had enough time to visit Kate though, which tells me all I need to know."

"I'm sure it must seem that way to you now. Give it time." Jane reached across to pat Suzie's hand and then abruptly changed tack. "So what happened to your ankle?"

Jane listened to Suzie's explanation and roared with laughter.

"Similar thing happened to me when I walked out on mine just before I brought The Grange. He went off with a younger model, but he was loaded and I fleeced him," she said cheerfully. "Best thing I ever did. Gave me enough cash to buy The Grange outright and indulge in the bohemian lifestyle I've always craved."

"And you rescue animals? I think that's wonderful."

"Then you're in a minority round her," Jane said bluntly. "There's some pretty dirty tricks going on, trying to get me out." Jane watched as Dazzle jumped onto Suzie's lap, turned in several circles, and then settled down, purring like a traction engine. "Anyway, let's have the other half, and then I'll organize supper. Can I use your phone?"

"Sure," Suzie said faintly, still not sure how she felt about being taken over but with no energy left to object.

A short time later three young people arrived. They brought with them a large saucepan, and its contents smelt delicious. Suzie's tummy rumbled, reminding her that she hadn't eaten all day. Even so, given her heartbroken condition, she was astonished that she could even contemplate anything as mundane as food. If she attempted to eat, it would probably stick in her throat and choke her.

"Right, you lot," she said to the newcomers. "This is Suzie. Suzie, this is Ellen." The taller of the two girls smiled and offered Suzie her hand. "Ellen is my niece and unpaid skivvy. And this is Pansy." The other girl shook Suzie's hand but didn't appear to be particularly friendly. "Pansy is the paid help. And last but not least we have Gordon, who also gets paid a pittance and has a roof, of sorts, over his head."

"Hi, Suzie."

Her hand disappeared into Gordon's huge paw. He was tall, probably in his late teens, with a mop of unruly brown hair, a friendly face, and capable appearance.

"Right, kids," Jane said, taking charge again. "Unload Suzie's car for her and then get that lot served up pronto. We'll eat in here."

Suzie was surprised when all three obeyed without question, even if Pansy did look a little put out and was the last to respond. Half an hour later Suzie was tucking in to one of the tastiest casseroles that had ever passed her lips. Her new friends helped her to dispose of a couple of bottles of the burgundy she'd appropriated from Mark's store as well. They had just finished when Sparkle jumped up and started his barking and wagging routine.

"I say, anyone at home?" A head appeared through the French doors.

"Oh, Jack, there you are," Jane said. "Come on in, don't mind the hound. This is Suzie, Flora's granddaughter."

Suzie looked up into the bluest eyes she'd ever seen. The face housing them wasn't too shabby either. The man must have been about Mark's age and was casually dressed in jeans, his blond hair tied back with a bootlace. He had a strong jaw that sported at least a day's growth of designer stubble, rugged features, and very white teeth. He shook Suzie's hand firmly. Pansy, who'd been quiet throughout their makeshift meal, perked up immediately when Jack appeared.

"Jack Simmons is our local vet," Jane explained. "Have you just been to check the piglets, Jack?"

"Yeah, all's well. The antibiotics have worked their magic. And I gave Billy his second shot whilst I was there. I left the certificate on your desk."

"Thanks."

"Not at all." Jack perched on the end of the sofa that Suzie occupied.

"There's room over here, Jack," Pansy said sweetly. "You wouldn't want to jolt Suzie's ankle."

Jack ignored her. "What have you done to yourself, Suzie?"

"It's just a sprained fetlock," Jane answered for her.

Jack laughed. "Well, if Jane's caring for you, then you're in good hands." He looked about him. "This is a very nice house. I've never been inside it before, but I get curious every time I drive past. Are you planning to stay with us for long, Suzie?"

"I'm not sure yet." She adroitly changed the subject. "How long have you had a vet's practise?"

"Oh, it's not my practise. I joined a few months ago when a vacancy for a junior partner came up. Worked in Basingstoke before that but fancied a taste of country life."

"Yes, Jack helps out at The Grange," Pansy said, galvanised into being agreeable now Jack was amongst them. "He saves us a fortune by giving us special rates."

Suzie suppressed a giggle at the sick-making gestures Ellen was making behind Pansy's back.

"Don't shout about it, or you'll land me in trouble with my partners."

Pansy stood and placed a hand on his arm. "I'd never do that to you, Jack."

"Suzie, mind if I use your cloakroom?" Jack asked, shaking off Pansy's hand.

"Sure, through the kitchen and into the scullery."

"Thanks."

Jack disappeared for a long time, eventually returning with Honey tucked under his arm. "Er, Suzie, did you know you had a rabbit in your scullery?"

Suzie laughed and stretched out her arms, taking Honey from him. "That's Honey, and she's not a rabbit, she's an honorary cat."

To prove the point, she placed Honey back on the floor. She hopped up to Dimple, who was sitting in front of the marble fireplace in stately splendour, washing his face. Honey engaged his attention by head-butting him. Dimple regarded her for several seconds through piercing green eyes before he abandoned his ablutions and curled up on the rug. Honey stretched out next to him, one floppy ear resting over the cat's body, which she used as a furry pillow. Everyone laughed.

"Heavens, Suzie," Jack said, "that rabbit seems to have an identity crisis."

"Not at all. She's just sensible enough to realize that cats have a pretty good time of it and has decided to join their ranks."

Pansy rolled her eyes and helped herself to another glass of wine without waiting to be asked.

The phone rang, startling Suzie. Just for a moment she'd let her guard down and almost forgotten why she was at Shalimar. It could only be Mark calling. No one else knew she was here. Panic and despair took turns to attack her insides. Before she could decide whether or not she wanted to talk to him, Jack got up and lifted the receiver. She wondered what Mark would make of a strange man answering her phone but decided that a taste of his own medicine would do him no harm.

"Mrs. Alexander's residence," Jack said in a plummy voice that made them all giggle. "To whom do you wish to speak?" He listened. "Just one moment, I'll see if she's available to take your call. Suzie," he said, loudly enough for Mark to hear him. "A man claiming to be your husband wishes to converse with you. Shall I tell him to call back another time?"

Suzie was sorely tempted to say *yes*, but if she did, she wouldn't put it past Mark to get in his car and drive straight down here. With a sigh, she hobbled across the room and took the receiver from Jack.

"What do you want, Mark?" she asked.

"Who was that?"

"A friend."

"Oh really? Who is he, Suzie?"

"None of your business. I repeat, what do you want?"

"I'm coming down, Suzie," he said tersely. "I need to see you. We have to talk."

"I don't want to see you, Mark."

"No, but you're happy to see your fancy man. How long has it been going on, Suzie?"

"Nothing's going on. Don't make the mistake of judging everyone by your own low standards."

Mark moderated his voice. "Please, Suzie, I have to see you."

"No."

An elongated sigh echoed down the line. "Look, I have to go to work tomorrow. There are too many meetings scheduled that can't go ahead without me. And I suspect I'll have to go to Brussels on Wednesday for a few days. Can I come and see you next weekend?"

It was her turn to sigh. "Phone me then, and we'll see."

"Thank you, Suzie." He paused. "I love you," he said, sounding utterly sincere. "Take care of yourself until I get there, sweetheart."

* * * *

Good as his word, Jim reported back to Annabel within the allotted time frame.

"Got a pencil?"

Annabel sucked in her annoyance. Of course she had a bloody pencil. What sort of imbecile did he take her for? The only calls she ever received required note taking. Friends never called because she didn't have any, nor did she need them. Friends traded secrets. Friends took up precious time. She had no intention of giving up the former or wasting the latter. She was too busy making money.

"Go ahead," she said briskly.

"Greenberg came up from nothing," Jim told her. "Started off as a brickie and finished up marrying the boss's daughter." Annabel elevated a brow. He hadn't mentioned that in any of his self-promoting interviews. "His wife's father is old money. He enjoys mixing in those circles but has never been accepted, other than as a convenient guy to tap up for a loan."

"I see." And she did, all too well. This was looking more and more hopeful. "What else?"

"They have three kids. The oldest, Reggie, works for his old man. Well," Jim amended, "works is probably stretching it a bit. He's a lazy little sod by all accounts and has been given a boot up the backside more than once by his father. But the mother spoils all the kids and always takes his side." Better and better. "Reggie has a couple of police cautions for possession of cannabis and a few points on his licence for speeding. The other two kids are still of school age."

"Anything on the wife?"

"Big on charity committees. Not so keen on coming across for the old man." Annabel didn't bother to ask how he'd found that out, nor did she doubt the veracity of the information. Jim's sources had always proved to be one hundred percent reliable in the past. "Greenberg has a high sex drive but worries about his public image and doesn't use prostitutes."

"What does he do then?"

"Well, the woman he kept until recently walked out on him. She worked for his company and for him personally. Her job's now being advertised."

"Don't tell me," Annabel said with a tight smile. "She was a junior partner at Greenberg's."

"How did you know that?"

"I'm psychic," Annabel said, cutting the connection.

Chapter Three

Suzie woke early on Monday morning, wondering why Mark's alarm hadn't roused her. Then she remembered where she was, and the pain kicked in with all the force of a bad-tempered mule. She lay back in her grandmother's huge tester bed, convinced that she would never be strong-willed enough to overcome the pain that was searing through her, ripping her insides to shreds with remorseless efficiency as she contemplated life without Mark. She experienced the gut-wrenching heartache associated with bereavement as she grieved for the death of a marriage that she'd naively believed would last forever.

In spite of her permanently broken heart, she'd managed to sleep rather well. Perhaps the invasion of Shalimar by her new friends was responsible for that. They'd certainly taken her out of herself, refusing to allow her the luxury of wallowing in her own misery as they saw her safely through the first lonely evening of her new life.

Hobbling downstairs, Suzie opened the French doors and let Sparkle and the cats out. She waved when she saw Gordon walking up the path from The Grange with a basket of fresh groceries over his arm.

"Jane's orders," he told her cheerfully. "She's worried you won't have any breakfast otherwise. She instructed me to cook it for you as well."

"Really, that's kind but quite unnecessary."

"Look, Suzie," he said, feigning fear, "you can defy Jane if you like, but I haven't got the guts to take her on. Breakfast she said I had to cook for you, and that's precisely what I'm gonna do."

And he did, most efficiently. He joined her for the meal, actually eating a lot more of it than she did. There was soft fresh bread, which Gordon informed her was home baked at The Grange, and lovely free-range eggs courtesy of Jane's hens. Even though it was delicious, Suzie only forced it down to appease Gordon. If she didn't eat, she wouldn't put it past him to rat her out to Jane, who would doubtless take matters into her own hands.

Gordon insisted upon doing the washing up and then offered to walk Sparkle.

"In a minute, Gordon. Keep me company for a while first."

"Okay." He resumed his seat opposite hers. "What do you wanna talk about?"

Before they could strike up a conversation, the phone rang.

"Let me."

Gordon crossed the room in two enormous strides and grabbed the receiver. Suzie knew it would be Mark. It was eight o'clock, which meant he'd already been in his office for at least an hour. She wondered idly how he'd react to her phone being answered by another strange man at this hour of the morning and grinned, taking comfort from this petty victory over him. Reluctantly, her heart beating ridiculously fast just at the prospect of hearing her husband's voice, Suzie took the receiver from Gordon.

"Yes, Mark," she said. "What is it?"

"I just wanted to be sure that you'd slept well."

Suzie merely grunted.

"How does your ankle feel today, sweetheart?"

"Fine."

"I'm glad," he said, seemingly undeterred by her monosyllabic response. "Is there anything you need?"

"No."

"I'm going to be in meetings all day, but I'll call again in the evening."

As Suzie listened to the lilting, hypnotically persuasive cadence of his voice, the familiar emotion that tugged at her heart caused her patience to snap. If she allowed him to control their telephone conversations, then she didn't stand a chance of holding out against his coercive charm when she next saw him in person.

"It's a little late to adopt the caring husband routine, Mark," she said, replacing the receiver with a loud clatter and shaking hand.

"Tell me more about the setup at The Grange," she said to Gordon, resuming her seat at the table and taking several deep, calming breaths.

"Well, Jane has a bark that's far worse than her bite. Beneath that stern exterior there's a heart of gold."

Suzie smiled. "Yes, I'd already worked that out for myself."

"She doesn't just rescue abandoned animals, you know, she does the same with people." Suzie elevated a brow. "Apart from Ellen, all of us came from care institutions or were scooped up off the streets by her. That includes me, by the way," he added cheerfully. "Used to be a right tearaway, I did."

Suzie leaned her chin in her cupped hand and smiled at him. "I find that hard to believe."

"Nah, it's true." A wide grin stretched across Gordon's face. "Not so long ago that posh car of yours wouldn't have stayed parked where it is for five minutes with me about. In and out of trouble all the time, I was. No father in my life, you see, so I had no role model." Gordon's casual attitude didn't fool Suzie, who guessed there must be more than a little of Jane's pragmatism behind his throwaway remarks. "But Jane changed all that," he said, as though reading her thoughts. "I was one of the first that she took in, over three years ago now."

"You fit in well."

"Yeah, that's a turn up for the books an' all. I'd never lived in the country before and thought I'd find it too dull. I didn't think anything ever happened out in the sticks, see." He rolled his eyes. "Dull? Huh, there's more scandal and intrigue in this small village than I ever got to know about in any city. That's because everyone here knows everyone else's business. It's a right hotbed of gossip and goings-on. Anyway, Jane made me appreciate the countryside for what it is and brought out a love for animals that I didn't know I possessed. I said I wanted to stay with her, and so she insists upon paying me a wage. Better than she lets on, too."

"Well, if this morning's effort's anything to go by, then she gets her pound of flesh."

Gordon shrugged off the compliment. "She ain't soft like most do-gooders though and won't take crap from any of us."

"I can well imagine."

"Yeah, when people turn up at her door, she tells them straight how it's gonna be if they want to stay. They live by her rules, work hard, and stay off drugs. In return, they get a leaky roof over their heads, as well as food, purpose, and direction. If anyone wants to try a career path that's attainable, she'll move heaven and earth to get them the training they need for it, too."

"You're fond of her, aren't you?"

"Yeah, we all love Jane and not just because she's given us a chance. We admire her down-to-earth attitude and the fact that she treats us as adults. She don't talk down to us all the time, making out that she knows best. She's very good at letting us make our own mistakes."

"She's certainly one in a million." Suzie couldn't imagine many rich divorcees ploughing their settlements into such a risky venture, and her respect for the woman increased. "How many of you are there at The Grange?"

"About a dozen at the last count, I think, but it don't look set to continue."

"Why not?"

"Locals ain't happy about the place. We're constantly being pestered by the council. Complaints about noise, lack of the right insurances, lack of proper licences…you name it, and someone's complained. Plus, Social Services are trying to get involved with the kids there. Christ, they're the ones who fucked…whoops, sorry, I mean, they're the crowd who failed in the first place with most of the kids who are now making a go of it with Jane. They seem to want to take the credit for that."

Suzie sighed. "I can't say I'm surprised."

"No well, Jane isn't about to take their crap lying down, but it's not going away. Noise pollution is their latest gripe."

"Who's having their peace disturbed? The Grange is too far away from the village to upset anyone there. Shalimar and, I suppose, that row of cottages on your northern boundary are the only places likely to be affected, and I haven't heard a peep out of anyone or anything since I've been here."

"Well, there you are. But someone's got it in for Jane, that's for sure."

Jane was clearly in urgent need of sound legal advice, and Suzie's mind automatically drifted toward Mark. He'd know exactly how to fight the bureaucrats, but she dismissed the notion of consulting him out of hand. Much as she liked Jane and her assorted rabble, she wasn't about to fall at the first hurdle in her bid for independence and run to her husband for help.

Gordon stood up and called to Sparkle. "I'll take him for a run, and then I'd better get back before I'm accused of skiving."

"Thanks, Gordon. What do I owe you for the groceries?"

"Oh, Jane said nothing. You're to consider it payment in lieu of rent for use of your paddocks."

Waving to the departing Gordon, Suzie phoned her grandmother's solicitor and told him she was temporarily in residence at Shalimar. He reminded her that the family needed to get together as soon as her parents returned for the formal reading of the will. Suzie promised to remind them, already dreading the moment. Hopefully their return would, as usual, be delayed by the more pressing necessities. That would buy her a little more time. She was in no hurry to tell them of her estrangement from Mark any more than she relished finding somewhere permanent to live and a means of supporting herself. All the time she was at Shalimar she could remain comfortably in limbo, detached from the stark reality of her situation, and delay facing up to the prospect of a future which didn't include Mark.

Suzie ached to start rooting through Shalimar, unearthing her grandparents' treasures and deciding which bits she'd like to keep. She could face the task with greater equanimity now, but frustratingly her ankle was still too painful for such strenuous activity. That put gardening out as well, she decided, looking regretfully at her grandfather's once pristine flower borders. But she had to do something. There must be some job she could cope with sitting down that would occupy her mind and prevent it from entertaining thoughts of her erstwhile husband. She hobbled aimlessly into her grandfather's library and was confronted with the obvious answer. She'd catalogue his books. There were many rare and valuable ones amongst his collection, including first editions. Her father would doubtless wish to sell them all, and so they would need to be properly listed.

Suzie happily set about her task, aided and abetted by a dog and two cats, distracted by one nosy rabbit. But still, it was a peaceful occupation, and Suzie found herself smiling at the memories stirred by the sight of those well-thumbed tomes. She could still see her grandfather's large frame, slouched in a chair in front of the library fire, open book on his lap. But it would be discarded the moment his granddaughter walked in, his face coming alight with pleasure. Inevitably, he would remember a really important story, some tale of his derring-dos of long ago, that he'd always meant to tell her. Suzie was convinced that he made most of it up but was enchanted nonetheless, and another evening would drift peacefully by without the need for television to keep them entertained.

Suzie was so wrapped up in her task that until Sparkle let forth with a volley of barks she didn't realize she had another visitor. Jack put his head round the door.

"Hello," he said. "I knocked, but I don't think you heard me."

"Oh hello, Jack. Sorry, I was preoccupied."

"So I see." He glanced round the disarray in the library. "Quite a task you've got yourself there."

"Yes, it's certainly going to keep me busy."

Jack strolled around the room, examining the bookshelves with a fascination that surprised Suzie. "If you need any help, I'm your man."

"Thanks. You're keen on books, too, I take it?"

"Yeah, and this lot look valuable."

"They are, but they're part of my grandparents' estate. I daresay my father will want to sell them."

"Shame." He was still examining the rows of books with avid interest. "Anyway," he said, turning away from them at last. "I'm here on Jane's orders, and of my own volition, to offer you lunch." He held up bags containing freshly made sandwiches and fruit. "I've just come from the kitchens at The Grange," he added by way of explanation.

"I'm starting to feel overwhelmed."

He chuckled. "If Jane decides to take someone under her wing, they don't usually have much say in the matter." He smiled at her properly then. It was a smile that lit up his whole face, illuminating his remarkable eyes and softening his craggy features into an engaging expression that she could imagine appealing to a lot of females besides Pansy. "Come on, let's eat in the kitchen. I'll put the kettle on." He handed her the walking stick she'd commandeered. It had been her grandfather's and was a beautifully carved, highly polished solid piece of oak. "I would suggest that we crack another of those excellent bottles of burgundy, but I've got a full afternoon's work ahead of me, so I guess we'll have to make do with tea."

Suzie's feigned expression of regret matched his. "Tea it is then."

Jack was good company. Unlike when they'd been in the library, she could tell that she had his full attention now. It was equally obvious that he was intent upon charming her out of her introspective mood. He chatted about his various four-legged patients, feeding the hovering Sparkle with pieces of his sandwich as he did so. At one point, he swooped upon Honey, rescuing her just before she munched contentedly through the electric radiator cable. Suzie discovered that Jack had a wicked sense of humour, a compassionate nature, and incisive brain. He appeared to enjoy her company and quickly put her at her ease, making her feel as though she'd known him for far longer than she actually had.

Jack didn't appear to be in any hurry to start his afternoon calls and returned to the subject of Shalimar with tenacious regularity, wanting to know more about her plans for living there. For some reason he seemed to think she owned it, and Suzie didn't bother to disillusion him. It was none of his business, and she had no intention of discussing the unresolved matter of her splintering marriage with someone whom she'd known for less than a day. She parried his questions with nebulous politeness until Jack eventually got the message and changed the subject.

"There's a quiz night at the local this evening," he said when he finally stood to leave. "Do you fancy coming along and improving our chances of actually winning for a change?"

"No, I don't think so." She shook her head. "Thanks, but it's not really my cup of tea."

"Nonsense, you'll enjoy it. It's just a bit of fun. Mind you, some of the teams that come from other areas are red-hot professionals and take it really seriously." He pulled a wry face. "Unfortunately The Grange team has a tendency to get plastered before the questions even start, as if we didn't have enough of a disadvantage already. Anyway, Jane said to get you involved, and if you don't come willingly, I ought to warn you that she isn't above using force."

Suzie knew when she was beaten and, smiling, agreed that Jack could pick her up at seven thirty. When he left, she wondered if she'd just accepted a date, not twenty-four hours after walking out on the love of her life.

She'd hardly settled back into the library when Sparkle's rumbling bark alerted her to another caller. This one was more conventional and chose to knock at the front door. By the time Suzie hobbled into the hall and wrestled the heavy door open, her visitor had already knocked twice and obviously given up. He was walking back down the drive, but when she opened the door, he turned to smile and raised his hat in acknowledgement. Suzie had never met anyone who wore a trilby before, especially in such warm weather. Perhaps it was supposed to give the impression of greater stature since its wearer was one of the smallest men Suzie had ever seen. He was neatly dressed, and his ingratiating smile put Suzie in mind of a Jehovah's Witness. She'd already experienced more than enough religious indoctrination during her lifetime, resented the intrusion, and made to slam the door in his face, careless of how rude it might appear.

"Mrs. Alexander?" the man asked, stopping her in mid-slam, his weasel-like face still wreathed in smiles. "I heard you were in residence at Shalimar. My name is Porter. I've written to you several times but not had the pleasure of receiving a reply."

His politely couched words sounded more like an accusation. Suzie's gaze drifted towards the pile of mail she'd picked up when she arrived and dumped on the hall table, meaning to sort though it later. The arrival of Jane and her clan had put it completely out of her mind.

"I haven't looked at the mail yet," she informed him, wondering why she felt the need to justify herself to this condescending stranger.

"No matter, you're here now, and these things are always best discussed in person anyway. Perhaps I could come in?" He moved forward expectantly.

Suzie hesitated, her instinctive dislike for the man making her cautious. Sparkle obviously shared her opinion and was still growling. That swung it as far as Suzie was concerned. Her friendly dog hardly ever displayed aggression and was a far better judge of character than she would ever be.

"Perhaps you'd just tell me what this is about?"

Porter showed no reaction to the rebuff. "Why, I thought you realized. I am from Watson and Porter, Estate Agents in the village." He puffed himself up to his full five feet four, clearly supposing Suzie would recognize the concern in question. When she made no comment and failed to look impressed, he ploughed on regardless. "We've been trying to contact you with exciting news. We have a client who would like to purchase Shalimar and is willing to offer a very generous price."

Suzie raised a brow at the odious little man. "I wasn't aware that Shalimar was on the market."

"Well, no, but no doubt—"

Suzie cut him off. "Anyway, no one in their right mind would offer for a house that they haven't set foot in." She wanted him to know that she had his measure. She'd read an article once about unscrupulous Agents pretending to have offers for vacant houses just so that they could get them on their books.

"Ah, but that's where you're quite wrong, my dear." His patronizing tone left Suzie fighting the urge to bop him one in the centre of his obsequious features. "You see, my client loves Georgian architecture and has fallen in love with Shalimar, sight unseen. He realizes of course that it has been grossly neglected over the years but wants the property so much that he's prepared to offer the full market value, as though the house was properly modernised." At Suzie's unfeigned look of surprise, Porter's visage became smug. "Yes, I thought that would interest you. Mr. Greenberg is prepared to offer a very generous sum for the freehold in return for immediate possession."

"How generous?"

Porter named a figure that rendered Suzie speechless. It was far more than the property was worth.

"Now then," he continued, stepping forward confidently. "Perhaps we could discuss this inside?"

Suzie pulled herself together. "I'm sorry, Mr. Porter, but you're wasting your time. At present Shalimar is not for sale." She paused and looked him straight in the eye. "At any price."

She should have made him aware that the property wasn't hers to sell and put him in touch with her father, but she'd had enough of his supercilious attitude. A severe case of *small man syndrome* if ever she'd come across one.

"Oh come, my dear, surely not. Perhaps if we could discuss the matter with your husband, he would see it in a different light? It's a very generous offer."

That did it! Suzie squared her shoulders and glared down at the top of his trilby. "Which part of *not for sale* is it that you don't understand?"

Without waiting for his reply, she slammed the swollen door in his astounded face.

* * * *

Annabel waited in an anteroom, along with the other half-dozen people shortlisted for the vacancy at Greenberg's. She cast a shrewd eye over the competition, three men and three women, but didn't attempt to engage them in conversation. She saw nothing to cause her undue concern and buried her head in a magazine, dismissing them as the irrelevance to her that they were. When she'd learned what extracurricular activities the previous holder of the position had engaged in, she'd hesitated to apply. She absolutely didn't want to know about anything like that. Then she recalled how she must appear to others, the pains she'd taken to appear efficient whilst ruthlessly suppressing any iota of femininity that might break through her protective shields. Greenberg would have to be desperate to look upon her as a sex symbol simply because she didn't give off those sorts of vibes. Now that she could see there were as many male applicants as there were female, she relaxed. If he was in the market for another mistress, he'd obviously looked elsewhere.

She was the last to be called to Greenberg's inner sanctum, which suited her just fine. The man who stood to greet her already seemed familiar because she'd spent so much time checking him out on line. He was probably six foot two. He was certainly overweight. His well-cut suit failed to conceal his considerable bulk, and his face lacked character. Even his mother would have been hard pressed to describe him as handsome, but he exuded an air of authority that would persuade most people to overlook his physical shortcomings. Clearly, Greenberg wasn't a man who suffered fools gladly, but then she already knew that about him. His close-set eyes missed nothing as they assessed her, and she guessed she'd have her work cut out to get anything past him. That was okay. She enjoyed a challenge.

They quickly dispensed with the usual interview questions and got down to the nitty-gritty.

"I see you've been with a big construction company in London for over three years, Annabel. You went to them straight from university, right?" Annabel confirmed the information he was reading from her résumé. "Why do you want to leave them? I happen to know that they look after their employees and offer good opportunities for advancement."

Annabel played on a carefully calculated hunch, born on the back of her research, and answered in a way that ought to have dismissed her application out of hand.

"Office politics," she said succinctly. Greenberg's large head shot up, and she now had his full attention. "Can't stand them, don't understand the rules, and don't see the point. If I'd wanted to get into all that stuff, I'd have gone into Human Resources."

"You're not a team player then?"

She met his gaze and held it. This was crunch time. "If being a team player means spending hours setting stupid targets that don't mean anything and wasting time discussing decisions that have already been made, then no, I'm not a team player."

"So how do you like to work?"

"Alone as much as possible, using my intelligence. I do whatever it takes to get the job done, no questions asked."

"Interesting."

He appeared not to know what to ask her next, so she helped him out.

"I stand by my decisions, Mr. Greenberg, and have yet to fail in *anything* that's been asked of me."

She fell silent, continuing to hold his gaze. But she knew, even before he offered her his hand, that she'd gotten the job.

Chapter Four

"I'm not so sure about this." Suzie poked her head round the door to the Frog and Ferret's main bar, disconcerted to see it so crowded. "I have no idea what to expect."

"You and me both," Jack said, chuckling. "No two weeks are ever the same, but at least life's never dull around Jane."

That wasn't what bothered Suzie. It was a long time since she'd been anywhere in the evening without Mark, and the delicacy of the situation made her anxious. But it quickly became evident that she needn't have worried. Jane had cornered the market in the local as effortlessly as she'd taken control of Suzie's life only yesterday. She greeted Suzie and Jack in her usual verbose manner and made sure that Suzie was supplied with a large G&T in double-quick time.

Loud voices and raucous laughter dominated in all but one small corner of the bar. On the opposite side of the room several teams clustered round tables, heads together, meagre halves of bitter in front of them.

"No chance of addled brains in their teams," Jane said, snorting.

Suzie laughed. "So I see."

"You don't know the half of it. They warm one another up by asking questions and debate the answers with the intense zeal of repressed academics."

"Oh dear! What have I let myself in for?"

"It's a bit like doing warming-up exercises before going jogging," Jack said, grinning.

"Well, just so long as they don't strip off."

Jack shuddered. "Now I'll never be able to get that image out of my head."

The Grange crowd, in contrast to the professionals, had sequestered the best part of the bar in front of the fireplace and were already well stuck into the booze. All the people she'd met yesterday were there, together with three more youngsters. Everyone treated her with friendly courtesy, with the exception of Pansy who'd been openly hostile since she'd arrived with Jack. Suzie ignored her. So, too, did Jack, causing Pansy to flop sullenly in a corner seat and sulk. Suzie didn't think Jane would tolerate that, but to her surprise, she did nothing about it. At one stage, Jane even offered the girl a smile and soft words of encouragement. Suzie couldn't help wondering why.

The Grange team weren't as hopeless as Jack had led her to believe. They certainly had more fun than their more serious rivals. They joshed one another for making stupid answers. Did Ellen really think that Andorra was in Africa? They also catcalled if they felt their efforts weren't being marked fairly. They insisted their answer was correct when asked the Christian name of Prince Charles's second son. The professionals looked smug, knowing it was Henry, but Gordon loudly shouted them down.

"Charlie only has one son," he yelled. "You only have to look at Harry to see that his father's James Hewitt."

They didn't get the points but chalked it up as a moral victory and consoled themselves with another round of drinks. The kids didn't know much about history and current affairs but were red-hot on pop music and entertainment. They led the laughter when the professionals proved themselves to be human, naming Gladys Knight's backing group as The Pimps. Jack and Jane were good lateral thinkers, and Suzie's knowledge of literature ensured that The Grange team finished a respectable third, their best result to date.

"Well done, team," Jane said as they tucked into the pub grub supplied for the contestants.

"We're not in danger of getting serious about this, are we?" Ellen asked warily.

"God no!" Gordon answered for them all. "Don't wanna be like that lot, do we, love?" He nodded toward the professionals, checking their scores and laboriously debating the answers they'd got wrong.

Jack resumed his seat beside Suzie and handed her another drink. Was it her third or fourth? She'd lost count but figured that since she wasn't driving it didn't really matter.

"Thanks."

"You're welcome. Did you enjoy it?"

"Yes, I guess so, but the professionals make me feel a bit thick."

"It's a deliberate ploy to belittle the opposition. We reckon they spend their whole week reading nothing but quiz books." Jack shrugged. "Sad really."

She laughed. "Yes, I've got better things to do with my time."

"Any room for me in those things?" Suzie looked at him askance. "I'm sorry, unfair question." He lowered his voice. "I know you've come down here to sort your life out, and the last thing you need is the likes of me making things more difficult. Just remember, if you need a shoulder, I'm there for you." He smiled directly into his eyes. "I don't bite, and I'm a good listener."

"Thanks." But she felt distinctly uneasy and changed the subject.

With Jack having made his interest in her plain, Suzie felt uncomfortable when he drove her back to Shalimar. He was attractive and available, and she should be flattered that he was so obviously taken with her. God alone knew, her battered ego could do with the boost, but she was still totally married to Mark. In spite of what he'd done, it was far too soon to even think about other men. Would Jack expect to be invited in, or at least try to kiss her? Suzie panicked, unsure how to handle either situation, unwilling to offend him. Jack, more intuitive than she'd realized, resolved the problem for her. At Shalimar, he got out of the car and helped Suzie to the door.

"I'd love to linger, but I have an early start," he said, offering her an economical peck on the cheek.

Suzie tried to smother her relief. "Yes, well, thanks, Jack. I enjoyed it."

"Me, too. Let's do it again next week."

Suzie watched him drive away before she let herself in. The phone was ringing, but she ignored it. Let Mark sweat on her whereabouts for a change. She let Sparkle out, hobbled up to bed, and applied herself to the task of falling asleep without thinking about her husband.

The following day started off in the same way as the one before it, only this time Suzie wouldn't allow Gordon to cook for her and sent him straight back to The Grange. She had to stand on her one good foot and not start relying on her new friends. She knew they meant well, but the only crutch she intended to lean on in future on was her grandfather's walking stick.

When the phone rang, she resignedly answered it, aware that if she didn't, then Mark was more than capable of descending upon Shalimar and demanding to know what she'd been up to. He sounded relieved when she answered herself.

"Hey," he said in a soft tone. "I tried to reach you last night, but you weren't answering."

"No."

"Are you okay? I was worried about you."

"I was out."

"Oh, anywhere nice?"

"Why would I go anywhere unpleasant?"

"You didn't mention that you had plans."

"Any reason why I should have done?"

He sighed, and Suzie could imagine how much effort it cost him not to ask more questions. Could it be that he was actually jealous? Now that really would be a turn up for the books.

"I have to go to Brussels early tomorrow morning," he said, "but I'll call you from there."

"If you like," she said casually, "but I can't guarantee that I'll be home."

"Then I'll keep ringing until I get you. Or I'll try your mobile."

"Do what you have to do, Mark. Now, you'll have to excuse me, I have things to do."

She hung up without saying good-bye, feeling that for the first time ever she'd gotten the better of a conversation with Mark. The realisation didn't bring much satisfaction, and Suzie returned to her grandfather's library feeling unsettled and out of sorts, as though matters were about to swing out of her control.

Mr. Porter phoned her, his voice full of oily insincerity.

"My client is so enamoured with Shalimar that he's willing to increase his offer by £20,000." Suzie said nothing. "Surely that must put a different light on matters, Mrs. Alexander?" he said. "After all, it's far more than the property's worth."

Suzie was irritated by the man's patronising attitude but intrigued as well that someone who'd never set foot in the place could want it so badly.

"I'm not interested, Mr. Porter," she said curtly. "Please don't bother me again."

"But—"

She hung up at him, more disconcerted than ever.

Time passed, and with routine came a gradual degree of tranquillity. She continued to catalogue her grandfather's library and spent time with her new friends, accustomed now to their habit of dropping in unannounced. Jack appeared at all sorts of odd times but usually when she was alone. He tried to inveigle her into going out to dinner with him, but Suzie steadfastly refused, annoyed by his tenacity when he knew she'd only just separated from her husband.

On Friday evening, Jack was one of the gang from The Grange who descended upon her, dinner in saucepans, and was the last to leave. He took her completely by surprise when he pulled her into his arms and kissed her. Too startled to object, she accepted his kiss but didn't return it.

"I think you'd better go," she said as soon as he released her.

"Suzie, I'm sorry, I thought you wanted to—"

"Good night, Jack," she said, opening the front door wide.

He left but didn't look happy about it. Suzie closed the door behind him, wondering why she couldn't take to him. There was something about Jack that made her wary, but she was damned if she knew what it was. She shrugged. Perhaps it was just her. She'd been married for too long to think like a single person, and any intimate contact with another man felt like adultery. Stupid, but there it was.

Suzie's contrived to make her days as busy as possible to prevent her mind from dwelling upon the subject of Mark. And it seemed to work, after a fashion. But at night, when she lay alone in her huge bed it was a different story. No matter what she did, she couldn't prevent herself from thinking about her husband. She'd be drifting off to sleep, thinking about something else, when suddenly her head filled with images of Mark's gorgeous melting brown eyes smiling into hers. She could actually feel his long, capable fingers stroking her body, whipping her into a frenzy of desire as his lips hardened upon hers. So real were these dreams that when she woke from them, she actually believed that Mark was beside her. Then she would remember, her heart would plummet, and the emptiness intensified. Sleep would be a long time coming after that, only attainable when she had cried herself to the point of exhaustion.

Suzie missed Mark so much that she couldn't imagine ever getting over the pain. In a constant state of jealousy, she wondered all the time who he was with and what he was doing. His glamorous assistant Rebecca was bound to be in Brussels with him. Not only was she gorgeous, but Suzie suspected she also had her eye on Mark. She'd never worried about it before because she trusted him, but now that Suzie had left him, it could easily be another story. Mark had a high sex drive, she wasn't there to see to his needs, he and Rebecca were staying in the same hotel…Damn it, she simply refused to think about it! Suzie bashed her pillows into a more comfortable nest and cried for all she'd lost.

In spite of her insistence that he not bother, Mark called her every day and continued to assure her that he wanted her back. But Suzie couldn't afford to relent. Something had come out of those sleepless nights, and she knew now that she wanted more than just exclusive rights to her husband. She wanted a more even partnership and a career of her own. That would never happen, no matter what promises he made now, and if she went back, she doubted if she'd ever find the strength to leave him for a second time.

Alone in her bed on the night Jack had kissed her, for the first time Suzie thought about something other than Mark. She thought about that kiss and all that it implied. It had been expertly executed, so why had she felt nothing? Even after ten years, Mark's kisses could still cause fire to rip through her. It was infuriating! But Jack's kiss had prompted no such reaction. Suzie wondered what was wrong with her. Okay it was still early days, her raw emotional state too volatile, but surely that wouldn't prevent her libido from responding to such an attractive man? Jack *was* an attractive man, and she'd noticed at the pub that Pansy wasn't the only one who had him in her sights. She was flattered by his interest in her but couldn't take their friendship to the inevitable conclusion. Not yet anyway. Perhaps not ever. And certainly not just to get even with Mark.

One particularly unpleasant experience marred Suzie's fragile contentment during her first week at Shalimar. On Thursday, Sparkle warned her of a stranger's approach, and shortly thereafter, the front door knocker sounded. Supposing it to be the tenacious Mr. Porter, Suzie hobbled into the hall much faster than she'd been able to manage a few days previously. She wrenched the door open, ready to give the irritating little man a piece of her mind. But it wasn't Porter. Instead, the sunlight was blocked out by a bull of a man wearing a well-cut suit that sat awkwardly on his large frame.

"Mrs. Alexander?"

"Yes."

"My name is Greenberg. Porter has been speaking to you about me. May I come in?" He took a step forward, seeming to assume that she would agree. Suzie got the impression that few people argued with this man.

"No," she said, folding her arms beneath her breasts and glaring up at him. "Unfortunately you've had a wasted trip. Shalimar is not for sale, Mr. Greenberg." She made to shut the door, but he jammed it open with a huge foot.

"Not so fast, young lady. Have you discussed this with your husband?"

He couldn't have said anything less likely to persuade her. Tamping down her rising irritation, she endeavoured to remain calm.

"Good afternoon, Mr. Greenberg," she said evenly. "Remove your foot from my door please, or I'll have my dog remove it for you."

Sparkle obliged by growling a little louder. Suzie was proud of him and made a mental note to give him some extra treats later.

"Look," he said, spreading his meaty hands in a conciliatory gesture, "I think we've got off on the wrong foot here. Porter's fault, I expect. Bloody little man," he added, almost to himself. "I like plain speaking, Mrs. Alexander, and I expect Porter procrastinated and didn't explain my position properly. Should have dealt with this myself. No matter. I want this house, I reckon you and your husband want to sell it, and I don't like mucking about. I can pay you cash. Name your price." He offered her a tight smile, revealing nicotine-stained teeth, clearly confident of victory.

Suzie disliked him even more than Porter, which was saying something. She would, she supposed, have to inform her father of the man's determination to purchase Shalimar at any price but was damned if she'd tell him so.

"If you're so keen on plain speaking, Mr. Greenberg, let me do some of my own. Again. Shalimar is not for sale at any price. Is that plain enough for you?" She placed her hands on her hips and looked him squarely in the eye without blinking. He was the first to look away.

"You should think carefully about that," he said, his expression darkening. "Everything in this life is for sale. And quiet villages can be dangerous places, especially for a woman on her own."

Suzie felt a chill run down a spine. The man was a thug, and if he was trying to frighten her, then he was succeeding better than he could possibly know. But she wasn't about to let him see it.

"Are you threatening me?"

"Not at all," he said unconvincingly, his words accompanied by a malicious little smile. "Just telling you how it is. I'll be in touch. Good afternoon."

Abruptly he turned away, walked back down the drive, and climbed into a flashy, top-of-the-range BMW.

* * * *

Greenberg tested Annabel by giving her all sorts of routine stuff to deal with. She'd expected that but almost died of boredom as she waited for things to change. Her opportunity came after three months when he told her that he wanted rid of some long-standing tenants in a large house he owned in Essex. He'd acquired them along with the property. Their controlled tenancy ensured that it went for a song, but now that he owned the house, he wanted them out. John offered her no advice about the tactics she should use but probably thought she'd go down the prescribed route of bribery. Annabel knew better than to leave the sort of trail that might lead back to her. Instead, she simply moved a gang of young tearaways-for-rent into the flat above the elderly couple. They systematically terrorised the sitting tenants with late-night parties, loud music, doors banging, and strange comings and goings at all times of night. Within two months, the tenants went to live with their married daughter and John had full vacant possession of his house.

His approach came over dinner in a fancy restaurant the following week. They had attended a business meeting together in London that resulted in the acquisition of a valuable office block. Annabel had single-handedly brought the deal to a successful conclusion by using unorthodox tactics to discover how high the competition had been prepared to bid for it.

"I like the way you play hardball with the big boys, Annabel," he said, watching her over the rim of his wine glass.

"Thanks."

"Do you have a boyfriend?"

"No."

"Any sort of sex life?"

"No again."

She knew what was coming and felt a moment's panic. She was doing well at Greenberg's. John left her alone to get on with things and didn't waste time asking awkward questions. She still had to work with others at times but didn't let their obvious disapproval of her methods stand in the way of her ambition. She never flirted with John, was all business, and gave him no reason to suppose that she wanted to step into his late mistress's shoes. The conversation they'd just had about her personal life was the only time the issue had been raised between them, and she thought he'd made arrangements for his sexual needs elsewhere. From the way he was observing her, his eyes drifting slowly down her body as though mentally undressing her, she had a feeling that her gravy train was about to run dry. Unless… She shook her head. Greed and ambition were making her think the unthinkable.

"I have a proposition for you," he said.

"I'm listening," she said calmly.

"My wife doesn't give out, and I have a high sex drive."

"Go to a whorehouse then."

"I'd get found out sooner or later. I don't want to embarrass my wife or ruin my reputation." He paused to drain his wine glass and refill it. "I'll offer you another twenty grand on top of your salary and give you a lease on one of the duplex penthouses we've just finished converting. In return, you'll see no man other than me and do whatever I ask of you without hesitation."

"No thanks."

His eyebrows disappeared skyward. He clearly hadn't been expecting rejection.

"Why not?"

It was her turn to rake his body with her eyes. "You don't attract me."

"No," he said, leaning toward her, his eyes intent. "I didn't imagine that I would. But money does, doesn't it, Annabel?"

She merely shrugged, toying with the stem of her wineglass, as she thought his proposition through. Twenty grand was a lot of money, but not enough.

"All right," he said, "I'll double your salary."

Annabel sat a little straighter. She was seriously tempted now. It would mean she could fulfil her dream of setting up on her own that much quicker. The downside was having sex with this thug, but Annabel knew how to distance her mind from distasteful tasks. She'd had enough practise. His bulk, thinning hair, flaccid cheeks, and bulbous nose meant as little to her as his legendary short fuse. When it came down to it, it was all about money, and her body was just a convenient way to earn more. To feel used or humiliated she would need to experience emotion, and that had long since been knocked out of her.

"Agreed," she said succinctly.

If he was surprised by her abrupt change of heart, he gave no sign. "Our relationship will remain confidential." Really, she thought, remembering how easily Jim had found out about the last one. "It won't interfere with my home life, and I won't cut you any slack in the office because of it."

"I would be insulted if you did."

"I like it rough, and I like it kinky." Annabel merely shrugged, already compartmentalising so that she didn't have to think about the commitment she'd made. "You ought to know that this is a business relationship like any other. I'm not sentimental, I don't get emotionally involved, I don't remember birthdays, and I don't react well to female histrionics."

Annabel merely nodded, wondering if she looked as bored as she felt. They'd agreed terms. What more was there to talk about?

"It depends, of course," he added, "upon whether you know how to fuck."

She remained perfectly composed. "There's only one way to find out."

He chuckled, causing her to suspect that none of his previous conquests had reacted quite so casually. "Why do you want to get involved with me?" he asked, glancing down at his bulk.

She quirked a brow. "It's mostly about money, you're right about that, but also power. You are a powerful man, John, intelligent, too, and I enjoy the combination." She looked him straight in the eye and treated him to a smile. "It turns me on," she lied.

"Come on!" He virtually salivated as he signalled for the bill. "I'll show you round your new flat."

Annabel suppressed a shudder, reminding herself that she'd just found a way to forward her ambitions by doubling her salary *and* getting a fancy place to live, rent free.

Chapter Five

"Hey, baby." Mark's voice echoed down the line. "I'm back from Brussels. Can I come down tomorrow?"

Suzie could tell from his tone that he was determined, but still she hesitated. "I'm not sure, Mark."

"I'll take you out to lunch somewhere nice."

"We need more time to adjust before we see each other."

"We also need to talk."

"We've said all there is to be said."

"We haven't even scratched the surface. There are a lot of things you don't understand."

"All right," she said with a sigh. "Come down but I'll cook."

"Great, see you about one then."

He sounded pleased, and she could imagine him arrogantly assuming that she'd already weakened. He would think she wanted to be alone with him, that a week on her own was more than enough to bring her scuttling back to him, tail between her legs.

He would be partially right on both counts, damn him! The idea of actually seeing him again was both thrilling and terrifying. She could already sense his compelling presence, the eloquent, persuasive charm he would deploy in an effort to entice her back. Unsure how prepared her battered heart was to withstand such a forceful assault she felt what little peace of mind she'd managed to gain over the past week literally draining out of her. Even so, if Mark expected the Suzie of old to simply play into his hands, then he was in for a surprise. She would cook lunch but not just for him. She'd invite Jane and some of the gang from The Grange as well.

Pleased with herself, Suzie issued the invitation to Jane when she dropped in that afternoon. She extended it to include Gordon, Ellen, and, reluctantly, Pansy. They were the mainstay of Jane's organisation and the people from The Grange whom she saw the most.

"Any special occasion?" Jane asked.

Suzie grimaced. "Mark's insisting upon coming down."

"Ah, so we get to meet the hunk at last."

"There's no at last about it. I've only been here a week. Less, actually."

"Well, it seems like longer."

"I'm not sure how to take that," Suzie said, pretending to take offence.

"And you don't want to be alone with said hunk?"

Suzie glowered at her. "Stop trying to analyse everything I do and tell me if you want roast beef and all the trimmings or not?"

"Absolutely." Jane grinned. "Just pointing out that I've got your measure. There's no such thing as a free lunch, but that's okay, I'm quite willing to play my part."

"That's what I'm worried about."

"Are you extending your invitation to include Jack?"

"Probably better not to."

"Whyever not?"

Suzie hesitated. How much did Jane know, or suspect, about Jack's interest in her. Before she could decide, Jane spoke again.

"A little healthy competition never did any man harm."

Suzie sighed. "I can't play those sorts of games, Jane. I'm no good at them."

"Then you should learn the rules. Give him a taste of his own medicine and see how he likes it. Anyway, Jack usually has lunch at The Grange on a Sunday, so if we're coming here, you can hardly leave him out. I'll tell him, shall I?"

Suzie nodded reluctantly, forced into a position that didn't sit comfortably with her. "Okay, I suppose you'd better bring him along."

"Good, that's settled then, and if nothing else, it'll please Pansy."

"I've been meaning to ask you about that," Suzie said as she spooned tea into the pot and put a plate of biscuits between them on the kitchen table. "How come you're so lenient with her? You seem to give her much more latitude than the others."

"That's because Pansy's a special case."

"She must be. I haven't noticed you letting the others get away with her sort of attitude."

"Pansy's mother sells herself to feed her drug habit, and Pansy's been in and out of care since she was a baby. Then she somehow slipped through the net and finished up living permanently with her mother. Last place she should have been because a number of her perverted clients set their sights on the kid, and her mother let them."

"God, how awful!"

"Quite. Pansy was ten the first time it happened to her. The men beat her as well. So did her mother if she wasn't compliant. Pansy ran away three years ago, when she was fourteen. She was picked up immediately by a pimp, of course. It was bound to happen to a vulnerable kid like her. Those sorts of men can recognize Pansy's type at a glance."

Suzie shuddered. "And there was me thinking I had problems."

"Worse things happened to her after that," Jane said, talking over Suzie's interruption. "I came across her by chance in a hospital where she was recovering from a suicide attempt and offered to take her in. She's the only one that was officially placed with me by Social Services." Jane snorted. "I'm not flavour of the month with the authorities anymore, but that's another story. Anyway, as Pansy is now over sixteen, they can't take her away. It took her months to trust me enough to tell me all that had happened to her and longer still for her to realize that she'd finally found safety at The Grange."

"That's really terrible. I'll try and ignore her truculent attitude in future and be nicer."

"Yes, that might help, but for God's sake, don't let her think you're being deliberately kind to her. That will freak her out." Jane stretched. "I'm not saying that what happened to her is out of the ordinary. That, and worse, happens to loads of kids. But she's the only one that's come into my care. All the others have less harrowing tales to tell."

"Yes, but still." Suzie sipped at her tea, lost in thought. "It beats me how any mother could put her own welfare before that of her child."

"That's because you've never been addicted to drugs."

"I suppose."

"Pansy was petrified of all men when she came to me and didn't want anything to do with the boys I take in."

"That's hardly surprising."

Jane reached for a biscuit and munched away. "It's taken her this long to regain some sort of confidence in herself," she said round a mouthful of crumbs. "That's what being used by men did to her. Her self-esteem was nonexistent. She was made to feel that she was good for only one thing, and I didn't know how to change that. But things unexpectedly took a turn for the better when she first set eyes on Jack. It's probably the first time she's ever reacted to a good-looking man naturally and shows she's recovering. Jack hasn't ever shown any partiality for her but that doesn't seem to deter her." Jane paused and smiled at Suzie to soften her next words. "Then you came along, and Jack appears to have fallen headfirst."

"But I don't—"

"I know that, but Pansy doesn't. Jack never misses an opportunity to talk to me about you, wanting to know if I think you'll go back to Mark." Suzie made to speak, but Jane silenced her with a gesture. "I know, I know, you didn't encourage Jack and aren't interested in him. But Pansy doesn't understand that yet. It's a hard lesson for her but one she has to learn. I just don't want to see her set back by it, that's all."

"Should I try and talk to her?"

"No, leave it to me. She'll come round. In spite of the only side of her you've seen so far, she's actually a nice kid."

"I'm sure she is."

"Well," said Jane draining her mug and standing up, "this won't do. See you on Sunday, if not before."

Suzie kept herself busy on Sunday morning, making preparations for lunch. She intended to push the boat out. Not to impress Mark, of course, but to thank her new friends for their collective kindness over the past week. Besides, she liked cooking, was good at it, and could move around now well enough to make more of an effort. She'd do traditional roast rib of beef. And not just because it was Mark's favourite but because she'd promised Jane. There would be smoked salmon and large prawns with a spicy dip to start with, and she'd make a Pavlova for dessert. She could prepare most of it in advance but still have enough to do when Mark arrived to prevent her having to sit alone with him for long.

As usual, Suzie was so organized that more than an hour before Mark was due she had already run out of things to do. She coaxed the reluctant boiler into life and took a long soak in the bath, forcing herself to relax. But she had still dried her hair and was dressed and ready half an hour ahead of time. Suzie examined her appearance critically in her grandmother's peeling pier glass. It was hot again, and she'd opted for a simple outfit, having no intention of letting Mark think she'd dressed up for his benefit. An old, floaty printed summer skirt, a simple black vest, and black wedges on her feet. Her hair she brushed and allowed to float loose, a touch of mascara and pale lipstick.

She ought to look pale and fatigued, given the amount of sleep time she'd given up to agonising about her wretched husband. Her eyes ought to have permanent bags beneath them, given the amount of crying she'd done. She ought to have lost weight, and her clothes should be hanging off her. But Suzie could see that the reverse was true. Her eyes sparkled, her skin looked fresh and slightly tanned due to the amount of time she'd spent sitting on the terrace in the sunshine, and thanks to her bossy new friends, she'd not been permitted to give up food and waste away. If Mark expected to find a shadow of her former self, then he was in for a surprise. The thought gave Suzie's confidence a much-needed boost, and she went back downstairs, Sparkle at her heels, taking deep, calming breaths as she awaited his arrival.

He was early. Suzie heard the distinctive sound of his car as soon as it entered the drive. She waited for him to knock rather than running to open the front door before he was even out of the car, as she would have done as recently as two weeks ago. The changes that she recognized in herself gave her courage. When he did knock, Suzie took her time traversing the hall, attempting to subdue the horde of butterflies that had taken up residence in her stomach. Sparkle, unhindered by finer feelings, reached the doorway before her, tail wagging in recognition even though he couldn't see through the solid oak.

Suzie paused with her hand on the latch, took a deep, fortifying breath, and wrenched the door open. The sight of Mark standing there, wearing blue Levi's, an open neck white shirt with the sleeves rolled back to reveal strong, tanned forearms, and deck shoes on his bare feet made her physically flinch. He looked devastating. He'd obviously had the roof down on his car, and his thick hair had been blown into curly disarray, only enhancing the beauty in his chiselled features. He removed his sunglasses, and the expression in those remarkable chocolate eyes melted as he regarded her.

"Hello, Suzie. You look ravishing."

"Come in," she said.

Suzie stepped back to let him pass her, wondering how she'd managed to keep her voice so even when her stomach was performing Olympic-standard summersaults. Mark hesitated for some time, his eyes not once leaving her face. Suzie met his gaze steadily, determined not to be influenced by it, or intimidated. The tension, the raw sexual attraction, the chemistry between them was palpable and hit her like a bolt of lightning. Mark felt it, too. Suzie could tell that much from the change in his expression. He appeared surprised, as though he hadn't expected it to be so brutal. She could understand her husband's confusion, she could even find it in her to sympathise with his predicament because she hadn't expected anything quite so cataclysmic either.

But it changed nothing, Suzie reminded herself, looking away first. It broke the spell, and Mark stepped into the house. He looked as though he wanted to touch her, but she flinched away from him, not trusting her treacherous body in its present state of heightened awareness to remain impassive to any form physical contact. Before the situation could become awkward, Sparkle intervened, jumping up at Mark and wiggling his whole body ecstatically. Suzie silently condemned her dog as a traitor but took advantage of Sparkle's diversionary tactics and preceded Mark into the drawing room where the French doors were open to the sun-drenched terrace.

Mark handed her a huge bouquet of her favourite white lilies, along with a large box of Belgium chocolates and placed several bottles of what she knew would be excellent wine on the table.

"Thank you."

"You're welcome." He looked at her for a long time, as though drinking in her appearance. "It's good to see you, Suzie." He paused and offered her his full wattage smile. She felt weak at the knees and fuzzy headed as she absorbed it, suddenly finding it hard to remember what madness was causing her to reject this gorgeous male specimen. "I've missed you."

"I'll just put these in water, and then we'll sit outside, shall we?"

"Sure, I'll open a bottle of wine." He followed her into the kitchen. "Something smells good."

Mark poured two generous glasses of wine and carried them out to the terrace. When he saw the long metal table beautifully laid up for seven with crisp white linen and her grandmother's best china, he stopped dead in his tracks.

"What's going on?"

"Lunch, of course," she said, not looking at him. "Isn't that what you came down for?"

He quirked a brow. "For seven?"

"Yes, a few other friends are coming."

"This was supposed to be just the two of us," he said, frowning.

"Was it?" She turned away from him, taking an unnecessary amount of time to settle into a chair. He loomed over her, large and powerful, looking annoyed. Too late she realized that by sitting she'd put herself at a disadvantage.

"You know it was. We have lots to talk about."

"So you keep saying, but I don't see it myself." She patted the chair next to her. "Do sit down, Mark, it's giving me neck ache looking up at you."

He complied with obvious reluctance. "Who are these friends then? I didn't know you knew anyone down here now."

She told him about Jane and the others, making no mention of Jack.

"Ah," he said, stretching his legs out in front of him and sounding relieved. "That explains all those mysterious men who answered the phone."

She flashed a circumspect smile. "If you say so."

"Don't, Suzie," he said in a snarl. "Don't play those games."

She wanted to point out that he'd started it when he couldn't keep his hands off Kate's plastic tits but knew it would sound juvenile. "They were a godsend," she said instead, "when I first got here and couldn't move about."

"I'm glad they've looked after you, but I could have done that if you'd stayed at home."

"What, from Brussels?"

"I could have made arrangements for someone to come in."

"Well, you didn't need to. I can look after myself."

Mark sighed. “I didn’t know you could be so stubborn.”

“There’s a lot you don’t know about me.” She shrugged. “I’m only just discovering a few things for myself as it happens.”

“What time are your new friends arriving?”

“One thirty.”

Mark consulted his slim gold Cartier watch. “Then we still have some time alone.”

Her turned toward her and attempted to take her hand. Suzie snatched it away, feeling as though her skin had been scorched where his fingers had briefly made contact. He didn’t pursue his attempts to touch her but smiled instead. It was a curling, glamorous smile that caused her insides to literally melt with a desire. But that was probably the point, and she mentally upbraided herself for being such a pushover.

“Suzie, what can I do to persuade you to come back to me? I promise you that things will be different in future.”

“Empty promises, Mark,” she said, her voice laced with sadness. “Oh, I know you want me back and that right now you mean what you’re saying. But it won’t last.” She expelled a long breath. “You’ll get caught up in the corporate jungle again and revert to type. You won’t be able to help yourself.”

“No, you’re wrong about that.” He shook his head emphatically, sending heavy locks cascading across his forehead. “Your leaving me has made me realize what’s important.”

“I don’t doubt it, for the moment. But in another month or two, when you’re stuck in some godforsaken hotel somewhere, temptation will get the better of you.” She waved his protests aside. “And even if it doesn’t, I’ll still be left at home imagining all sorts of terrible things going on.” She turned to look him fully in the eye for the first time since he’d arrived. “I can’t trust you anymore, and I’ll never feel a moment’s peace when we’re not together.”

“I’ve been thinking about that and—”

“I’m not as religious as my parents, you know that, but my

marriage vows meant something to me, and I've never broken them."

Mark sighed. "I know that, angel. That's one of the many reasons why I love you so much."

He succeeded in capturing her hand in a firm grasp this time and looked straight into her eyes, his expression candid and full of unadulterated love. She felt her resolve wavering under the full force of his sincerity. She called upon the images, never far from the surface, of Mark and Kate together, but just when she needed them the most, they were slow in materialising. When they finally did arrive, they weren't as sharp as usual and the ensuing pain was far less acute. Nevertheless, she struggled to renew her determination. Before she could do so, as though sensing the fact that she was wavering, Mark went in for the kill.

"I love you, Suzie. I'm so sorry I hurt you." He kissed the back of the hand he was holding, allowing his tongue to linger as it swirled intricate patterns on her skin. "Come back home to me."

Suzie pulled her hand away and looked at her husband through tear-filled eyes.

"I can't," she said. "I won't put myself through that agony again. I deserve better than that."

Disappointment was etched in his expression. "You don't believe I can change the way I live?"

"I believe you want to try." She attempted a smile that would convince no one, least of all Mark, who knew her so well. "But it isn't just that. It's a question of the life I want for myself. There's nothing for me in Epsom anymore. It was different when I had a job, when Granny was still alive, and I had…" Her voice faltered, but she ploughed on. Had to find a way to say what she felt. She owed him at least that much. "When I had friends." She was thinking of Kate, and they both knew it. "Kate's children gave me a purpose, but obviously I can't see them now." She starred off into the distance. "I expect they're wondering what's become of me."

Mark ran a hand through his hair. "Suzie, don't—"

"I don't know why she did it," she said reflectively. Seeing his surprised expression, she smiled. "Oh yes, I've had all week to think about it, and I realize now that you were telling the truth, at least about that. She obviously set you up, wanted me to see you together. The problem that's been plaguing me ever since is why. I thought we had a special friendship. I thought she and Graham were happy together. Why would she want to jeopardise all that and hurt her children into the bargain? What sort of mother, what sort of friend, could do that?"

"So you don't blame me?" Mark looked as though he couldn't quite believe what he was hearing.

"Did I say that? I believe Kate was being deliberately malicious for some convoluted reasons of her own, but you didn't have to go along with her."

"I know, and I did try to walk out. I didn't—"

"Quit whilst you're ahead, Mark," she said tightly. "Don't make it worse by lying."

Suzie reach for her stick and stood to pace the terrace, too agitated to sit still and let this arrogant charmer woo her with his clever words.

"If I could have moved with my job to the new surgery, there would have been more for me in Epsom." She eyed her husband. "But you didn't want me to do that."

"It was full-time," he said. "You don't need to work at all, much less full-time."

"God, do you know how old-fashioned that makes you sound?"

"I just want to look after you, Suzie. Is that so bad?"

"No, it's not bad," she said, sighing. "But have you stopped to consider how much time I spend on my own? You're away during the week more than you're home. Perhaps I need something worthwhile to fill my hours."

"I thought you understood about my work," he said quietly. "It won't always be this crazy."

"No, it won't because in the end you'll burn out."

"You didn't complain about being bored or unhappy."

"What would have been the point?" she asked, resignation in her tone. "And anyway, I wasn't—until recently. I know how important your job is to you and how hard you work. But you didn't seem to realize that simply keeping house for you and waiting patiently for you to return home wasn't enough for me. I have a brain, too, but it's dying from lack of stimulation."

"Oh God, Suzie, I didn't have a clue!" He dropped his head into his splayed hands and shook it from side to side. "Why didn't you say?"

"Say what? That I want a baby? That I want to see more of you?" She squared her shoulders and held his gaze. They both knew how often she'd suggested the former. "What do you think my recent depression's been about?"

He stood and reached for her but she moved out of range. "I'm sorry. I don't know what else to say. It was never my intention to make you unhappy."

"I know that, but since I've been down here, it's given me time to do some thinking. I love the countryside, and no," she continued, holding up her hand, "Epsom isn't really countryside. It's just part of the widening suburban sprawl. I love this house, too. Oh, I know it'll have to be sold soon, but I can stay here for the months that takes and get things sorted for my parents. Don't suppose they'll want to do it themselves. Anyway, perhaps afterward I can buy myself a small cottage down here and find work. I'd like that."

"You don't have to worry about money, Suzie. I'll always look after you, no matter what."

She sighed. "You just don't get it, do you?"

"Get what?"

"I want to be my own person. Be self-supporting and prove to myself that I can make a difference, however small, in an area that's important to me."

Mark caught her arm as she paced past him and placed his hands on her shoulders. “Suzie,” he said fiercely, “look me in the eye and tell me you don’t love me anymore.” He offered her a curling smile, full of love and unfulfilled promise. “If you can do that, then I’ll stop fighting you and let you go. I’ll even help you to find your cottage.” He placed his index finger beneath her chin and tilted her head until she was forced to look into his face. “Well, come on then,” he said, when she didn’t immediately take up his challenge, “let’s get this over with.”

Suzie was in a quandary. She had never lied to Mark in her life. If she did so now, then she’d be free and could start to get over him. It was easy. All she had to do was to say those few simple words. “*I don’t love you anymore, Mark.*” That was all it would take, and he’d release her.

She simply couldn’t do it. Even though she hadn’t yet spoken, she could see from Mark’s guardedly triumphant expression that he knew he’d won.

“Tell me, Suzie,” he said, increasing the pressure he was placing on her shoulders.

“I can’t, I don’t know what I—”

“Hello there, trust we’re not interrupting anything?”

Jane’s strident voice caused them to move apart like guilty lovers and turn in unison to face the gang striding up the garden path.

“Fuck it!” muttered Mark under his breath. “We’ll continue this conversation later.”

With lightning speed, he dropped a gentle kiss on her lips. Suzie, completely unprepared, gasped in astonishment at the way her treacherous body reacted so enthusiastically. Annoyed that Mark had noticed, cheeks burning with embarrassment, she turned away and hobbled toward her friends.

* * * *

Greenberg drove her back to the flat in silence, removed his jacket, poured himself a brandy, and settled in an armchair. Annabel glanced about, with no particular interest in the luxurious space. It was expensively yet spartanly furnished, with no additional little bits and pieces to make it seem like home. It would remain that way. Annabel had no sentiment to waste on transient living quarters.

"Like it?" John asked.

Annabel was probably supposed to gush, but gushing was something else she didn't do. "It's fine," she said with a marked lack of enthusiasm.

Her response clearly unsettled him, but to comment upon it would imply that he cared what she thought. That, presumably, explained why he said nothing more on the subject. "Undress," he said, scowling.

This was it, her last opportunity to back out. But backing out wasn't an option. Slowly, she removed her clothes.

His eyes never left her, and she could imagine what he was thinking. Annabel was no oil painting, and she knew it. She'd worked on downplaying any bits of her that might attract attention. She wanted to blend in, not make an exhibition of herself. At five foot two, she was short enough to pass through life unnoticed. At seven stone, she was thin enough to slip through its cracks.

"You need to put on at least ten pounds," he said as though reading her thoughts. "I like meat on my women's bones. Hopefully that'll fill out those tits. Can't be doing with those fried eggs of yours."

Annabel made no response but had absolutely no intention of putting on weight. She had taken obsessive care over the years, using the same iron self-control over her diet as she did over every other aspect of her life. Fat women with pendulous breasts got more attention than Annabel could handle. John had bought her, but he didn't own her and never would.

She cupped her small breasts in her own hands and tweaked the nipples as she walked toward him, knocking his hands away as he reached for her.

"Wait!" she commanded.

Annabel knelt in front of him and unzipped his fly. A huge erection, angry red veins prominent along its length, sprang out to greet her.

"My, my, what a big boy we are!"

She had to bite her lip to stop herself laughing at such a ridiculous statement, but he seemed pleased by the praise. Men were *sooo* predictable. She brought him to a swift climax and swallowed his sperm without any show of distaste, wiped her mouth with the back of her hand, and beckoned to him with that same hand. Might as well let him see what he was getting for his money.

"Come on," she said. "Show me the bedroom."

"Christ, Annabel," he said, almost tripping over as he stood up and his unfastened trousers crumpled round his ankles. "I had you pegged right all along."

"And me you," she muttered beneath her breath.

As they walked through the flat, he continued to lay out his terms. "Just remember what I said, I like it rough and kinky," he warned her. "If I feel in need of a submissive missionary, I'll go home to my wife."

"I thought you said she was off sex."

"She's off the sort that I like, which is why between us nothing's taboo." He patted her naked rear but needn't have bothered because she'd already got the message. "Nothing at all. I don't kiss, I don't dole out meaningless endearments, I seldom give gifts, and I expect complete obedience for my money. Oh, and a word to the wise, if you see someone else, I'll know about it and you'll be out on your ear." He paused. "That's out of a job as well as a flat," he said. "But if after five years you've stuck to your side of the bargain, then this flat will be yours outright and you'll be free to go your own way. Deal?"

"Deal," she agreed dispassionately.

"There's some stuff in that cupboard," he said, shedding his clothes. "Put it on."

A latex cat suit with a split crotch, boots with four-inch heels, *and* a mask. She rolled her eyes and pulled it all on, feeling absolutely nothing. When she emerged, he was lying naked on the bed, another erection and a stupid grin his only adornments.

"Walk on me," he said, his voice thick, his eyes bulging in anticipation.

By the time he'd finished with her, Annabel no longer felt quite so in control. He'd had her through every orifice and taken his time about it. His staying power was remarkable, and she could only hope that his initial enthusiasm would wane. Whatever, she remembered the ridiculous amount of money he was paying her and decided it was worth a bit of discomfort.

"I've wanted you like this since that first day when you walked in for that interview, all buttoned-up tight and businesslike. I kept wondering what you'd be like." He snarled at her. "You don't disappoint," he said, burying himself in her yet again.

Finally, he'd had enough and reached for his cigarettes.

"I've got a job I need you to do for me off the books," he said. "And it's right up your alley."

"Tell me," she said, taking the cigarette he offered her.

"There's a place in Malton called The Grange. I want possession of it. I gave the job to Reggie, but he's made a balls-up of it, and the people are sitting tight. Hopefully you can do better."

That shouldn't be too hard. "Why do you want it?" she asked.

He told her.

"I see. What's in it for me?"

"My god, you're a mercenary little bint, aren't you?"

"Everything in life's about money, John, you told me that yourself."

"Okay, do this and there's a four-figure bonus in it for you."

"Consider it done," she said, putting out her cigarette and heading for the shower.

Chapter Six

Mark switched to full social mode and held out his hand to Jane before the introductions were even completed. His irritation at having their conversation interrupted at such a vital point was obvious only to Suzie.

"Well now." Jane elevated her brows and cast a wicked sideways glance at Suzie. "There was obviously nothing wrong with Granny's eyesight." Suzie winced. What was supposed to be a quiet aside came out at full volume. "Nice to meet you, Mark."

"And you." He oozed charm, the conniving rat. "Suzie's told me a lot about you."

She shot him an accusatory look. Naturally, he ignored it.

"Really? Funny that, she hasn't told me anything about you."

Suzie could have kissed her.

Pansy greeted Mark with a display of overt flirtatiousness.

"Jack's still with the piglets, but he'll be up here soon," she said with a devious glance at Suzie. "Said he couldn't wait to see you. Always seems to be in a hurry when he's coming here, does our Jack."

"Jack?" Mark looked mildly interested.

"Oh, didn't Suzie explain?" Pansy jumped in again. "He's our local vet." She accepted the beer Suzie handed her with a nod of thanks. "He took Suzie to the pub quiz on Monday."

"He drove her there to join the rest of us because of her ankle," Jane said.

Suzie took one look at the set to Mark's features and beat a hasty retreat. "I'll just get the vegetables going," she said.

"We'll help," Gordon and Ellen said together.

Suzie dealt with the vegetables and sent her helpers back outside to have a drink. She delayed her own return for as long as possible, finding excuses to linger. Never before had a piece of beef been coaxed through the cooking process with such assiduous care. Only the sound of Jack's voice stirred her reluctantly into action.

As she stepped onto the terrace, Mark and Jack were shaking hands, sizing one another up. Suzie viewed them in speculative silence, convinced she could sense the animosity radiating from them in waves. Mark was several inches taller than Jack, but they were both extremely good-looking men. The fact that they were both taking more than a passing interest in her worked wonders for her low self-esteem. They noticed her at the same time and both turned toward her, smiling. Jack walked up to her and kissed her cheek. Avoiding Mark's eye, Suzie asked him what he would like to drink, and the tension eased.

The meal was a success, at least as far as the food was concerned. Everything was perfect, apart from the fact that Mark assumed the role of host. He ensured that the wine flowed, carved the meat, and kept the conversation on an even keel. He was naturally good at such things, probably due to all the time he spent living in hotels and dining with colleagues. Today she was grateful for that skill. Her emotions were in turmoil, and she was unequal to the task of paying her guests proper attention. All she was aware of—the only person who engaged her attention—was the formidable figure of her husband. He was completely at his ease, laughing at something Jane had said to him as though he didn't have a care in the world, whilst she was a bundle of nerves. She could cheerfully have throttled him.

As dessert was being cleared away, Jack's mobile rang.

"Sorry, Suzie," he said, hanging up, "emergency at Clay Farm. Have to dash. Are you up for the quiz tomorrow?"

Suzie hesitated, about to refuse. But something in Mark's expression caused her to change her mind.

"Yes, why not? But I can make my own way there now. See you at the pub."

"Great!"

He kissed her cheek again, thanked her for lunch, and was gone.

Jane despatched the kids, including a truculent Pansy, to clear up the kitchen and make coffee. Grateful to Jane for not leaving her alone with Mark, Suzie forced herself to relax. If Mark didn't feel under any strain, why the hell should she?

"Are you settled permanently at The Grange, Jane?" Mark asked.

"Well, that was my intention."

"But…"

Jane sighed. "The locals, well, some of them anyway, don't seem to like me very much."

Mark quirked a brow. "Why? Who are you hurting?"

"No idea, but someone's got it in for me. In the two years I've been here, I've had the tax inspectors put onto me because someone told them I was running a business selling animals. Then Charity Commissioners accused me of running an Animal Charity without charity status or proper licensing. I've had Social Services skulking about because I was reported for taking in underage kids." Jane ticked the points off on her fingers. "Those are the more serious complaints to date, but since they've failed to budge me, I daresay someone will dream up more before too long."

"Aren't people vindictive!" Suzie was outraged by the pettiness of it all.

Mark covered her hand with one of his own. "I reckon Jane gives as good as she gets."

"Too right! I never intended to run a business and sent that slimy little tax man away with one of the dog's fleas in his ear."

Mark chuckled. "I'd like to have seen that."

"The animal charity's a different matter though." She took a long sip of wine, presumably using it to quell her resentment. "That was my original plan, but when I discovered just what rigmarole was involved—the licensing, the insurances, the health and safety aspects—I decided not to bother. Should have looked into it all first before jumping in and buying The Grange, I suppose, but then I've always been impulsive."

"There are probably ways round all that."

"There would be if people left me alone and minded their own bloody business."

"Point taken."

"Anyway, the only serious problem was Social Services. The bastards neglected most of the kids that finished up with me in the first place, too busy with their red tape to listen to their problems. But there was never going to be an easy way round that one, and so I stopped taking any kids under sixteen." She shrugged. "Shame, but it's the only way."

"It doesn't make any sense," Suzie said. "The kids would be much better off with you than in care. Just look at Gordon and some of the others you've turned round."

"I agree with you." Jane stretched her arms above her head and sighed. "But meddling, pen-pushing little Hitlers are a fact of life in this nanny state we've created."

"Are you being left in peace now?" Mark asked.

Jane harrumphed. "Don't be daft. That's never going to happen. There have been niggling problems from day one. People sneaking onto the land and leaving gates open, bricks through windows, damage to cars, my water supply accidentally cut off, that sort of thing. Fortunately no one has deliberately tried to hurt the animals. If they did, I'd really get mad. Anyway, the latest thing is a notice from the council regarding noise pollution."

"Who's being disturbed by your noise? You're in a pretty isolated location."

"Good question. Apart from Suzie here, the only people who can hear us are the residents of the cottages to our north."

"Are they owner occupied?"

"No. There're two terraces of half a dozen cottages each, and they're all let. Some of the kids that live with their families there are real tearaways, always causing mayhem, so I don't see how anyone there could have the gall to complain about us."

"If their kids are wild," Mark said, frowning, "then Social Services would know about them and be on their cases. Why draw attention to themselves by complaining about distant neighbours?"

"That's what I'd like to know."

"What noise do you supposedly cause?" Suzie asked, this being the first she'd heard of this latest problem.

"Well, there are twelve of us living at The Grange, plus we have about a dozen rescued dogs at the moment and—"

"How do you home the dogs if you're not allowed to set up as a charity, Jane?" Suzie asked.

Jane grimaced. "Not easily, mostly word of mouth. No money changes hands, and anyone coming onto the land to look at the animals signs a disclaimer, so if they break their necks tripping over a bucket of pig shit, then we're not to blame."

Mark smiled. "Very sensible."

"Yeah well, I've never been one to back away from a fight. Anyway, Suzie, you asked about homing the animals. If someone wants a dog or cat, we check out their home to make sure it's suitable and then let them take their new pet. It's funny," she said with an impish smile, "but when they hear about our impecunious state, they offer a donation. We can't accept, of course, just in case someone has been deliberately sent to catch us out. What we can legitimately do is accept reimbursement for vet's fees. Every cat or dog has to be fully vaccinated and neutered before we home it. That's where Jack helps so much. He gives us receipts for the full amount but charges us less, and we make a little bit back that way."

"Is it the dogs that are accused of making a noise?" Mark asked.

Jane grinned. "And the cockerel, but he's a daft idiot with a wonky body clock. If we waited for him to wake us up, half the day would be gone."

"Yes, I heard his dawn chorus at eleven o'clock this morning," Suzie said, smiling.

"There you are then." Jane spread her hands and then used one of them to reach for the bottle and top up her glass. Mark anticipated her and did the honours. "Thanks," she said, taking another healthy swig. Suzie wondered what it took to get her tiddly. She drank like a fish, and it never seemed to affect her. "And as for the dogs, as we've only got a dozen, I can't bear to keep them outside in runs. They live in The Grange along with the rest of us. They all get along well enough. Obviously they bark sometimes but never for long and not late at night unless a stranger comes anywhere near."

"Have you received a written complaint from the council?" Mark asked.

"Unfortunately yes."

"Was it an official abatement notice?" Jane shrugged. "What did it say?"

"Not too sure on either count either. It was in officialese, you see."

"Ah, I do indeed see." Mark was silent for a moment, and Suzie knew that his incisive brain would be processing the problem, looking for an angle. "Noise abatement rules can vary widely between town and country and from council to council. If I remember correctly, local authorities can evoke individual bylaws, peculiar to their particular area. The problem is that some of them have been on the statute books for centuries and don't have any particular bearing on the way we live today."

"But surely, Mark," Suzie said, "as this is definitely country, having relatively few animals on a large piece of land can't be construed as a nuisance?"

"Quite right, sweetheart." Mark took her hand and squeezed her fingers. "But unless we know what bylaw they're seeking to invoke, it's difficult for me to say." He looked at Jane. "I'll look into it for you, if you like. Get the notice you received to me, and I'll see what I can do."

"Would you really?" Jane brightened. "Thanks. Pansy, be a love," she said to the teenager who'd chosen the wrong moment to re-emerge from the house, "pop back to The Grange and get that wretched letter the council sent about noise."

Pouting, Pansy complied with obvious reluctance.

"Could it all be a ploy, do you suppose?" Mark asked. "Someone wants you out so they can purchase The Grange cheaply."

"Same thought had occurred to me, but I don't think so. The property had been on the market for a long time before I bought it. It was so dilapidated that no one wanted to invest in it."

"But if you've done it up—"

"Ha, don't get carried away. I've done some basics, but it's still a dump."

Smiling at Jane's cheerful description of her ramshackle home, Mark refilled everyone's glasses and relaxed back in his chair. Denim-clad ankle crossed over his opposite thigh, he gazed across the gardens.

"Shame about your grandfather's gardens looking so neglected," he said to Suzie. "I remember them always being pristine."

"Yes, I feel guilty about them. I should have thought to have a gardener come once granny went into care."

"No matter." Mark's smile was exclusively for her. "Still got that ride-on contraption?"

"Yes, I think so. It's in the outhouse."

"Any petrol for it?"

"Ah, I don't know about that."

"Come on, Gordon." Mark sprang athletically to his feet. "There's work to be done."

Ten minutes later, Jane and Suzie, alone on the terrace and nursing oversized glasses of wine, heard the ancient mowing machine grumble reluctantly into life. A lot of rather worrying clanking, laughter, a few choices curses, and then plumes of exhaust smoke emanated from the outhouse.

"Should we be concerned?" Jane asked, sounding completely unconcerned.

"No, it always makes that noise. Mark will sort it."

As if to prove her right, Mark drove the old machine sedately out of its shed, steered it toward the lawn and started cutting the long grass. Gordon trailed behind him with long-handled sheers. He winked at them as he trimmed the edges of the overgrown flower borders. Sparkle darted about in hot pursuit of the mower. The cats peered aristocratically down on the proceedings from a shady area further along the terrace. Honey sulked on Suzie's lap because she wasn't allowed to get involved.

"Quite a man, your old man," Jane remarked. "Hope you don't mind me taking up his offer of help."

Suzie had been trying to decide how she felt about that. Obviously she wanted Jane's problems solved, but was Mark using Jane's situation to spend more time at Shalimar?

"Right now I'm not sure how I feel about anything," she said.

"If you want my humble opinion," Jane said, not pausing for long enough to let Suzie say whether she did or not, "then I reckon that man is deeply in love with you, has received the fright of his life, and will mend his ways PDQ."

Suzie sighed. "If only it were that easy."

"I could be if you stop letting your pride stand in the way."

"I don't have any pride. Not anymore. Mark and Kate saw to that."

"Perhaps not right now, but Mark will make sure you feel good about yourself again." Jane levelled her eyes on Suzie's profile. "If you let him."

"Whose side are you on?" Suzie snapped.

"Just playing devil's advocate."

"Well, don't! Have another glass of wine and be quiet."

"Thought you'd never ask!"

Suzie watched in reluctant appreciation as Mark, stripped to the waist, worked his way round the large garden. Gordon, also shirtless, lifted the heavy grass box from the back of the mower and manhandled it in the direction of the old compost heap. Bulging, flexing pecs, titanium glutes, and washboard abs were the order of the day, and, unlike Suzie, Jane wasn't pretending not to be impressed. Pansy reappeared and did a double take when she saw the men. Her vapid expression turned to one of surprise and fascination, but it soon became obvious that it wasn't Mark's naked torso that held her attention. Jane rolled her eyes and took yet another swig of wine.

A couple of hours later everyone had left—with the notable exception of Mark. But by now Suzie was ready for him. She felt more composed, less inclined to be swayed by his compelling entreaties. When he renewed his demands that she tell him she no longer loved him, Suzie simply went with the truth.

"I'll always love you, Mark. I don't think I could stop if I tried." She paused and looked him directly in the eye. "And I know because I've tried." She let her breath out slowly, unaware that she'd been holding it in. "But it's not enough. I've told you how I feel. I can't go back to the way things were, and I can't ask you to change. Where does that leave us?"

"Suzie, I—"

"No, Mark, don't say anything else. Just go home and think about what you want."

"I don't need to think about it. I already know."

Suzie sighed. "I don't think you do, not really."

He tried to take her in his arms, but she pulled away and put distance between them. She couldn't allow him to touch her. Her resolve wasn't that strong.

"I'll be in Brussels again for most of the week, but can I come and see you again next weekend?"

"There's no point," she said wearily.

"Nevertheless, I intend to come." He patted the pocket containing

Jane's noise notice and grinned. "I should have some answers for Jane by then."

"Oh all right then." She capitulated with bad grace, knowing he'd come no matter what she said. If she was completely honest with herself, she wanted him to come. Not that she had any intention of being honest. She didn't need any reminders of just how pathetic she actually was, still clinging to the hope that they would somehow resolve a situation that was insoluble. "Come down if you must but don't expect me to have changed my mind."

* * * *

Annabel pulled herself up against the headboard and winced. John had been especially rough tonight, and she'd have trouble moving tomorrow. He'd probably bruised her again. He'd certainly bitten the inside of her thighs, and her breasts, too. He enjoyed being cruel, but she refused to give him the satisfaction of showing any reaction. It was probably why he'd warned her that he disliked female histrionics. Not many women would be able to take what he dished out without crying. That's probably what caused her predecessor to quit. What he didn't know about her was that she hadn't cried since she was fourteen.

She lit cigarettes for them both.

"We have a problem with The Grange," she told him, in business mode just seconds after being fucked so hard that he'd almost split her in two, or so it felt right now.

"Tell me," he said, drawing smoke deep into his lungs.

"The woman has got a fancy lawyer acting for her. He's written to the council demanding details of the complaints against her so he can construct her defence."

"You stupid bitch! I told you to go easy." He blew more smoke straight in her face. "Bloody hell, I should have left it with Reggie."

"It was your precious Reggie's actions that brought this about, not mine. I haven't done anything yet. If he'd been a bit more subtle—"

"Yeah okay, you've made your point."

"I have something up my sleeve that ought to work better than Reggie's heavy-handed tactics."

"Who is the lawyer?"

"Guy called Alexander."

John jerked his bulk upright. "Mark Alexander?"

"Yes."

"You stupid fuck!" He slapped her face hard.

"Ouch, what was that for?" She rubbed her cheek. "That hurt." She glowered at him. "Don't blame me for your son's inadequacies. He did this, not me."

"Go get the ropes," he snarled, erect again. "And the whip."

Annabel ground out her cigarette, resisting the urge to put it out on his fat gut—he'd probably enjoy the pain—and did as he asked.

"Tie me up," he said. "And bring that whip down hard across my arse. I wanna really feel it."

"My pleasure," she said, putting every ounce of strength she had behind it. If she lived to a hundred, she'd never understand why he enjoyed pain so much, both giving and receiving it. She'd be on the receiving end soon, when he got fed up with flagellation. It didn't matter. He could hurt her body, but he'd never touch her mind.

Chapter Seven

"We need a routine," Suzie told Sparkle at the start of the following week. "What do you think? Gramps's gardens are looking very sorry for themselves."

Spurred on by the sight of the beautifully cut lawns, she reckoned her ankle was now strong enough to support her through a couple of hours of gardening each morning. She took a hoe to her grandfather's once pristine flower borders and gently turned the rich loamy soil. She showed no mercy to the weeds that had the audacity to flourish in this previously forbidden territory and ruthlessly pruned the shrubs that had gotten well above themselves over the past couple of years.

It was a therapeutic occupation that required only gentle physical exertion as opposed to the cerebral variety. With her mind free to wander, Suzie tried to make sense of her situation. Was Jane right? Had she given Mark the shock of his life, enough to keep him faithful? Somehow, she doubted it and was angry with herself for finding it so difficult to resist his lethal charm offensive. He knew exactly how to play her, knew where all her weaknesses lay, and used them against her. Wearily, she conceded that to stand a chance of holding out against him she needed to make up her mind about the rest of her life. If she had a goal, perhaps she'd be able to forget about Mark. The nebulous plans floating through her mind were useless when pitted by Mark's implacable determination to lure her back.

Time wasn't on her side either. Her parents were due home soon, and when they arrived, she'd no longer be able to hide away at Shalimar, prevaricating, hoping for… Hoping for what exactly? What was it that she really wanted to do with her life?

Much to her annoyance, her mind refused to move beyond Mark. But not Mark as he was now—successful, personable, universally popular, impossibly busy, and never with her for more than a few days at a time. The Mark she craved wouldn't be the corporate wiz she was so used to sharing her life with. Instead, he would be softer, less stressed, prepared to live his life in the slow lane, more in tune with her own aspirations. A doting father to the baby she so desperately wanted.

Leaning on her hoe, Suzie shook her head, blaming the sunshine for prompting such fanciful notions. Mark could no more live that sort of life than she could fly to the moon. The situation was hopeless. Sighing, she readdressed her attention to the flower borders, unsurprised to sense her grandfather hovering about her like a celestial bodyguard.

"What should I do about him, Gramps?" she asked aloud at one point.

But any advice her worldly grandfather might once have offered had been buried with him ten years before, and Suzie was left to face the brutal realities of her life alone. No one could help her, and so she'd just have to pull herself together and help herself.

During the afternoons, Suzie continued to steadily work her way through her grandfather's books. Progress was slow because she kept discovering new treasures that required immediate investigation. She lost count of the number of times she was distracted by old favourites as well as authors hitherto unknown to her. The steadily growing pile of books she intended to read when she got the time was now in danger of toppling over.

Mark phoned every day, and just the sound of his voice with its hypnotic, persuasive undertones was enough to make her feel weak at the knees. She forced herself to be brisk and businesslike when she spoke to him. It was hard on her, and if the phone rang at a time when she was feeling especially vulnerable, she didn't answer it. He seemed to be able to sense her mood and used his charm to batter away at her defences. After the first time it happened, she no longer trusted herself to remain steadfast when her heart was screaming at her to do just the opposite.

The Grange crowd were giving her a bit more space now, but she still saw them regularly. Far from putting Jack off, meeting Mark had made him more persistent than ever. Suzie still refused to go out alone with him. She liked him, he was good company, but she found it relatively easy to resist his charm. She even began to wonder if he had some sort of hidden agenda. She'd made it obvious that she wasn't interested, but it didn't seem to make a blind bit of difference.

Early on Wednesday morning, Suzie decided to visit the out of town supermarket and restock her depleted supplies. As she headed for her car, still parked crookedly in Shalimar's driveway, she stopped dead in her tracks and gasped. Both of the near side tyres had been savagely slashed, and there was a deep gouge all along one wing. This was clearly malicious damage, and Suzie's mind turned unbidden to the occupants of the cottages behind Jane. Surely someone wasn't trying to make trouble for her as well? What could they possibly have to gain by acting so spitefully? Perhaps they knew she was friendly with Jane. It seemed tenuous, but she didn't know anyone else in the area, and so if it wasn't them, who else could it be?

Back in the house, Suzie thumbed through an out-of-date copy of the Yellow Pages and eventually found the number of a local garage. The man they sent out confirmed what Suzie already knew. The damage had been deliberate.

"Don't know what the world's coming to," the middle-aged mechanic said. "Should garage your car in future if I were you, love. Can't trust anyone nowadays."

The tyres were replaced easily enough, and the helpful man suggested a local mobile car repair service that would come out and re-spray the wing. By the time she'd phoned them and arranged for them to call on Friday, it was already midday. Still intent upon her shopping trip, Suzie was about to leave the house when her mobile rang.

"Ah, there you are, Suzanne. Where have you been? I've been trying to reach you at home all the morning."

Suzie's heart sank. "Hello, mother," she said. "Welcome home."

"Never mind all that. Where are you?"

And I love you, too! Suzie really had hoped that as usual her parents' return would be delayed by a few weeks. Just her luck, for the first time ever they were home on schedule.

"I'm at Shalimar," Suzie said reluctantly. She knew her mother would find out soon enough anyway but had no intention of admitting that she'd left Mark. She didn't have the strength right now for the argument that would inevitably ensue. "Mark's away this week." Well, that was true enough. "I thought I'd make myself useful by tidying the garden and starting to sort through things."

Suzie heard her mother sniff, temporarily outmanoeuvred, but it was a short-lived victory.

"Hmm, well I hope you haven't removed anything. Your father will want to see exactly what's what."

"No, mother," Suzie said, struggling to contain her temper. "Of course I haven't."

"All right then, you might as well tell the solicitors that we're back and can sign whatever is necessary to take the property over. I think it's a good time to sell, and we can certainly put the money to good use." Before Suzie could reply, her mother said she couldn't waste any more time talking to her. "Derek is due here any moment, and we have so much to tell him about our latest venture."

Suzie hung up in a foul temper. Not so much as one word of endearment from a mother whom she'd not seen for over six months. No enquires about her health—or Mark's. No voluntary information for Suzie's ears about their activities. But the moment her mother mentioned Derek, her voice changed from shrill inquisition to tolerant affection. Suzie didn't know why she should feel so deflated. It had always been that way, but somehow, today, it mattered. To know there was someone out there who cared about her welfare would have been a fillip.

With a heavy heart, she lifted the phone and called the solicitors. Mr. Latimer was delighted to know that matters could be resolved at last and asked Suzie if she and Mark, her parents, and brother could attend his office together at eleven o'clock on Monday morning. Suzie's heart plummeted to her toes. So soon? Events were starting to overtake her, and it was with tears in her eyes that she called Mr. Latimer back and confirmed her parents' availability. But why did he need to see Mark? She explained that her husband was abroad, blatantly lying when she said he wasn't contactable. The last thing she needed was the added complication of Mark's presence at a time when her ragged emotions were bound to be wound taut. He would know it and turn his instinctive empathy for her plight into a deadly temptation she'd be hard-pressed to resist. He could have no reason to be there any more than she or her brother needed to be, unless Granny had left them small bequests. That was probably what it was. It would be typical of the lady whom she'd loved considerably more dearly than her own mother.

Tossing and turning on Friday night, unable to sleep, Suzie started violently when Sparkle suddenly sprang up from his basket in the corner of the room and let forth with a volley of barks. He ran to the door and scratched at it. Disorientated, Suzie struggled to sit up, surprised by Sparkle's display. He rarely needed to relieve himself at night. She switched on the bedside light and groped for her robe, pulling it round her naked body. As soon as she opened the bedroom door, Sparkle flew down the stairs ahead of her and barked frantically at the front door. He jumped up at it, his barks now interspersed with rumbling growls. Suzie staggered down the stairs slowly in his wake, and as she did so, a distinctly unpleasant smell assailed her nostrils. Confused, still half-asleep, it took her a moment to realize that something had been posted through the letter box. Cautiously she bent down. There was a carrier bag dangling from its spring, dripping its slimy contents onto the floor. Almost overwhelmed by the noxious smell, Suzie was horrified to find that the bag contained wet dog excrement. What the hell was happening? Who had done this? And why?

Suzie shivered in spite of the warmth of the night, afraid and perplexed. But the longer she stood here the harder it would be to get rid of the smell. Resigned to the unpleasant task that faced her, she went into the kitchen, donned rubber gloves, grabbed a stout bin liner and kitchen towel, and started to clear up the mess. As she did so, the lights she had turned on to counter her shock at this horrible prank abruptly went out, and the house was plunged into total darkness.

Fear rendered Suzie temporarily motionless. Was someone in the house, or was it simply the unreliable power circuit playing up again? She felt Sparkle's reassuring presence at her side and held on to him tightly. It seemed that she stood frozen in the hall, her hand resting on Sparkle's collar, for an eternity. In actual fact, it couldn't have been more than a minute or two. Forcing herself to think rationally, she decided that local kids, fuelled by alcohol, had played a cruel joke with the dog shit. As for the lighting, that surely that was just a coincidence? She took a firmer hold on Sparkle and encouraged him to lead her towards the kitchen. Aware of the vagaries of the electrical system at Shalimar, she kept a strong torch there. She located it and, more confident now that she could see her hand in front of her face, followed its beam into the scullery where the fuse box was located. She breathed a sigh of relief. It was just as she had suspected. The main fuse had tripped out—again. It wasn't the first time it had happened since she'd been here, but it crossed her mind to wonder why it should happen in the middle of the night when nothing was switched on that could overload the system. Shrugging, she pushed the switch back up and relished the flood of light from the hall.

A noise drew her attention to the scullery window. It had swung wide open, squeaking as it rocked on its worn hinges. Her blood ran cold. She knew for a fact that the window had been closed before she went to bed. The scullery was Honey's domain, and to such an inquisitive rabbit, an open window would spell irresistible temptation.

Honey! Where was she? Suzie panicked for a moment as her eyes wildly scoured the room. No, it was all right. She was in the corner, contentedly munching on a collection of dandelion leaves Suzie had picked for her earlier. She barely bothered to look up at Suzie and Sparkle.

Suzie went into the drawing room and poured herself a substantial measure of brandy. If sleep had been difficult before, it would be impossible now. There could no longer be any doubt. Someone had been in the house, trying to frighten her. And whoever it was, he was doing a damned good job of it.

She returned to bed, resisting the temptation to call Mark and tell him about her problems. He would know exactly how to deal with them, but she *had* to look out for herself now and not rely on him. It was only kids being evil, probably targeting her just because she was a friend of Jane's. But by Saturday afternoon, other niggling incidents had frayed her nerves to frazzles, and she gave in and rang on the pretext of asking him to bring a few things down when he came.

But it wasn't Mark who answered the phone.

"Hello, Suzie, is that you?" She froze when she heard Kate's voice, refusing at first to believe it, unable to say a word. "Mark isn't here yet. Can I give him a message?"

"What? Who is this?" Like she didn't already know.

"It's me, Suzie." Kate put on the phony laugh that had always irritated Suzie. "Don't tell me you've forgotten your old friends already?"

* * * *

Annabel thought the meeting would drone on forever. For once, she was not giving the matters in hand her full attention, missing opportunities to shine in front of her colleagues or to expose the weaknesses in their arguments. Worse, John had to repeat questions aimed specifically at her because she was too preoccupied to realize he was addressing her. She felt her colleagues' astonished glances resting upon her, noticed their raised eyebrows and the exchange of significant looks between them. Annabel always had her fingers on the pulse and they must be enjoying this rare sloppy performance from her. The notion that they might consider her star to be in the decline forced her to concentrate. She was more than capable of out-performing all of them, even with only half her mind on the job, and hell would freeze over before they got the better of her.

The meeting did finally come to an end. Relieved, Annabel was one of the first to head for the door. She'd almost escaped when John's voice halted her.

"Annabel, a word please."

Reluctantly she turned back and waited whilst everyone else collected their papers together and shuffled out.

"What the fuck is wrong with you today?" he asked as soon as they were alone.

"Sorry, John, I'm not feeling too good. But I'll get onto the Brooker thing straight away."

"Don't worry about that. I've given it to Reggie."

"To Reggie!" Annabel was appalled. "After the way he botched something as straightforward as The Grange, you give him our best client to sweeten."

"I'll keep an eye on him. I need you to sort The Grange thing without any distractions. What do you intend to do?" She told him, and he nodded his approval. "Okay, but go easy. I don't want any more screw-ups. Now, come here and tell me what's really wrong."

Reluctantly, she walked round to his side of the desk and stood in front of him. He ran his beefy hand up her thigh, producing a sharp exclamation of pain from her.

"Sorry, Annabel, I guess I got a bit carried away yesterday, but you did ask for it. You should know better than to get me angry."

"It's okay," she said in her usual cool manner.

His face darkened, and she knew she'd played it wrong. He hated it when she attempted to put herself above him, but pain and abhorrence had, for once, made her incautious. He grabbed her by the wrist and pulled her onto his lap.

"Don't forget who you've sold yourself to, Annabel," he said in a deceptively mild voice. "Tonight we'll eat in. Order something for us." He patted her bruised rear in dismissal. "You're one hot chick, and I can't get enough of you." Annabel nodded, not trusting herself to speak. "It's your call tonight," he told her. "I'll leave it to you to devise some way to entertain me. Be inventive, you know the sort of thing I like." He grinned at her. "I'll be thinking about it all day, wondering what's in store for me."

Annabel's heart plummeted. She wouldn't normally expect to see him two nights running and knew he'd only suggested it to make a point. She'd angered him, and he was punishing her by reasserting his authority. She reached the door, only to be stayed once again by his voice. "Nothing too tame, mind," he warned, running his hand crudely over a very visible erection.

Annabel finally escaped and made a beeline for the ladies' cloakroom, ignoring the startled gazes of her fellow employees. None of them liked her. She'd thwarted the women's initial attempts at friendship, making it clear that she wasn't the type to enjoy girly nights out. They now considered her to be stuck-up and humourless. The men, some of whom had made advances of a different kind, had been handled with equal disdain. It must be obvious to them all that she was suffering today. The bruise on her face couldn't be completely concealed, even with the thickest of base makeup. No doubt they were enjoying themselves at her expense, but what did she care for the little people? Still, it was just as well that they couldn't see the heavy bruising John had inflicted on her thighs and stomach, the gouges, angry red wheals, and bite marks on her breasts. She had been the last to arrive at the meeting, unable to walk steadily across the room without wincing. John had noticed, of course, and she saw satisfaction flash briefly across his face.

He was a mean, vindictive bastard. She'd known that from the outset but hadn't been deterred. She'd learned long ago to displace herself from her body when it was being abused. It was only a body, and it could take anything Greenberg threw at it. But she'd underestimated his desire to humiliate her and understood now that he wanted her to show fear. He gained some sort of perverted satisfaction by breaking through the protective wall she'd taken such pains to construct around her emotions.

She'd admired him at first and thought they'd make a good team. Brash, loud, and self-opinionated he might be, but he was still a self-made man, even if he had given himself a leg up by marrying into money. Annabel was hardly in a position to throw stones. He'd still worked ceaselessly to get where he was today, not caring who he trampled on it the process. Determination and single-mindedness were qualities Annabel could relate to since she had an abundance of both.

John's son Reggie was proving to be a real thorn in her side. Unlike his father, he'd had it easy all his life, but he'd never bothered to take advantage of his expensive education and compensated for his lack of nous by throwing his weight around in the office. He countermanded Annabel's orders, for no reason other than that he could, leaving her to pick up the pieces. John had a blind spot when it came to Reggie, and he was never blamed for his errors. The Grange was a prime example. Annabel rolled her eyes. How hard could it be to get a middle-aged woman and a crowd of homeless kids out of the place?

Annabel swore softly as she continued to inspect her injuries. John Greenberg was a perverted bigot, and he'd pushed her too far this time.

Chapter Eight

Suzie slammed the phone down, tears of disillusionment pouring down her face. Bitterness and anger joined the party, and she downed a huge swig of brandy to drive them away, almost choking as the fiery liquid hit the back of her throat. She didn't want to cry. She absolutely refused to shed any more tears over her erstwhile husband. He didn't deserve them.

She slumped in an armchair and cradled her glass against her chest, trying to make sense of it all. Mark wanted her back. Until Kate had answered their home phone, she would have put money on it. She'd never seen him so contrite before, so sincere in his determination to win her round. She had almost weakened, too, almost fallen for his smooth assurances, but all the time he wanted to have his cake and eat it, too. She wondered why she was so surprised. Hadn't she always wondered what he got up to on those endless business trips? But how could he have hoped to keep up both relationships if she returned home? Was she such a doormat that he assumed she'd turn a blind eye? Probably. She'd never once voiced any doubts about him in all the years of their marriage and had behaved like a trusting idiot. She scoffed in disgust. The Suzie of old really was that feeble, but the new, improved version was altogether a different proposition, as Mark would soon discover for himself.

Still slumped in the drawing room an hour later, dry-eyed and composed, Suzie came to a decision. As soon as she got through the torment of the reunion with her parents on Monday, endured the agony of seeing Shalimar signed over to her father's control and placed on the open market with an alacrity that spared no time for sentiment, she would start house and job hunting. She would also contact a local solicitor and start divorce proceedings. She had no idea what settlement she could expect, no idea how affluent they were—she'd always left that side of things to Mark—but now urgently needed to know where she stood. Once she found that out, she would have to decide what type of work she wanted to do. Her requirements weren't extravagant, and so if he treated her fairly, perhaps she'd be able to buy a small cottage locally and work voluntarily for Jane? Now that was something she would enjoy.

Driven by rage and jealousy as she considered her next move, Suzie didn't move when she heard Mark's car pull into the driveway. It was the sound of the doorbell that snapped her out of her reverie, but she ignored it until it rang for the third time. She didn't want to see anyone right now. It sounded for the third time. Whoever it was had pressed a thumb on the bell and left it there. Resigned to the fact that her caller wasn't about to go away, she walked into the hall and opened the door cautiously, Sparkle at her side. She kept it on the chain, just in case someone was hand delivering a further nasty message. Mark was the last person she expected to see, and she was unable to prevent a small gasp from slipping past her lips. In spite of her anger and resolve, for a brief moment her heart soared. Then common sense reasserted itself, and she attempted to slam the door in his face. She couldn't manage it because Sparkle was trying to squeeze through the gap and get to Mark.

"What do you want?" she asked, not removing the chain.

"To talk to you."

"We have nothing to talk about."

"You know that isn't true. Let me in. Suzie."

He obviously wouldn't go away until he'd said his piece. Reluctantly, she released the chain and turned her back on him. She heard the door shut behind him and the sound of Sparkle's claws scrabbling as he ran after the ball Mark must have thrown for him. He followed her into the lounge. Only then did she look at him, taking some comfort from his ravaged expression. He placed both of his hands on her shoulders and looked directly into her face.

"Suzie, I can imagine what you're thinking but you're wrong."

"Oh, please, spare me—"

"At least listen to me. Let me explain, and then, if you still don't believe me, I'll leave. You have my word on that."

"Okay, get it over with." She folded her arms beneath her breasts and looked everywhere except at him.

"I got home from Brussels, dreading going into the empty house, but when I opened the door, I thought I was going mad. I was sure I could smell cooking. Suzie, I thought you'd come home to surprise me."

He looked as though he was in physical pain. Suzie wasn't about to be deceived by his lies but couldn't help admiring his audacity. If she hadn't known better, she would have thought he was sincere. But, of course, she knew much better. The old Suzie might have been desperate enough to believe this half-cocked explanation, but that Suzie had grown up over the past few hours.

"Save it, Mark, I'm not interested."

She half turned away, but Mark's hands, still on her shoulders, turned her back to face him. "Suzie, do you really think I'd do something so stupid? That I would even want to? Apart from the fact that Kate repels me, what would it do to us, to say nothing of my career?"

"Yes, your career would have been your first concern," she said with a sad little shake of her head. "Don't try and pretend that I come first."

"She was in the house, waiting for me, wearing one of your dresses." He looked desolate at the memory, but Suzie hardened her heart. Whatever game he was playing, she wanted no part of it. "Just for one moment I really thought she was you."

She looked into his eyes, and the naked pain they reflected confounded her. She allowed herself to wonder.

"You must believe me," he said quietly. "Apart from anything else, I haven't a clue how she got in."

"She had a key," Suzie said, her voice sounding as though it was coming from a long distance away. She regretted speaking as soon as she realized that the admission implied belief in his ridiculous story. "I guess she never returned it."

"That's what I imagined. I got a locksmith out. That's why it took me some time to get here." He turned to the hall dresser, picked up Suzie's keys, took off her old house key, and replaced it with a new one. "Here's the new alarm code." He slid a piece of paper into her bag.

"It doesn't matter. I won't be using it."

"You do believe me though, darling?"

"I don't know what to believe or why you should think it matters to me."

"It was a surreal experience. She seems determined to turn herself into you."

Mark poured Suzie a refill and then one for himself. He downed his quickly and poured a second.

"You haven't answered me," he said after a prolonged silence. "Do you believe me?"

Suzie expelled a long breath. "Why is it so important whether I believe you or not?"

"Because I can't bear to have you think that I'd lie to you."

Suzie harrumphed. He obviously wasn't going to leave until he got his answer. Incapable of lying about something that shouldn't matter to her, she told him that she believed him.

"Thank God!"

"So, you can go now."

"Go? Don't be silly." He drained his glass again and refilled it. Too late to stop him, she realized what he was doing. "I can't drive after all this brandy," he said, a tiny smile tugging at the corners of his mouth.

"Then go and get a room in the local pub."

"It's gone eleven o'clock. They'll be closed."

"Well, you can't stay here." She was annoyed at the way he was able to manipulate her but also thrilled and a little afraid to be beneath the same roof as him. At least if her phantom saboteur called tonight, she wouldn't have to deal with him alone.

"I'll stay in the spare room." He flashed the puerile smile that never failed to get a reaction from her.

"Oh, for God's sake!" She swirled away from him. "All right, you can stay here tonight, but tomorrow I want you out of here."

"We were going to spend the day together tomorrow," he reminded her. "Anyway, I have to be here on Monday."

"Monday?" She narrowed her eyes at him. "Who said anything about Monday?"

He pulled a letter out of his jacket pocket and waved it in front of her face. "When were you going to tell me that Mr. Latimer wants me involved with the probate?"

"There's no reason for you to be there." She would have a few choice words to say to Mr. Latimer when she saw him. If she'd wanted Mark there, she would have told him about it herself.

"There must be," he said with infuriating calm. "Latimer wouldn't have asked me otherwise."

She treated him to disdainful glare and stomped wordlessly ahead of him up the stairs. She flung clean sheets and towels into the spare room furthest from hers, wondering if he'd ever had to make his own bed before. Well, he was an intelligent guy. He'd figure it out without any help from her. She wished him a curt *good night* and flounced off to her own room, making a loud show of locking the door behind her.

Suzie slept badly yet again, and it was all Mark's fault. She could hear him moving about down the corridor and using the bathroom for what seemed like an eternity. He hummed as he passed her locked door and called out a cheerful *good night* as he did so.

She refused Mark's offer of Sunday lunch in a posh riverside restaurant, made a covert call to Jane, and wangled them both an invitation to The Grange instead. The usual suspects were present, and Jane could be relied upon to keep the conversation off sensitive topics.

The meal over with and only Jane, Mark, and Suzie left at the table finishing the excellent wine Mark had provided, Mark fished in the pocket of his jacket and produced a sheaf of papers.

"Now, Jane, about your noise problems."

"But I thought you'd been in Brussels all the week. How have you found time—"

Mark winked at her. "Always got time for things that matter. Anyway, it's pretty much as I thought. There's a cumbersome beast entitled The Environmental Protection Act, which gives the local authority wide-ranging powers to tackle noise problems. But the terms of the act are nebulous and open to a variety of interpretations. For instance, antisocial behaviour in built-up areas, such as excessive noise from motor vehicle exhausts, loud music late at night, noisy machinery, that sort of thing—"

"But we're not guilty of any of those crimes. Anyway, this isn't a built-up area."

"I know, but, as you rightly said, someone's got it in for you. Apparently, several complaints have been received."

"Who from?" Suzie asked.

"They're not saying, but it can only be from those cottages. Seems they're upset about some sort of farm machinery making noise late at night."

"We were making hay in the lower paddock."

"The one closest to the cottages?"

"Well, yes, but it went on for less than a week. We worked late because the weather was due to break and we had to get the hay in." Jane looked angry enough to hit something. "Christ, Mark, this is the countryside. What else can they expect?"

"It was countryside, but the council virtually have *carte blanche* to interpret their powers in any way they wish."

"Bloody little Hitlers," Jane muttered.

"Well, these local authorities do enjoy their bit of power. As they see it, those cottages, and the rest of the village for that matter, has gradually encroached on the open land over the years, and the council are now claiming that it's a built-up area."

"But that's ridiculous!" Suzie and Jane spoke together.

"Course it is, but it gets worse, I'm afraid. The local authority has the power to bring proceedings in the magistrates' court and impose hefty fines on domestic dwellings and even heftier ones on trade or business premises if they flout the law. They're claiming to have received protests, not just about the hay making, but about barking dogs and noxious smells, too. Bottom line, they're planning to treat The Grange as business premises and levy fines if things don't improve."

"Lord above, the dogs don't bark much, and the smell they're probably referring to is from the manure we topped the paddocks with." Jane looked as though she was struggling to hold on to her temper. "Mark, it's all part of living in the country, for heaven's sake. Anyway, they can't have it both ways. The powers that be have prevented me from running a business, so these are domestic premises."

"I know. Don't worry about it. They're pissing in the wind but two can play at their game. Here's a copy of a letter I've sent to the council on your behalf. That should spike their guns for a while."

Jane and Suzie read the letter together. It was produced on Mark's personal, impressively thick embossed headed paper. It referred to him as a Barrister at Law and had a bewildering array of letters trailing behind his name. The letter itself was written in splendidly confusing legalese, containing ambiguous referrals to the implementation of environmental law in general and local bylaws in particular. It finished with a politely couched demand for access to all the documents relating to the case against Jane in order that Mark, in his capacity as her legal representative, could form what he implied would be a spirited defence against their questionable accusations. The missive informed the council that any action taken against Jane would be robustly defended.

"Wow," Jane said, finishing reading it before Suzie. "Wouldn't like to get on the wrong side of you, Mark. Thank you! But how did you manage all this whilst in Brussels?"

"One of my minions did the research and spoke to some pompous bod on the local council. He drafted the letter on the back of what he'd learned, e-mailed me his proposed response for approval, and then my secretary sent the letter out on my behalf." Mark leaned back in his chair and grinned at the two ladies. "Piece of cake," he assured them. "That bit about rigorously defending any action taken against you should put the wind up them. Always fight fire with fire, that's my motto. Anyway, I think it's time to strike back now, don't you?"

"Absolutely," Jane agreed. "But how do we do that?"

"Keep a log of all noise disturbance *you* get from those cottages. Log dates and times and duration of noise from motor bikes, loud radios, car engines running late at night, that sort of thing."

"Thank you, Mark," Jane said, topping his glass up. "What would I have done without you? Should Suzie do the same thing?"

Suzie flashed a warning glance at Jane, but Mark was too astute to miss the implication, and the damage was done.

"Suzie?" He turned toward her, frowning. "Have you been having trouble as well?"

"Not really." She had no intention of permitting him to inveigle himself further into her new life on the pretence of helping her.

Jane flashed a brief smile. "Now, that isn't strictly true, is it?"

Suzie knew when she was beaten. If she didn't tell Mark what had been going on, Jane almost certainly would. Sullenly, she outlined the damage to her car, the excrement through the door, the broken window in the scullery, and the deliberate switching off of the electricity. Mark was appalled.

"Why the hell didn't you tell me?"

"I can handle it," she snapped. "I'm not as helpless as you seem to think."

"You must have been terrified." He reached for her hand, but she snatched it away.

"I've had the car repaired, and Gordon replaced the scullery window for me yesterday."

Mark flashed a smile of thanks in Jane's direction.

"What about the alarm? Didn't that go off?"

"I don't set it at night. It's not a sophisticated system and doesn't separate the zones. Anyway, the scullery isn't linked up to it."

As she'd started, she thought she might as well tell them everything and went on to explain about Porter and Greenberg.

"You can't stay here on your own, Suzie," Mark said, looking convincingly concerned. "It's not safe."

"I won't be able to stay for much longer after tomorrow anyway," she said tightly.

"Just as well." Mark still frowned. "I don't like the thought of you here on your own when someone's out to cause trouble for you both. This needs looking into."

* * * *

Reggie took pleasure in taunting Annabel for the rest of the day.

"Juvenile little prick," she muttered under her breath as he kept swanning in and out of her office, asking loudly enough for the papers on the Brooker deal to ensure that everyone heard.

He assumed that she gave a damn, and in this case, he'd be right. The Brooker deal was big time, and Reggie would cock it up, ruin all her hard groundwork, just as surely as he messed up the simple business of The Grange. Had Jim got it wrong? Her investigator had implied that, unlike his wife, Greenberg didn't indulge his kids. He'd have to be blind not to realize what a useless waste of space Reggie was, so why was he doing this to her? And to himself. The deal meant as much to him and his precious public image as it did to her. Annabel just didn't understand it.

Worse, it now looked as though she had nothing important to do. The Grange was equally important to John, but he'd told her to deal with everything to do with it herself and not even involve the two associates who reported to her. They were now twiddling their thumbs in the open-plan office, making her removal from the Brooker case seem even more humiliating. And they were enjoying her fall from grace every bit as much as Reggie.

"Oh, Annabel." Reggie put his head round her door for at least the tenth time that morning. "Not interrupting anything important, am I?"

"Something I can explain to you?" she asked sweetly.

"No thanks, everything's back on track now," he said, implying that she'd somehow cocked up. "It's just that there's a lot to get through, and Greg and Marcia look as though they've got time on their hands." He smiled, unable to resist glancing over his shoulder to make sure he still had the attention of the entire outer office. "Don't suppose I could borrow them for a day or two, could I? We're snowed under, and I could use the help."

"Yes, Reggie, I don't doubt your need to have your hand held—"

"That's not what I—"

"Be my guest," she said, waving in dismissal. "They won't let you make any mistakes."

No longer looking quite so cocksure, Reggie left her office and told her two associates to report to him for a briefing. Annabel retreated to the same place inside her head that she went to when John was fucking her and felt absolutely nothing at all.

Chapter Nine

As Suzie and Mark left The Grange, the sky turned dark and heavy rain clouds gathered, threatening to drench them before they reached Shalimar.

"Looks like Jane was right to predict rain." Suzie glanced up at the sky. "Hope she'll be all right. Her roof is hopelessly inadequate, and it looks as though it's going to bucket down."

"She was marshalling the troops before we left."

"Yes." Suzie smiled, recalling how everyone had been dashing about, clutching anything that would catch the rain. "I had no idea commodes were still in vogue."

"The plumbing at The Grange is even less reliable than Shalimar's, so I suspect they're used for their original purpose. Anyway, Jane is quite capable of looking after herself. But you, Mrs. Alexander, are entirely another matter." He looked down at her. "Why didn't you tell me?"

"Because it's none of your concern."

"You can't mean that. Of course I'm concerned."

They were still arguing about it when they got back to Shalimar. It dawned on Suzie that the whole evening stretched ahead of them and she would have to share it with Mark. She stole a glance at his face as he leaned casually against the kitchen surface, arms folded across his chest, devastatingly and dangerously male. His presence in the huge kitchen made it feel as though the walls were closing in on her. She let out a deep breath, blushing beneath his close scrutiny. She fed the hovering cats, just to avoid his gaze. She'd seen that look too many times over the past ten years to doubt its meaning.

"Don't even think about it!" she said, not looking up.

"About what, darling?"

Suzie had never been more pleased to hear a car pull into the driveway in her entire life. Any distraction from Mark's complete mastery of the situation and her inability to refrain from responding to him would be welcome. It was probably the old minivan that Jane used. They needed more saucepans to catch the rain at The Grange. She glanced through the hall window and groaned aloud. Just when she thought the day couldn't get any worse. It wasn't Jane's van. Instead, an ancient Fiesta had come to a careful halt beside Mark's Mercedes. Given a choice, she'd take her chances with Mark after all.

"What are they doing here?" she muttered, watching as her parents climbed inelegantly from the car. "They're not due until tomorrow."

"I guess we'll soon find out." Mark opened the front door and slid an arm round her waist. "Have to keep up appearances," he said smugly, raising a sardonic brow. "I assume you haven't told them yet?" He was so infuriating that she wanted to hit him. She couldn't, of course, and instead had to endure his vicelike hold as he pulled her against his side, his thumb circling her hip in a provocative declaration of intent. It felt so wonderful, so intimately and blissfully personal that just for one magical second she closed her eyes and surrendered to his sensual touch. "Try and put up with it, darling," he said, amusement in his tone. "It won't be for long."

She pulled away from him, mortified that she'd briefly lost control. "Too right it won't." She glared up at her husband. "There's no need to look so pleased with yourself either because if you think this changes anything—"

"Suzanne, where have you been? We've been ringing all the afternoon."

"Hello, mother." Suzie dutifully pecked her mother's papery cheek. "We were invited to lunch with some neighbours."

"Well, that was hardly considerate, was it?" She harrumphed, the sharp features of her small, birdlike face pinched with disapproval. "We thought to come this afternoon and have a good look round the place, see what's what. Instead, we had to fill the time by going to Evensong in the village."

"What a drag," Mark said drolly.

"It certainly was." Suzie's mother clearly mistook Mark's sarcasm for sympathy. "I must say, I don't care for that new vicar at all. Far too modern in his ways for my taste. He came out in favour of gay marriages, didn't he?" She paused for breath but didn't appear to expect an answer. "Hello, Mark, I thought you were away?"

"Obviously not any more, Mrs. Watson," he said in a cool tone. Suzie's mother had never asked Mark to address her by her Christian name, and Suzie knew he'd never deign to call her *mother*. Suzie couldn't blame him for that. She'd quite like to be relieved of that responsibility herself. Mark took her bag and shook hands with Suzie's only slightly less irritating father.

They trooped into the house. Suzie made tea for her parents and served it in the drawing room. Whilst they were drinking it, she bolted up the stairs, removed all signs of Mark's presence in the spare room, and placed his things with hers in the master bedroom. She refused to think about the consequences, preferring to suffer though a night in the same room as her husband than endure the inquisition and ensuing lecture from her parents if they found out Suzie had left him. First though, she had to get through the evening.

"Wine, darling?" Mark asked, waving a newly opened bottle as she reentered the drawing room.

She was about to refuse, knowing that her parents didn't drink and thoroughly disapproved of those that did. Then she caught sight of the frown on her mother's brow and a devilish instinct made her accept the proffered glass. If nothing else, it might help her to relax. If it also stopped her fertile imagination anticipating the night to come and running off in directions it had no business taking, she wouldn't put up too many objections.

The evening dragged on interminably, and Suzie had never been more appreciative of Mark's presence. He disliked her parents, especially her domineering mother, but hid it well enough to keep the conversation ticking over. Whenever Suzie was with them, she felt like a crass schoolgirl all over again. She had nothing in common with them and was a married woman in her own right but perversely still craved an approval that would never be forthcoming. Mark felt no such restraints and played them at their own game. They lacked the intellect to get the better of him and so treated him with an indulgent affection they had never once displayed toward their own daughter.

Mark sat beside Suzie on the gloriously comfortable, overstuffed sofa and encouraged his in-laws to talk about their time in Sierra Leone. Not that they needed much encouragement. It was a clever ploy since almost no contribution was required from them, and they listened with less than half of their combined attention. Suzie was aware of the expectation, the sexual tension building inextricably between them. Her husband's close proximity made it increasingly difficult to deny that the spark was rapidly assuming the proportions of a raging fire. Mark fuelled its intensity by taking every opportunity to touch her hand, her arm—any part of her that he could. It was a perfectly natural way for a husband to behave toward his wife, and there was no way she could take exception to it.

"Suzanne, are you listening to me?"

Her mother's voice pulled Suzie's attention away from the delightful fantasy she was lost in. The one in which Mark was…well, never mind what he was about to do to her.

"Sorry, Mother, what did you say?"

Her mother expelled a long sigh. "I said that since you've given up your silly job at that vet's you could be of help to us for a change. I can't think why you allowed her to work there anyway, Mark. Still, since you have nothing better to do with your time, I'll tell the chairman that you'll be available to type up the reports for the board following our trip. It will save us having to pay someone else to do it and will give you a worthwhile occupation. You could also help with the fundraising campaign for the fresh water pipe we're planning to have laid. Oh, just think!" She clapped her hands and threw back her head in delight, looking almost girlish. "Just think of the difference it will make to those poor people's lives."

"I'm sure it will," Mark said smoothly. "But I'm afraid you'll have to manage without Suzie's help. We have other plans."

Suzie didn't know whether to be grateful or annoyed. She certainly didn't want to help her mother, but if she was going to be independent of Mark, then she needed to stand on her own two feet. If she couldn't even take her mother on, what hope did she have?

Something about the determination and finality in his mildly spoken words stopped Suzie's mother in her tracks, and she made do with a disapproving tut. An uncomfortable silence ensued, and Suzie was damned if she'd be the first to speak. Dredging up suitable topics of conversation for the entire evening had drained her, and a headache threatened. Her father gazed through the window as torrential rain pounded relentlessly against it.

"Looks like we're in for quite a storm," he said, stating the obvious.

Suzie tensed and felt the reassuring touch of Mark's fingers on her arm. They both knew she had witnessed the destruction of several animals, caught beneath a falling tree that had been struck by lightning in the field next to this house when she'd been a small child. She had told Mark once that the sound of thunder always brought back the terrified screams of the dying cattle and her feelings of helplessness because there was nothing she could do to help them.

It was bedtime at last. Suzie fussed around the drawing room, clearing up the clutter. She let Sparkle out and checked for at least the third time that Honey was safely locked in her domain, protected from the storm. Mark leaned against the kitchen surface, watching her, an infuriating smile playing about his lips.

"Ready, darling?" he asked innocently.

She wouldn't look at him. "You go ahead."

"Wouldn't think of it."

"Oh, you!" Suzie pushed past him and rushed for the stairs.

She dashed into the bathroom and returned after an eternity, her bathrobe pulled tightly about her. Smiling, Mark casually headed for the bathroom himself.

"Won't be long," he said, dropping a light kiss on the top of her head before she could move out of range.

"Take all the time you need. I'll make you up a bed on the settee."

Chortling, which told her more than she wanted to know about his opinion of their sleeping arrangements, he left the room. He clearly didn't think she was serious. Well, he was about to learn just how wrong he was. When he returned, he glanced at the settee, now adorned with pillows and blankets and screwed up his nose as he threw himself down on it.

"It's lumpy," he complained. "And too short. See?" He waggled his toes, drawing attention to his feet hanging over the end.

"Too bad!" Suzie refused to feel sorry for him. "Hope it puts your back out."

Mark stood up again. She'd been so focused on their battle of wills that she only just noticed he was wearing his boxers—and nothing else.

"Oh, well, if you insist." He started to take them off.

"What are you doing?" Suzie shrieked and backed away from him.

"Getting ready for bed, such as it is." He smiled at her. "Come on, baby, you've seen it all before. It's far too hot to wear anything in bed."

"Well, at least I don't have to sleep next to you." She nodded towards the settee, just in case he thought she'd changed her mind.

"Have a heart, love!" He glanced at the enormous tester bed that occupied half the room. "There's more than enough room for us both. We don't have to get up close and personal." He waggled his brows.

"Unless you want to, of course."

"Oh no!" She pushed her hands toward him as though warding off an attack. "You needn't think…"

"Don't you trust me?"

"Not an inch."

"You wound me, Suzie," he said, clutching at his heart. "I'd never take advantage. We're both tired and need a good night's sleep if we're to deal with your parents tomorrow." He offered her a languid grin. "Tell you what, why don't we have a demarcation line? I remember seeing something like it on an old black and white film once. They hung a blanket down the middle." He took the pillows from the couch, pulled back the covers, and arranged them neatly down the centre of the bed. "See? This is my space, and that's yours." He winked at her. "Make sure you don't encroach on my side now." Without preamble, he climbed into the area he'd designated for himself, stretched full length and signed with contentment. "Don't worry, Suzie. There are no strings attached. I promise I won't let my rampant desire get the better of me." He paused for a beat. "Unless you want it to, of course."

Suzie tossed her head, sending her hair cascading down her back.

"You're enjoying this, aren't you?" she said, removing her dressing gown.

He spread his hands, his expression suspiciously innocent. "As if I…good God, what in the world are you wearing?"

"One of Granny's nighties."

Mark chuckled. "Granny was a couple of sizes smaller than you, darling." He continued to observe her in the flannelette nightdress buttoned right up to the neck. It had full-length sleeves tied at her wrists in bows. Intended as a full-length garment, in ended halfway down Suzie's calves. It was way too small, and her breasts strained against the awful material, no doubt accounting for the lust that had crept into Mark's expression. She should have kept the dressing gown on. "You'll roast to death in that thing," he warned her.

"No I won't." She dashed across the room, leapt into bed, and wished him a curt good night.

"Don't I get a good-night kiss? After all, I did save you from your bossy mother."

"Thank you for that, and no, you don't get anything. Just remember to stay on your side."

She turned on her side, facing away from him, and thumped her pillows as though she bore them a grudge. Sleep would be next to impossible to achieve, what with her errant husband so close, naked and ready to pounce at the least sign of encouragement from her. If she relaxed her guard, he'd know it, and she'd be in danger of forfeiting the tiny wedge of independence she'd carved out for herself.

What if she fell asleep and accidently rolled toward him? She'd done it so often over the past ten years that instinct might well win out over caution. She was overwhelmed by his presence, by the masculine smell that was so uniquely him, by the even rhythm of his breathing, his glorious physique hers for the taking. Her fingers itched to reach out and touch his chest. She tucked both hands under her pillows to prevent them from developing a mind of their own and tried to think about something else. Mathematical equations ought to do the trick, but she couldn't remember any. Animal cruelty—but no, that would make her cry, and Mark would think she was crying over him.

She must have drifted off and was woken an hour later when the storm broke directly overhead. The sudden crash of thunder caused Suzie, half-asleep and disorientated, to sit up and cry out. Mark reached for her. She was sodden with sweat and trembling violently.

"It's okay, darling, I'm here." He pulled her close, and she made no effort to push him away. He stroked her back gently, soothing her as though she was a child, and she leaned against him until her trembling subsided.

"Don't let me go!" she said when he relaxed his hold. "I can't stand it. Please stop me hearing it."

"Shush, it's all right." He whispered the words into the top of her head. "Nothing can hurt you. I won't let it."

He continued to soothe her, and it made her feel so safe, seemed so natural, that she didn't pull away.

"Darling, you're soaked," he said gently. "Come on, you can't wear this thing."

He unbuttoned the neck of her nightdress, but her mind had shut down and she barely noticed. He pulled her closer and kissed her. Suzie knew Mark was kissing her, that much certainly registered. She started to kiss him back, her tongue tangling with his in the way that it always did. All the while something was nagging at the back of her brain. She shouldn't be doing this, but she couldn't remember why. The storm and all the painful memories that came with it had deprived her of the ability to think straight, but she knew there was something important that she ought to remember. But it couldn't be anything to do with kissing Mark. He was her husband. Why shouldn't she kiss him? Besides, something that felt so right couldn't possibly be wrong.

Mark kissed her again, and it was as though someone had suddenly turned a switch inside Suzie's head. She sat up, wound her arms round his neck, and took an active part in proceedings. Mark eased the flannelette away from her body, his forefinger gently tracing the outline of her breasts. Suzie subsided onto her pillows, responding with the tiny moans of pleasure.

"Do you want me?" he asked her.

"You know I do. I always want you," she said dreamily. "Why are you even bothering to ask?"

He seemed surprised by the question, but Suzie barely noticed. Instead, she grabbed his hand and returned it to her breast.

"All right," he said, chuckling. "I get the picture."

Suzie had never been with anyone but Mark, so she had no gauge by which to measure his performance. Even so, she instinctively knew that she'd struck lucky. He aroused her, keeping her teetering on the edge until passion boiled over and she reached her first climax before he'd even touched her clitoris.

"Greedy!" he said, chuckling as she bucked against his hand.

"Can't help it," she said, running her hand down the length of his erection. "But I want more."

"Music to my ears, Mrs. Alexander," he said.

He really went to work then, his fingers and tongue bringing her to orgasm time and time again. Waves of pleasure washed through her body, but he appeared to be in no hurry to actually enter her.

"Mark, you haven't—"

"Shush!" He rubbed the finger that had just been inside her across her lips. She could taste her own juices on it. "This is for you, just to show you how sorry I am."

"Sorry?" What was he sorry about? There was something—something important—but her brain was now addled with desire and she still couldn't remember. "Come on, Mark. You need to be inside me."

"Yes." She could sense his glamorous smile in the darkened room. "That's what I need. It's all I've ever needed. I know that now."

He guided her hand to his prick, and she gasped in astonishment. He was a well-proportioned man at the best of times, but tonight he was swollen to gigantic proportions.

"It's frustrating being a bachelor," he said as he eased himself into her.

A bachelor? This made no sense. They'd been married ten years. But as his distended prick stretched her wide and he slid home so she stopped trying to figure out what he meant. As soon as she wrapped her legs round his neck, he thrust more deeply still and, with a guttural moan, came in an endless stream. As too did she. The thrill was more piquant, more intense than it had ever been before. Her body seemed to spasm and tremble forever, even after the sensation faded.

Spent, Mark fell onto his back pulled her into his arms. Only then was Suzie's memory restored to her, and she realized the enormity of her error. As soon as Mark's even breathing told her that he'd fallen asleep, she pulled away from him and curled as far away from him as she could. This was a disaster! He'd used the storm to take advantage of her and presumably thought that everything was right between them again.

He would wake up in the morning with his usual erection and expect her to take care of it. Well, he could think again. She would be up and out of this room long before he woke, and they wouldn't refer to the incident ever again.

* * * *

Things went from bad to worse for Annabel. Reggie continued to swan about the office, full of his own self-importance as he mishandled their biggest deal to date. She didn't want to care. It was none of her business now because she was off the case. Whenever Annabel didn't want to care, she knew just how to insulate herself and let the world pass her by.

But the bugger of it was that she *did* care. She hated inefficiencies, especially when her name was all over the initial papers dealing with Greenberg's bid. She hung back at night after everyone had left, going through the documents that Reggie left strewn about his office, checking up on him. Greg and Marcia were worried about his cavalier attitude, too, she could see that. She almost wished that she'd made an effort to cultivate their friendship now. If they respected her enough to confide their fears, then perhaps they'd have found a way between them to pull Reggie back from the brink of blowing the entire deal. She tutted as she read his latest e-mails. It was easy enough to do because he never bothered to log out of his account. He'd taken completely the wrong approach. Brooker needed firm facts with figures to back them up. He wasn't interested in being wined and dined at fancy restaurants and subjected to sycophantic flattery. The way things were going, Greenberg's didn't stand a hope in hell of gaining the Brooker contract.

Annabel was given small, humiliating tasks to deal with at the office. Stuff that the least motivated associate could have done unsupervised. The rest of the staff didn't bother to hide their pleasure at her fall from grace, but Annabel barely spared their reaction a thought. She had a pretty shrewd idea why it was happening. She'd stuck rigidly to John's terms in respect of their personal relationship, and from the odd remark he'd let drop, she got the impression that was a first. John wanted a reaction from her, and Annabel refused to oblige.

"You're a cold fish," he'd said to her just the night before. "Don't you ever climax?"

She quirked a brow and blew smoke at the ceiling. "Is that part of the deal?"

"Have you ever had an orgasm?" He shook his head, not appearing to expect an answer. "No, of course you haven't. That would require emotion, and you hate being out of control, don't you?"

"You bought my body, John, not my mind."

"But I'd give a lot to know what's going on in it. What makes you tick, Annabel Burton?"

She shrugged. "Why do you care?"

"Money, isn't it? You hate what we do but you do it anyway and think about the money." She flashed a humourless smile, like his pegging her secret was no big deal. She really didn't want to have this discussion, but if he realized that, he'd never let it go. Act cool, she told herself, or find a distraction.

"You set the rules," she said offhandedly.

"I'll get a reaction out of you if it's the last fucking thing I ever do," he said, his face reddening.

And then he hit her.

Chapter Ten

Suzie's parents never stayed in bed beyond six a.m., and for that she was grateful. It meant that when Mark came down at six thirty, they were already seated at the kitchen table, demolishing the food she had prepared for them, and Mark couldn't cross-question her about her abrupt departure from bed. She refused to look at him as she placed his breakfast on the table. Obviously not about to be put off by her remote attitude, Mark stood behind her as she fussed needlessly over the Aga, lifted her hair from her nape, and kissed the back of her neck. She reacted as though she had been stung by a bee and moved away. The only sound was Celia Watson's tut of disapproval.

The agony of breakfast over with, Suzie's parents disappeared into the study to pore over the books that Suzie had so laboriously catalogued. She poked her head round the door and watched them as they fingered their spines and attempted to guess at their value. She'd seen enough and quickly moved away, straight into Mark who'd just emerged from the kitchen.

"What's the matter, darling?" he asked. They both knew he wasn't referring to her parents.

She glowered at him, feeling fit to burst with the injustice of it all. "Nothing in particular," she said, her voice oozing sarcasm. "The house I love is about to be taken away from me, my parents have been ganging up on me again this morning, trying to get me to work for them and…and you took advantage of me."

"Is that what you really believe?" He looked as though she'd physically attacked him.

"What else am I supposed to think?" She angrily snatched up a piece of kitchen towel and noisily blew her nose. "You know how I feel about storms."

"But I thought you wanted me to—"

"I didn't mean like that."

"I did ask if you were sure."

"You knew I wouldn't be thinking straight."

He stood very close to her and ran strands of her hair through his fingers. "But you enjoyed it, didn't you? I would have stopped if you'd asked me to. I thought I was helping."

She met his gaze and somehow managed to hold it. "Yes," she said quietly, "that's just it, don't you see? I did enjoy it."

"So what's the problem? I—"

She absolutely didn't want to have this conversation. Besides, there was nothing more to be said. "I'm going to take Sparkle for a walk. Alone," she added, when it looked as though he intended to join her.

She stayed out for over an hour, trying not to think about anything other than putting one foot in front of the other. Trying not to dwell upon how fulfilled she felt after a night of Mark's expert ministrations. She returned to the house more composed, ready to face whatever the day had to throw at her.

At ten o'clock Derek and Sheila arrived. With barely a word for Suzie or Mark, they were soon engrossed with her parents in a zealous discussion about Sierra Leone and the best way forward for their ambitious plans. When it was time to leave for the solicitors, Celia decreed that she and her husband should travel with Suzie and Mark.

"As you have these ghastly, environmentally unfriendly gas guzzlers," her mother said pompously, "we might as well make full use of them."

"If you disapprove so much," Mark said evenly. "You might be more comfortable using your own transport."

"Come on, time's getting on."

Mark raised his eyes to Suzie and shuttled everyone out of the house. Derek and Sheila set off in their ancient Renault, and Mark opened the front door of Suzie's Jeep for her. Before she got to it, Peter Watson clambered in and fastened his seat belt with deliberating care. Suzie almost giggled. Anyone would think they were about to embark upon some sort of off-road race. With a second roll of his eyes, Mark opened the back door for the ladies and drove Suzie's car toward the village.

Mr. Latimer invited them all into his office as soon as they arrived. Suzie was grateful that there would be no delay.

"Come on, Mr. Latimer," her mother said impatiently, "we haven't got all day. What do we have to sign to transfer ownership of Shalimar to ourselves?" Seeing the solicitor's puzzled gaze, she pounced. "Surely everything's arranged?"

"Indeed, Mrs. Watson, but first I am obliged to read the will."

"Read the will? What are you talking about?"

"You weren't here at the time of Mrs. Watson's demise, and it really does have to be done."

"Perhaps she left the children some small bequest," her father said. "That would account for the need for them to be here."

"Oh, very well, just get on with it then." Celia puffed out her cheeks and fiddled with the tattered handbag on her lap. "Why does everything need to be so complicated?"

Since no one seemed inclined to answer her, Mr. Latimer cleared his throat and after the usual preamble came to the crux of the matter.

"To my grandson, Derek Watson, I leave the sum of fifty thousand pounds in the profound but probably futile hope that he will use it to increase his family's comfort and provide for the future of his children."

"Good heavens!" Derek exclaimed, his bland features lighting up with surprise and pleasure. "Where ever did the old man get that sort of money?"

Celia patted her son's knee, obviously pleased for him.

"To my son Peter I leave the Russian Icons currently hanging in my library that he always admired and a heartfelt wish that they bring some pleasure into his austere life."

"Well, really!" Celia cried. "What a thing to say."

Suzie noticed Mark hiding a smirk behind his hand.

"To my beloved granddaughter Suzanne I leave the contents of this envelope, all of the contents in the house known as Shalimar, and the heartfelt love and devotion of the grandparents who will continue to look after her from the next life."

"What!" Celia, Peter, and Derek gaped at one another like fish suddenly starved of water.

Ignoring them, Mr. Latimer handed the envelope to a quietly sobbing Suzie and closed his file. "And that, ladies and gentlemen, is the content of Mr. Watson's will."

"Don't be ridiculous!" Celia snapped. "What about the house?"

"The house?" Mr. Latimer seemed bemused. "What house would that be?"

"Why, Shalimar, of course," Suzie's father said. "My parents' residence for the past thirty years."

"Oh dear, there must be some misunderstanding." Mr. Latimer scratched his head but appeared to Suzie as though he was having trouble maintaining his puzzled expression. "Shalimar hasn't belonged to your parents for some years, Mr. Watson." Suzie was as shocked as everyone else appeared to be and glanced at Mark in confusion. He merely shrugged, clearly as much in the dark as she was. "I thought you knew."

"Didn't belong to them?" Celia pursed her thin lips, the light of battle glinting in her eyes. "You must be mistaken."

"I can assure you, there's no mistake."

"If it didn't belong to them," Derek said in a tight voice, darting frequent malevolent glances at Suzie, "then whose is it?"

Mr. Latimer took his time responding. "It belongs to Mr. and Mrs. Alexander," he said, smiling at Suzie.

Pandemonium broke out in that tiny office, everyone shouting everyone else down, Celia's voice clearly audible above them all. Only Suzie remained quiet and detached, too stunned to take it all in. She twisted the bulky envelope Mr. Latimer had given her round and round on her lap, mesmerised by the unexpected turn events had taken and mourning the loss of her beloved grandparents all over again. Everyone else appeared too consumed with greed to spare a thought for them. Mark reached for her hand and squeezed it.

"This can't possibly be correct," Celia said, glaring daggers at her daughter. "Explain yourself, man."

"Gladly, madam." Mr. Latimer took a drink of water, apparently enjoying himself. Suzie almost didn't blame him. He'd had to deal with her insufferable mother for years. "Shortly after Mr. and Mrs. Alexander married Mr. and Mrs. Watson Senior transferred ownership of Shalimar to them." Silencing protests with an outstretched hand, he continued. "It's a common enough practise to avoid inheritance tax and perfectly legal. The Deed of Transfer allowed Mr. and Mrs. Watson uninterrupted residency at the property for their joint lifetimes, after which it reverted to its new owners. That's why there is no mention of it in the will."

"This can't be legal!" protested Peter.

"I can assure you that it is, sir. It's done all the time. As long and Mr. or Mrs. Watson survived the transfer for a minimum of five years, all obligations to the Inland Revenue ceased. Thankfully Mrs. Watson survived for much longer than that."

Celia rose abruptly to her feet. "Come along, all of you. We'll return to Shalimar and discuss this fiasco in private." She turned to face Mr. Latimer. "But you haven't heard the last of this, I can assure you of that. We shall, of course, contest this ridiculous parody of a will. And as for you, young lady." She glared acrimoniously at her daughter. "You have some explaining to do. You must have known all about this but let us carry on thinking the house was ours. Of all the selfish, self-centred, greedy—"

The argument seemed to go on for hours, but Suzie, still feeling numb and unable to absorb all she'd just learned, barely heard what was being said. Mark poured her a brandy and sat beside her, rubbing her hands between both of his.

"Sip your drink, darling," he said, raising the glass to her lips as though she was a small child. "You've had a shock."

When the recriminations showed no sign of abating, Suzie was subconsciously aware of Mark taking control.

"Enough!" he said in a voice so full of authority that everyone fell silent. "Latimer was right. If the transfer happened as he said it did, then it's legal."

"They must have been senile," Celia said. "No one in their right mind would disinherit their own flesh and blood. We'll challenge the will on the basis of their state of mind."

"It won't get you anywhere," Mark said calmly, "especially after all this time. You'll just be pouring good money after bad."

Mark's words briefly silenced them, but it wasn't long before they turned as one on Suzie, blaming everything on her.

"You must have known," her mother said, "and deliberately kept us in the dark."

"It must have been you, Mark," Derek said sullenly. "You're the hotshot lawyer. You must have advised Gramps that this was the best way to arrange his affairs."

Mark cast him a chilling glare. "I'd strongly recommend that you think before you start throwing unsubstantiated allegations around." He paused. "Especially in front of a hotshot lawyer."

Even Celia appeared to realize her son had gone too far. "We're upset," she said. "It's all come as such a shock. We were so depending upon that money to do some good. Peter's mother and father must have been losing their minds when they changed their will. They couldn't have meant to leave their only son destitute."

"You and Mark have so much, Suzie," her father said. "What need could you possibly have for this white elephant of a house? The proper thing, the only Christian thing would be to sell it and give the proceeds to us. We could put them to so much better use."

After two hours, Mark stood up and fetched their coats.

"Suzie and I need time alone to talk about this," he said. "Believe it or not, we're as shocked as you are."

They left without protest but Suzie knew it wasn't the last she'd heard of their grievances. As soon he closed the door behind them, Mark was back at her side. She hadn't uttered a single word since leaving the solicitor's office, but Mark was the only one who seemed to have noticed her catatonic state, or to care about it. Being alone with him and the sole focus of his concern brought reality crashing in on her.

"I had no idea," she said, her eyes wandering round the room as though seeing it for the first time.

"It's just typical of your grandparents. They did love you very much, you know."

"Yes, I do, but I suppose it does seem a bit unfair."

"I think your grandfather was a wise old coot and knew very well just how much those parents of yours made you suffer over the years." He smiled at her. "It also explains why you've been pestered by those men wanting to buy the house. They knew what you didn't."

"How?"

"They'd only have to look it up at the Land Registry."

"Oh yes, I hadn't thought of that." She paused. "I wonder what made Granny and Gramps do it?"

"Perhaps if you open your letter, you'll get some idea."

"Do you know, I'd forgotten all about it."

Suzie inserted her thumb beneath the seal, inexplicably nervous. The first thing she extracted was a sheaf of bank statements for an account set up in the Channel Islands. She opened them and gasped. They slithered through her open fingers and fell to the floor. Mark picked them up and seemed almost as astonished as she was. The balance was for well over half a million pounds.

"I don't understand," she said weakly.

"The letter," he reminded her.

Suzie took a deep breath. "I think I'd like to read it later, when I'm on my own. I don't think I can take any more emotional upheaval right now."

"I was going to stay tonight. In the spare room if you like but I can't leave you like this."

"You must. I'll be fine. Anyway, it's getting late, and I dare say you'll have to be at the office early tomorrow."

"Bugger the office!"

"No, Mark, please, I'd like you to go. I need time alone to think. Come down again next weekend, and we'll talk then."

"All right, if that's what you really want."

"It is."

He reached for his keys. "Just don't let your mother talk you into anything stupid whilst I'm not here."

Suzie offered him a wan smile. "I can't. We're joint owners of the property, remember?"

"Yes, I hadn't forgotten."

Mark pulled her into his arms and kissed her, releasing her again almost immediately.

"Take care, sweetheart. I'll call you later."

"Good-bye, Mark, and thank you."

"For what?" he asked, turning back from the open front door.

"For saving me from my rapacious family."

"All part of the service," he said, blowing her a kiss and closing the door quietly behind him.

Left alone, Suzie was finally able to dwell upon the remarkable events of the day, her mind full of a thousand unanswered questions. For starters, where had all the money come from? The fifty thousand pounds for Derek and the astonishing amount put aside for her. Why had they left Shalimar to her and Mark jointly when they had only been married for a few months before the will was drawn up. Gramps hadn't known he was dying, had he? And even if he had, there was no telling how much longer his wife might go on. Gramps hadn't been naïve about modern-day marriages and their likelihood to endure. What possible reason could he have to imagine that she and Mark would still be together when Shalimar passed into their hands? Technically speaking, they weren't.

Suzie wanted to open her letter so badly it was like a physical ache, but something held her back and she went in search of displacement activities. She tidied away all signs of her parents' presence, throwing their sheets in the laundry basket. She took Sparkle for his second prolonged walk of the day, her grandfather's letter crackling in her pocket with every step she took. Back at home again—and it was only just starting to sink in that Shalimar really was her home now if she wanted it to be—she made a fuss of Honey, who was sulking because she'd been locked up and ignored for the greater part of the day. Then she scrubbed the bathroom clean, dusted the drawing room, and tidied the pristine kitchen. Her movements were rigorous, impulsive, and bore no particular heed to sequence or necessity.

Exhausted, Suzie finally collapsed between clean, crisp cotton sheets. Her grandfather's letter was now propped on her bedside table, his familiar, spidery handwriting a comfort to her. She burned to know why he'd done what he did. Gramps saw things that mostly escaped others and seldom acted without a sound reason, but was she strong enough to withstand his home-grown wisdom right now? She was tired and emotionally drained, so the answer was probably *no.*

Suzie turned the light off. She would deal with the letter tomorrow, after a good night's sleep when she was bound to feel more in control. First she needed to adjust to the startling turn events had taken.

Five minutes later, swearing with frustration, Suzie put light back on. She wouldn't be able to sleep until she knew what it said. With trembling hands, she broke the seal and pulled out two sheets of paper, covered closely with her grandfather's distinctive hand.

My darling Quzie, she read, tears already blurring her eyes at an affectionate derivative of her name that only he ever used. *By the time you read this, your grandmother and I will have turned up our toes and moved on to a better place, so I hope for all our sakes it will be a long time from now. Now stop it, Quzie, you're crying, aren't you?*

Suzie nodded, sniffled and smiled. Even in death, her grandfather could second-guess her.

Please don't be sad for us, darling. We have led long and interesting lives that have been greatly enhanced and enriched by your presence in them.

Suzie gave up her unequal struggle and allowed the tears to flow freely. Unable to find a tissue, she dashed to the bathroom and returned with a complete toilet roll. She had a feeling she was going to need all of it.

We want you to have Shalimar, darling. You are the only one who fully appreciates its unique value and understand why it's so special. You are well aware what it meant to us, and we know you won't view it simply for its monetary value. Whatever decision you make about its future will be an informed one. We trust your judgement completely and hope you will eventually come to see the gift as the blessing it's intended to be rather than a tiresome burden. You will have a difficult time of it with the rest of them, I know. There will be jealousy and resentment, and great pressure will be put upon you to do things their way. Trust your own judgement, darling, and be guided by Mark. He isn't afflicted with your soft heart or ridiculous feelings of duty to two people who have never shown you an ounce of affection.

I don't know how things will stand between you and Mark when you read this letter, but let me give you one last piece of advice, my Quzie. I have seen how comprehensively you love him and that your love is more than reciprocated. Mark is intelligent and ambitious, and those factors might well get in the way of your relationship, in the earlier years, anyway. He is a driven man who can't help but act out his ambitions in the competitive, dog-eat-dog world we've created for ourselves. Try and understand that men in general view things very differently from you softer-hearted women. What to you might seem the ultimate betrayal would, to a man such as Mark—or any man, come to that—be viewed as nothing more than an irrelevance. What I'm trying to say in my clumsy way, darling, is that there are times when even the most intelligent of men don't think with their brains.

Suzie stopped reading and blotted her face. To her astonishment, she discovered that she was smiling. The crafty old devil had understood, all that time ago, how things might come to be between her and Mark. It didn't excuse anything, of course, but it did stop her feeling that she'd somehow been to blame because she wasn't sophisticated enough to retain his interest. Suzie sat bolt upright. It was the first time she'd even realized that she felt culpable. Clever old Gramps!

You are wondering about the money, of course, and when you learn the truth, I suspect you will feel the full burden of our gift every bit as much as it's played upon my conscience all these years. I'm not proud of how I amassed my fortune, and that is why, apart from purchasing Shalimar, I haven't touched a penny of it. Now perhaps you will understand why the house is falling down around you when all the time I had the means to put it right. The trouble was, I couldn't bring myself to do so. I think, when you know the truth, you will understand that. Insufferable old coward that your grandfather is, he's left that decision to you. Forgive me, darling, please, but of us all you are the only one with sufficient conscience and moral fibre to do what's right, with Mark's pragmatic hand to guide you, of course!

The decisions one takes in one's life are seldom straightforward.

There isn't always a right and wrong course to take. Sometimes, when one sees the horrors that man inflicts upon his fellow man, it leads one to wonder how we can possibly suppose ourselves to be the superior species on this wonderful planet of ours. That's my only excuse for what I did. That and the completely inhumane madness of the situation that confronted me at the time.

The events to which I refer took place long before you and Mark were born. I can only hope that given the passage of time you will see the solution to this knotty problem, (for surely there must be one?), which has doggedly escaped me. One that will allow you to act appropriately and live peacefully with your consciences.

The situation is too volatile, even after all this time, to document in a letter that could conceivably fall into the wrong hands. Now you're really curious, aren't you? Don't worry, Quzie, and don't panic or think too badly of me, I beg of you. Just think about our favourite pastime during those winter evenings we enjoyed together when you were still small. Swallow your reservations, look further in the direction I have indicated, and all will be revealed.

We love you both, darling, and will comfort and guide the two of you from the next, hopefully more compassionate, life.

With our love always, Granny and Gramps.

Suzie wept uncontrollably. Heaving, wracking sobs of sadness that shook her entire body. She curled defensively into a foetal position and cried for all she had lost, for everything that had gone before and could never be recovered. Her grandparents, Mark and her marriage, the tenuous relationship she had maintained with her parents for so long. After all the terrible accusations that had flown today, it would probably be unsalvageable.

When her tears ran out, Suzie felt surprisingly calm. She reread her grandfather's letter, dry eyed this time, her curiosity well and truly piqued. What on earth had he done that had impinged so dreadfully upon his conscience, and how was she supposed to find out what it was? He implied that it was something dishonest, but she refused to believe that. For the life of her, she couldn't detect any of the clues, the supposed keys to the mystery he had left for her to discover. *Think, Suzie, think! Put yourself in Gramps's place. What is he trying to tell you? How exactly did we pass our evenings together?*

* * * *

At the start of their relationship, Annabel knew that John had her watched closely. She suspected that he even monitored her telephone calls. She didn't much care because she toed the line. She had no life away from him and work, and there was nothing sinister for him to discover. He eventually came to realize that and slowly relaxed his guard.

She'd never actively sought a relationship with a man, unless it was for profit, which is why Patrick came as a complete surprise. John was wrong about her. She could feel emotion and had experienced orgasms, but only with Patrick. He came into her life by accident after she met John and turned it on its well-organized head. He was a landscape gardener and lived in a small cottage just outside of Malton. Annabel met him when she called to see one of John's tenants who had grievances to air. Patrick was working in her garden, and that chance meeting caused her to rethink her entire attitude toward men.

Annabel had been determined to amass enough money to start her own business so she needn't be beholden to anyone ever again. But Patrick's green eyes, sparkling with lazy amusement as they passed the time of day, chatting about nothing in particular, caused something inside her to change. She noticed him in the way that a woman's supposed to notice a man, and when he invited her to have a drink with him later in the week, she surprised herself by accepting.

They met several times in out-of-the-way pubs where she was unlikely to see anyone she knew, but sooner or later an arrangement to meet Patrick would clash with John's need to be with her. He was unpredictable, telling her not to expect him and then turning up unannounced, expecting her to be pleased to see him. So far she'd always been there, but how long could her luck hold? She'd never risk bringing Patrick back here, but for the first time in her life, she actually wanted to go to bed with a man, purely for pleasure.

It happened a week later when he took her to his cottage. The feeling was unimaginable, and she knew then that whatever the risks to her arrangement with John and the collateral damage that would cause to her future plans, she wouldn't be able to stay away from him. Patrick made things easy by asking few questions about her work. He believed her when she told him that she was on call twenty-four-seven and often had to attend meetings at a few moments' notice. Why wouldn't he? Presumably, he hadn't met many liars as accomplished as she was. Annabel didn't want to think about the consequences if he ever discovered the truth. Fortunately, Patrick didn't like the fancy restaurants where she was likely to be recognized, couldn't afford them, and wasn't prepared to let her pay.

Annabel bought a pay-as-you-go mobile that John knew nothing about to keep in touch with Patrick and invested some of her precious savings a small, nondescript Fiat. She kept it in a private garage, well away from the penthouse, and used it to visit him whenever she could. On those occasions, she left the flat impeccably dressed and headed for the shopping centre. In case John had someone watching her, she then dived into the nearest lavatory, changed into jeans and the sort of top that would blend in with the crowd, hid her hair beneath a baseball cap, and headed for the Fiat.

Patrick's only drawback was that he lacked of ambition. His scrupulously clean but nevertheless tiny cottage wasn't anything to shout about either, but that didn't deter Annabel. It was only a matter of time before she'd be able to put that right. There was now no question of her completing her five-year arrangement with John—an arrangement that now seemed sordid and cheap. But she'd stick it a bit longer, amass a bit more cash, and then surprise Patrick by offering him the necessary funds to expand his business. Then perhaps they'd be able to live together, somewhere more prepossessing.

Patrick never displayed curiosity about her activities when she wasn't with him, much as she didn't know what he got up to when she wasn't around. If she asked him, he deflected the question by taking her to bed. Once there she forgot about everything except the exquisite feel of his hands and lips exploring every inch of her body. He was a skilled and thoughtful lover, and Annabel couldn't get enough of him. In bed after the act with John, it was champagne and cigarettes. With Patrick it was more likely to be cold baked beans straight out of the tin. Her, Annabel Burton, eating baked beans! What would once have been unthinkable was now the highlight of her life.

When Annabel was in bed with John, instead of locking herself away in her private place, she now thought about Patrick. Images of his compelling smile as he lay in knee-high grass, his arms reaching up for her, kept her sane. She longed for him with a desire that burned. She was doing this for him—for them—but he would never know what sacrifices she'd made to bring about their future financial security.

Annabel's phone rang, bringing her back to the present. She'd been sitting at her desk, lost in a reverie about Patrick for too long. People would notice and think she was feeling sorry for herself. Pity from the insignificant people in the office was something she definitely didn't need. She answered her phone more brusquely than usual, then picked up her bag and left the office. She needed to see her contact at Malton Council face-to-face and try to recover some ground with The Grange fiasco.

Chapter Eleven

Wednesday and Suzie had thought of little except the startling contents of her grandfather's letter. But she was no nearer to unravelling the mystery or solving the clues he'd left her.

News of her good fortune spread like wildfire, even though she hadn't mentioned it to anyone. The Grange crowd had descended upon her en masse on Tuesday. Never ones to miss out on an excuse for a good party, they all seemed to be genuinely delighted for her. Jack had been especially attentive. He redoubled his efforts to get her to dine with him alone, but Suzie would have none of it. They all wanted to know if she intended to stay in the property, but she was unable to tell them because she didn't yet know herself. It was too early to make such a big decision. She told no one about her grandfather's letter, not even Jane. Nor did she mention the huge amount of money she'd inherited. Until she understood the mystery behind its acquisition, it was something she would keep to herself.

What she did share with Jane was her hope that Mark would agree to sign over his share in the property to her.

"I'd then give up all claims on the Epsom house," she said. "It makes perfect sense all round."

"Hmm."

Suzie glowered at her. "And what's that supposed to mean?"

Jane answered her question with one of her own. "How did you get along with Mark over the weekend?"

Suzie was furious with herself for blushing, which clearly told Jane all she needed to know. When she flashed an infuriating grin, she received a well-aimed cushion in her solar plexus, and that ended the discussion.

Mark continued to phone twice daily. Suzie wouldn't talk about her grandfather's letter over the phone but agreed to let him read it when she saw him next. If nothing else, she'd need his assistance in locating that damned explanation. It was just the sort of problem that Mark, with his annoying ability to think laterally, would solve easily.

All of a sudden, her parents were her bosom buddies and she could do no wrong in their eyes. They, too, phoned daily, and Suzie tried not to resent the fact that she'd spoken to them more in the past three days than she had in over three years.

Wednesday afternoon was especially warm. Suzie, exhausted from a hard morning's gardening, dozed off on the terrace. All of the animals, including Honey, were doing the same thing, until a persistent knock at the front door brought them all back to full consciousness. She cursed the interruption, thought about ignoring it, but eventually got up to see who it was.

"If it's that awful Greenberg man again, then I won't even open the door," she told Sparkle as he trotted into the house ahead of her.

It wasn't Greenberg though. Suzie looked through the hall window and encountered three small, very familiar heads bobbing up and down. Panic welled up within her. Kate and her kids were standing, bold as brass, on the doorstep like nothing had happened to drive a wedge between them. What was she supposed to do about that?

As the initial shock receded, Suzie straightened her shoulders. She would *not* skulk about here as though she was the guilty party. She hadn't done anything wrong and was damned if she'd give that impression. She took a deep breath, opened the door and was almost bowled over as the children made a collective beeline for her. Unable to resist, she crouched down and accepted their kisses. She hugged little Jenny tightly, enjoying the feel of the puppy fat on her podgy arms as they wormed their way round her neck. She didn't even mind the sticky fingers that clutched at her hair.

"Aunt Suzie, you're squishing me," Jenny protested, giggling.

"Sorry, sweetheart." She let the little girl go.

"Aunt Suzie, we've come to see you!" the older ones said unnecessarily.

"So I see." She tousled their hair.

"Did we surprise you? Mummy said we would."

"Yes, you three are a delightful surprise."

She didn't know what else to say and was grateful when Sparkle whirled round them, attempting to round them up. Suzie transferred her attention to Kate, still unable to believe the nerve of the woman. She didn't trust herself to utter a word, not with the children within hearing, and left it for Kate to speak first.

"Suzie, I had to see you."

"That was a mean trick." Suzie nodded toward the children as they clustered round Honey.

"Would you have seen me if I hadn't brought them?"

Suzie snorted. "What do you think?"

"Well, there you are then." Kate paused, having the grace to look unsure of herself. "I know I have no right to ask you to listen, but there's something I have to say."

The children were now looking at them in confusion, sensing the tension in the atmosphere perhaps. It brought Suzie to her senses. Whatever their mother had done, they didn't deserve to be caught up in it. She opened the door and led them onto the terrace. The children tumbled about on the lawn like energetic puppies, Sparkle in the middle of them all as they chased balls and screamed with laughter. Honey hopped round in lopsided circles, keen to be included. The cats scarpered.

Without asking Kate if she wanted a drink, Suzie opened a bottle of white wine and plonked it on the table. If ever a situation called for alcohol, then this was it.

"Speak," she said succinctly.

Kate drew a deep breath, clearly apprehensive.

"Suzie, I don't know how to start apologizing for what I tried to do to you."

Suzie gaped at her. "Tried to do!"

"Yes, look, I know it sounds impossible, but I had my reasons."

"This I must hear," Suzie muttered, taking a huge gulp of wine.

"I wanted to apologize, even though I realize I can never make things right between us again." When Suzie remained stonily silent, Kate ploughed on. "You see, I was envious of you."

Suzie had no idea how Kate intended to defend her actions, but claiming jealousy was the last thing she'd expected. She glanced at her, her eyes wide with shock. "Of me!"

"Yes." Kate contemplated her in silence for a moment. "You don't get it, do you?" she said acerbically. "You had everything you could possibly want. For starters, a ridiculously successful and highly intelligent husband who just happens to be a hunk into the bargain. A beautiful home, money, lovely clothes, exotic holidays." Kate counted the points off on her fingers. "The freedom to do whatever you liked whenever you wanted to but you…well, you just didn't seem to appreciate it. You annoyed me, always whinging about kids—"

Roused to a fulminating anger by the injustice in Kate's words, Suzie found her voice. "But you had all those things, and so much more, too." She encompassed the three romping children with her eyes.

"Yes." She sighed. "I know that now, but I didn't then."

"I think you'd better explain." Suzie's words were precise and clipped.

"I was always the runt, you see."

Suzie blinked at her former friend. "The what?"

"In my family. I'm the youngest of six. All the others are tall, good-looking, successful, and much older than me. My father always referred to me as an afterthought, never took me seriously, and I could never compete with my siblings on any level. Nothing I did could ever eclipse their achievements, you see. It had all been done before by one or other of them, and however hard I tried I was unable to impress the father I adored."

Suzie, against her will, experienced the first stirrings of sympathy. She knew how it felt to be ignored and unappreciated. To distract herself, she refilled their glasses. "I didn't know," she said. "Why didn't you ever say anything?"

"I know you didn't. I tried to tell you once or twice, but you were always distracted by the kids. Or banging on about Mark and how much you hated him being away so much, about not having children of your own. It was always about you, Suzie, and in the end, I came to resent it. You just didn't seem to appreciate how lucky you actually are."

Suzie was silent for a moment. Had she really been so wrapped up in her own problems that she hadn't appreciated her friend was wrestling with a different set of demons?

"Kate, I didn't—"

"Anyway," Kate said, cutting across Suzie's interruption. "That's why I mucked myself about so much with plastic surgery. The tits and the other stuff. I wanted to stand out, be noticed and admired. Is that so bad?"

"No," Suzie said. "I could never understand why you did it. I always thought you were fine as you were, but when you put it like that, it makes more sense."

"Oh, I know you thought I was being self-indulgent, but once I started, I couldn't seem to stop. And Graham was so passive, so amenable to anything I wanted to do to myself that I thought he didn't like me the way I was either. Anyway, once I'd reinvented myself, I tried flirting with all the men I met, testing out my new look." Her gazed was now fixed on the paving stones. "Don't get me wrong, I didn't once betray Graham. As soon as I was confident that a man wanted me, I moved on to my next victim. Seeing the lust in their eyes was enough for me.

"But Mark was different. He flirted with me, but then I reckon he flirts with most women. It's just his way. He wasn't interested in getting into my knickers, not like all the others had been, and that made me all the more determined to have him. You see, if one person didn't want me, then I was a failure again." She sighed, still not meeting Suzie's gaze. "And that's when I started to resent you. It grew steadily worse, and in the end it drove me so demented that I had to do something about it. That's when I hatched my plan. I would have Mark, prove to myself that I was attractive and desirable, and put you in your place."

"My God!" Suzie raked a hand through her hair, wondering if Kate was a few fish short of a shoal.

"I think I must have been inflicted with temporary insanity," she said, finally looking directly at Suzie. "Not only did I risk everything I have, but I also ruined your relationship with Mark."

Suzie let out a long breath, unable to hazard a guess as to why Kate felt the need to bare her soul all of a sudden. "Kate, why are you telling me all this now?"

"I was getting to that bit." Her cheeks flamed with colour. "It all backfired rather spectacularly. Mark was disgusted by what I did. I tricked him into coming round, but he was disgusted by my antics and tried to walk out on me."

Suzie choked on a gulp of wine, all the hurt and feelings of betrayal she'd worked so hard to bury once again swamping her. "I noticed," she said contemptuously when she was able to speak again.

"No, really, it's true, but I wasn't having that. I knew he was aroused, and so I figured it would be easy enough to persuade him. When you walked in, he was in the process of fighting me off."

"What!"

"It's true. I swear it on the children's lives. I unzipped him, which is what you saw. He was so intent of getting away without being emasculated—I had a tight hold on his balls, you see—that he didn't know you were there."

"I see."

Suzie's brain whirled. Could it really be true? Had Mark been honest about what happened all along? He kept trying to explain, didn't he? But she wouldn't listen.

"I found an excuse not to go to Graham's parents with him and the kids last weekend." Kate's voice brought Suzie's mind back to the present. "I laid in wait for Mark in your house, convinced that he would be pleased to see me if only because he was feeling horny, but he was furious. He threw me out. I was dumfounded, humiliated, and blinded with rage. I drove around for hours, fuming. I'd been rejected yet again, you see."

"Is this where I'm supposed to express sympathy?"

"Hardly that, but I thought you ought to know the truth."

"Well, now I do. Thanks for telling me."

"Slowly that night, as I began to drink myself into oblivion to cover the hurt, I started coming to my senses," Kate said, ignoring Suzie's sarcasm. "I realized just what I had in Graham and the kids and was appalled at the risks I'd taken. I could have lost it all. And for what? I decided that when Graham got home, I'd make it up to him and work harder at our marriage. He's always been so malleable, and I thought it would be easy. But when he got home, he was a different person. It was like I was seeing him for the first time. He didn't believe that I'd been ill over the weekend and thought I'd just made an excuse so I didn't have to go to his parents'. He said he'd had enough of my selfish ways and of looking after the children all the time."

Suzie cast her a withering glare. "Can you blame him?"

"I couldn't believe the change in him. He was so masterful. He'd always been considerate when making love, putting my needs before his own. Suddenly he was a different man, demanding, dictatorial…" Kate sighed, but Suzie guessed it wasn't because she'd been left frustrated. "We talked forever after that. You see, when I married him, I was already pregnant with Sophie. After that, I started on my never-ending list of improvements and squashed two more pregnancies in as wel. Family life took us over, and we never really got used to being together just as a couple." She shrugged. "Didn't really understand each other, I suppose."

"You were still almost a child yourself when you married him, so that's not surprising."

"True, I was only seventeen." Kate flashed a conspiratorial grin that took Suzie back to their long cosy chats round the kitchen table. Those days were gone, spoiled by Kate's impulsive behaviour, and for the first time, Suzie realized how much she missed them. "Do you know, Graham told me he never really wanted me to have any of those operations. He said he'd fallen in love with me just the way I was and thought I was perfect." Her eyes shone. "Can you imagine it? Someone wanted me just because I was boring old me."

Sympathy and guilt at her own failure to detect Kate's previous unhappiness caused most of Suzie's resentments to melt away. "Of course I can. I just wish that you could learn to love yourself. You have a lot to offer."

"Anyway, we really started to open up to one another then, in between mad bouts of lovemaking," Kate said, giggling. "Graham confessed to a guilty secret. He told me he's been regularly seeing another woman for years. He felt I was too fragile to withstand his baser requirements and so went elsewhere to satisfy them. He thought I'd be horrified by the things he likes to do. That's partly why he's been so lenient about my selfishness. I couldn't believe it!"

Suzie could understand that. She was having problems getting her head round the mild man she thought she knew having raging sexual appetites.

"He begged me to forgive him and, of course, I did. I'm now more than capable of satisfying him, and he doesn't need the other woman anymore. It's like we're newlyweds all over again but without a tiny baby getting in the way."

"I'm glad," Suzie said, meaning it.

"Since we were clearing the air, I told him what I'd done to you and Mark. He didn't seem that surprised and was wonderfully supportive. He said it explained why he hadn't seen you recently. He'd been wondering. He also said I ought to find the courage to come and apologize to you face-to-face and try to explain. He's going to collar Mark, tell him he knows, and try and mend bridges there. We thought if we could start again with a clear deck, it would make things easier for us."

"I'm sure it will, Kate, and I'm pleased for you, really I am."

"I'm more comfortable with the children now, as well. They seemed a bit confused by the change in me at first. I'll be the first to admit that I wasn't the world's best mother." Kate turned at looked directly at Suzie. "Suzie, I am so, so sorry. I don't expect you to forgive the unforgivable, but I do hope you can find it in your heart to understand."

"I do understand, Kate. I just wish you'd told me about your problems before now. Was I really so wrapped up in myself that I didn't read the signs or take the time to listen?"

"Maybe. Who knows?" Kate paused. "What will you do about Mark? He really does love you, you know."

"Yes, perhaps he does, but I'm not sure yet what I'm going to do. I know you say you trapped him, but he didn't need to let things develop so far before walking out." She paused, voicing a question that had only just occurred to her. "How did you get him to call round? He was supposed to be going to the airport."

"I rang him on his mobile, said I wanted to talk to him about you. That I was worried about you."

She gaped at Kate. "And he believed that."

"Yeah, because he was worried about you, too. You hadn't been acting like yourself."

Suzie sighed. "No, I suppose not. I had a lot on my mind."

The children tumbled onto the terrace, demanding drinks. In short order, Suzie watered and fed them and then organized an energetic game of rounders on the lawn. Kate astonished her by joining in, laughing, never once chastising them or seeming bored.

When Suzie waved them off, she was glad Kate had found the courage to call. It felt as though a huge weight had been lifted from her shoulders. Mark hadn't been having an affair with Kate, but there were still issues to be resolved. Kate painted him as an innocent victim, but Suzie couldn't view him in the same light. The hurt was still too raw, and the doubts about his activities on his frequent business trips refused to go away.

* * * *

Annabel left the council office, not having achieved very much. She resolved to move to Plan B. The sooner she could resolve this minor problem for John, the quicker she'd be given a proper assignment to sink her teeth into.

She stopped in the local shop for a paper and packet of cigarettes. An attractive woman of about her age had engaged the shopkeeper in conversation, and Annabel waited impatiently, drumming her red talons on the counter. When the woman paid for her purchases and the shopkeeper addressed her as Mrs. Alexander, Annabel's curiosity was piqued. It would be a coincidence, but stranger things had been known to happen.

Annabel made her purchases in a rush and without waiting for her change dashed out of the shop in time to see the woman disappear into the multi-story. Annabel, who had parked her little sports car illegally on a double yellow, jumped into it before a gimlet-eyed traffic warden could finish writing her a ticket. The Alexander woman drove out of the car park in a bright red Jeep. Annabel followed her at a safe distance and watched from across the road as she pulled into the driveway of Shalimar, the dilapidated house close to The Grange.

There could no longer be any question that this woman must be somehow connected to the lawyer of the same name. But if she lived at Shalimar, why was John getting so upset? He had no interest in that property that she was aware of. It didn't impinge on their plans in any way.

Thorough as ever, Annabel headed back to the council offices and consulted the Land Registry computer. Yep, it was as she had supposed. Shalimar belonged to Mark Alexander and his wife Suzie.

As Annabel drove away, she churned her fledgling plan over in her mind, assessing the risks, searching for flaws. If she played her cards right, she could get her revenge on John Greenberg, feather her own nest, and bring her future with Patrick a little closer.

Chapter Twelve

"I'm sorry, Suzie, but I can't make the weekend."

"Oh." She tried not to let her disappointment be apparent in her voice.

"I'm so annoyed about this," Mark said. "I really wanted to see you."

"It doesn't matter."

"I have to make an unscheduled trip to Brussels to sort out some cock-up over last week's negotiations. I can't get round it, I'm afraid."

"I said it doesn't matter," Suzie repeated, more acerbically than she intended.

"I'll be back late on Saturday, and we'll still be able to spend the day together on Sunday."

As Suzie hung up, she told herself she was relieved. She'd been agonising over the sleeping arrangements. After all the help Mark had given her recently, she could hardly banish him to the local pub. Besides, he owned half of this house now and didn't need to claim squatters' rights. Did she really want him to spend the night in the spare room? Her head said yes, but from somewhere in the vicinity of her heart she received a very different response. She'd hurt him when she accused him of taking advantage of her, especially since they both knew it wasn't true. The memory made her flush with a mixture of embarrassment and unadulterated pleasure.

If she allowed him into her bed again, he would have a right to assume that she had forgiven him. In view of Kate's confession, perhaps she had. He'd told her the truth, at least about that, but if she did agree to take him back, what happened then? Would things go back to the way there were before with Mark travelling all the time and her with nothing meaningful to do to fill the long hours until he returned? Would he expect her to put Shalimar on the market and move back to Epsom?

Suzie didn't want to think about her complicated situation with Mark and concentrated upon solving her grandfather's puzzle instead. She absolutely refused to be defeated and thought back to their activities when she was young. They had played cards, word games, completed jigsaws, and read aloud. She'd already scoured the library, tipped jigsaw boxes upside down, pulled books at random from the shelves, and even moved the rugs to examine the floorboards for hiding places. Nothing had come to light.

Frustrated, she had turned her attention to the two attic rooms and spent the previous two days rummaging through her grandparents' accumulated possessions. It was an emotional roller-coaster ride that made her feel like an intruder as she uncovered a veritable cornucopia of fascinating treasures. The temptation to examine them was compelling. There were old theatre programmes dating back to before the war, letters between Granny and Gramps written when he'd been off on one of his wild adventures. Other papers that she found meant nothing to her and didn't appear to shed any light on Gramps's secret. She cast them aside with an increasing sense of frustration.

Her mood improved when she discovered a box full of sepia photographs, faded with age. There were shots of Granny when she was young and of Gramps as a strutting peacock in a striped blazer and straw boater. Suzie smiled as she wiped the tears from her face and disciplined herself to keep searching.

A one-eyed rocking horse that she remembered well from her childhood held no secrets in his worm-eaten tummy. Nor did the discarded teddy bears, the old dollhouse, and the half-deflated space hopper.

On Saturday evening, Suzie finally admitted defeat. Perhaps if she stepped back and emptied her mind of anything to do with Gramps, a solution would slip into her mind. Failing that, she'd just have to pass the problem over to Mark when he arrived tomorrow.

"If he spots the answer immediately without even having to think about it," she told an attentive Sparkle, "then I swear I'll kill him."

Sparkle tilted his head to one side and let out an ambivalent little moan, confirming Suzie's belief that he understood every word she said. As she stroked his scruffy head, Sparkle's hackles rose beneath her hand. He leapt to his feet and rushed to the French doors, barking loud enough to wake the dead. The barks gave way to cautious whines of recognition as Jack put his head round the door.

"Hi." He entered the drawing room and offered Suzie a fulsome peck on the cheek. "Good, you're not doing anything. Jane tells me you need cheering up because hubby isn't coming down today."

Jane needed to learn to keep her damned mouth shut. "Hmm, not really."

"Yes, really, and I've been detailed to pick you up and take you to join the rest of them in the pub. So come on, chop-chop, no arguments, get yourself ready."

Suzie smiled, suddenly grateful for his cheerful persistence. An evening alone at home was just what she didn't need. If that happened, she was bound to dwell upon her grandfather's conundrum.

"Okay," she agreed, jumping up. "I won't be a minute. Help yourself to a drink."

When Suzie returned to the drawing room just fifteen minutes later, there was no sign of Jack. She stepped out onto the terrace, excepting to find him enjoying the last of the evening sun, but he wasn't there either. Perhaps he was in the lavatory. Several minutes later, she was still waiting for him to reappear. If he was in the smallest room, he was certainly taking his time. Then a sound from the library alerted her. She made her way toward that room, curious to know what he was doing. Obviously not expecting her to return so swiftly, Jack was taking a leisurely look round. She leaned against the doorjamb, but he didn't detect her presence and continued pulling out books, looking at the papers on her desk, even carefully lifting pictures away from the wall.

"What do you think you're doing?" she asked acerbically.

The sound of Suzie's voice made him jump like a scalded cat. Whisky slopped from his glass and spilled over his hand. "God, Suzie, you gave me a fright!"

"Then perhaps you shouldn't snoop."

"I love books," he said with a disarming grin, "and have always wanted to look at this collection. Sorry, should have asked if you minded first. You look great," he said, changing the subject with an alacrity that made Suzie uneasy. "Come on, the others will be wondering where we've got to."

When they entered the pub, they were greeted with loud guffaws and unseemly speculations about what had taken them so long. Only Jane, Ellen, Gordon, and Pansy were there. Pansy had desisted with her doomed pursuit of Jack and transferred her affections to Gordon. They were sitting together, a little apart from Jane and Ellen, holding hands and talking quietly to one another. Suzie raised a surprised brow at Jane, who grinned back at her as if to say she had guessed it would happen all along. She probably had.

A large gin and tonic in front of her, Suzie relaxed in the company of her friends and joined in the gentle banter directed toward Gordon and Pansy. She barely noticed how quickly she downed her first drink, or that a second had appeared in its place.

"We're having a serious discussion about the healing properties of alcohol," Jane told her. "Can't think how people who don't indulge manage to unwind at the end of a long day."

"Puts one in mind of that old W.C. Fields's quotation," Jack said. "The one where he comments that a woman once drove him to drink and he never had the courtesy to thank her."

Everyone laughed. "Maybe that would be a way to raise funds for The Grange?" Ellen said halfheartedly as she took a healthy swig of white wine. "We could go on a sponsored detox."

"Yeah, and how long do you reckon we'd last? And more to the point, who would sponsor us?"

"Most people in here that know us, I should imagine," Jane said briskly. "They know their money would be safe." More laughter. "My own record before falling off the wagon is two days, three hours, and seventeen minutes. Not that I was counting, of course." Jane sounded quite pleased with herself, and everyone looked suitably impressed.

"I've been meaning to ask," Suzie said. "How did the roof stand up to the storm?"

"Oh, we got through it okay, but it was a case of all hands to the commodes. It's forced me into getting a quote for reroofing. We really can't go on like this, but the cost is frightening. Don't think I can run to it quite yet because I haven't got a pot to piss in."

There was a collective groan at this corny reference to the commodes.

Gordon drained his glass. "Pansy and I are going for…er, for a walk," Gordon said, colouring as he held out a hand to Pansy.

Four pairs of eyebrows disappeared beneath hairlines as the pair beat a hasty retreat. Jane stood as well.

"Come on, Ellen," she said. "We really must make a dent in that paperwork."

Suzie shot Jane a beseeching glance. She really didn't want to be left alone with Jack. But Jane either didn't see or chose not to understand.

"See you tomorrow," she said.

And with that they were both gone.

"Did you get me here under false pretences?" Suzie asked Jack, trying to sound stern. The effect was ruined due to the amount of gin she'd hastily consumed on an empty stomach, and her words didn't sound entirely coherent.

"Hey!" He raised his hands in a gesture of innocence. "I was only obeying orders. How was I to know that our scintillating company wouldn't hold them all spellbound?"

"I suppose you couldn't have."

"Indeed not." He offered her a broad, infectious smile, and Suzie was quite affected by it. She blamed the gin for the fact that she also noticed just how good-looking Jack actually was. "Since you refuse to set foot in a restaurant with me, why don't we eat something here?"

"Okay."

"You will? Great!" Jack grabbed two menus before she could change her mind.

In spite of her misgivings, Suzie relaxed and found herself enjoying Jack's company. As they ate, she barely noticed how little Jack was drinking, or that she consumed most of the bottle of claret he'd ordered with their food. Everything he said sounded witty and hilariously funny, but she had to concentrate hard to understand what he was on about. Currently he was regaling her with details of a doomed affair he'd almost had at his previous practise. At least she thought he was.

"She was a pretty girl, and I might have been tempted. Only problem was, she was petrified of animals and couldn't stand them anywhere near her."

"Yes, well I can see that might have caused a bit of a conflict."

"To her credit, she made a good stab at hiding her fear, but you can tell immediately when someone isn't an instinctive animal lover. She cringed when so much as a cat crossed her path but insisted upon accompanying me one evening when I was called out to deliver a calf." He smiled across the table at her. "I knew it would end in tears. She threw up repeatedly, and I spent more time attending to her than I did delivering the calf."

Suzie laughed. "So what happened to her after that?"

"We agreed to go our separate ways, and six months later she married a farmer!"

Suzie thought it was hilarious and cracked up.

"Did you know that your eyes change colour when you laugh?" Jack asked, watching her intently.

"Jack, don't."

"Don't what?" He looked convincingly innocent. "I was only remarking."

"Don't make me feel uncomfortable."

"That's not my intention. You are a very sensual woman, Suzie, I've told you that before." He met her gaze steadily. "And I want you."

"Jack, I—"

"Sorry, forget I said that. I'm acting like an ass." He waved both hands in the air. "I finally get you to myself, and then I frighten you off."

"Let's change the subject."

"Okay, about your books. I'm sorry I was snooping. It was rude of me. But I really do love books and would enjoy having a closer look at your grandfather's collection. Not that I get much time to read, mind, but I've got an interesting collection of first editions of my own. Perhaps you'd like to see them?"

"Oh, Jack!" Suzie howled with renewed laughter. "Is that the best you can do?"

Jack grinned ruefully. "It did sound a bit on a par with 'come up and see my etchings' I suppose. You bring out the worst in me, Suzie Alexander."

Suzie's mobile rang, and she was grateful for its intrusion. This conversation was getting too personal. She excused herself and extracted her phone from her bag.

"Suzie, it's Mark. Where are you, darling?"

"In the local with the gang. Are you home?"

"No I'm bloody well not. We missed our flight because of last minute holdups with the contract and had to book ourselves on a later one. Now we're at the airport and the bloody French Air Traffic Controllers have decided to stage a twenty-four-hour lightning strike. We won't be able to get out of here until Monday, I shouldn't think."

"Oh dear, I'm sorry. Still, never mind, there's always next

weekend."

"I desperately wanted to see you."

"It can't be helped. Anyway, you're not on your own. Who's there with you?"

"Just Rebecca."

"Oh."

"I put an investigator on things down there," he said.

"You did!" Suzie could hear the surprise in her own voice and was glad she'd moved away from Jack to take the call. She didn't want him eavesdropping. "You didn't say."

"I wasn't sure what he would turn up."

"Well, what did he find?"

"John Greenberg's a self-made man, married into old money, father of three, managing director of a publicly quoted property company Greenberg Enterprises, based in Basingstoke. He's sailed pretty close to the wind once or twice, but no mud has stuck. Reading between the lines, it seems that he's either been exceedingly fortunate or has managed to grease the right palms."

"So he's a property developer. Is that why he wants Shalimar, do you think?"

"I suppose so, but I haven't figured out why he's so desperate to get his hands on it that he'd offer so much more than it's worth."

Suzie didn't doubt that he soon would. "What else?" she asked.

"Well, the entire row of cottages behind The Grange is owned by a subsidiary of Greenberg's called Forestline."

Suzie shook her head. Fuzzy from the effects of alcohol, she had trouble absorbing Mark's news. "I don't understand any of this," she said weakly.

"Nor do I, darling, but I shall introduce myself to Mr. Greenberg when I get back and let him know I'm on to him. That should put an end to his little game."

"Let's hope so but—"

"Sorry, darling, I have to go. Rebecca's managed to grab a cab.

We need to get back to the hotel and see if we can reclaim our rooms. The place is full of EU officials on some sort of junket, and we might have a problem. I love you, Suzie, and I'll talk to you tomorrow."

"Good-bye, Mark."

"Problem," Jack asked as she hung up and returned to their table.

"Yes, air traffic control strike. He's stuck in Brussels."

"Oh dear."

"Your sympathy is quite underwhelming."

But Suzie wasn't concentrating upon Jack. Instead, she struggled to dispel the image of Mark alone in a Brussels hotel, time on his hands and the voluptuous Rebecca to while it away with. Along with that image, all her doubts about him returned tenfold.

"Sorry, perhaps I'd better change the subject." Jack smiled at her. "We were talking about books. As a kid, I was never to be seen without my nose in one. I was—

"Suzie, are you all right? You've gone very pale."

"What, oh yes, I'm fine. Just a bit too much to drink. Perhaps you'd better take me home?"

"And tuck you up in bed?"

She sighed. "Don't push it, Jack. It's getting tedious."

She had trouble standing. Jack helped her to his car, opened the door for her, leaned over from the driver's seat and fastened her belt. She barely noticed. He drove her to Shalimar, stopped in the driveway, released her belt, pulled her into his arms, and kissed her. She let him because she was too preoccupied to do anything about it. Suzie was in shock. It had worked out just as she'd predicted. She had emptied her mind, got plastered, relaxed completely, and a chance comment of Jack's had unlocked the Pandora's box.

She knew now where her grandfather had hidden his explanation.

* * * *

Annabel didn't tell John about her chance encounter with Suzie

Alexander. He hadn't told her why he was interested in Shalimar, but she knew why he wanted The Grange, and so she could guess. There were two options open to her. She could either arrange for the Alexanders and the people at The Grange to discover exactly what John was up to and scotch his plans once and for all, or she could apply her mind to acquiring Shalimar for her boss and ensuring her star was once again firmly in the ascendency. The thought of the satisfaction she'd feel at blowing John's pet project was compelling, but Annabel never took decision based on sentiment or personal gratification, and wasn't about to start now.

She mulled the situation over. The Alexanders were obviously the key to it all. If they supported the Grant woman's bid to remain at The Grange, it followed that they wanted to hold on to Shalimar. Presumably, John had tried throwing money at the situation, but the direct approach wasn't always the best way to go. Everyone had skeletons in their cupboards, and the Alexanders would be no exception. She picked up her phone and called Jim.

"Get me everything you can on Mark and Suzie Alexander," she said, giving them Shalimar's address as a starting point.

"You're looking for dirt?"

"Why else would I call you?" she asked with a weary sigh.

"I assume you also want it all by yesterday."

"Naturally."

"Then it will cost you."

Annabel rolled her eyes. "When doesn't it?"

Chapter Thirteen

As soon as Jack left her, Suzie let herself in, downed a couple of aspirin, and drank several glasses of water, hoping to ward off the inevitable hangover. She was in no fit state to seek out her grandfather's explanation, but it had been hidden for years, so another day wouldn't make much difference. She let Sparkle out, checked on Honey, and then trudged up to bed.

As she wobbled out of her clothes, Suzie dissolved in a fit of alcohol-fuelled giggles. What an idiot she'd been! She just thanked goodness she'd solved the mystery before asking for Mark's help. It was so blindingly obvious, and he would have cracked it without breaking a sweat.

What was it that Gramps had said? *"Swallow your reservations….Think about our favourite pastime during the winter evenings when you were still small."*

Gramps frequently read aloud to her and Derek, enthralling his young listeners with the adventures contained in old favourites like *Treasure Island*, *The Railway Children*, and *Huckleberry Finn*. His deep, gravelly voice could resonate with fear, excitement, or danger, changing cadence in the blink of an eye and lingering for just enough time to build on the tension, ad-libbing shamefully as he made the characters come alive for Suzie and her brother. And their favourite book of all time?

Swallows and Amazons!

Suzie, alert and thankfully hangover-less the following morning, headed for the library. Ruthlessly suppressing the fear that her grandfather's letter had generated, trying to dispel the uneasy feeling that she would be better off walking away and leaving things as they were, she headed straight to the shelf that contained Ransome's work. She didn't have to think about where to find the volume because it was just where it had always been. She took a deep breath and pulled the book toward her, expecting an envelope to fall from between the pages.

Nothing.

Suzie was puzzled. She knew she'd interpreted her grandfather's clues correctly, but there was definitely nothing there. A more thorough search confirmed that. She pulled several more books from the shelf at random. Perhaps something had been hidden behind them. Again, there was nothing. Determined not to be beaten, she stood on a stool and ran her hand along the back of the shelf. That was how she detected a slight indentation in the otherwise smooth back surface. Pulling further books out of the way, she could now see that some sort of compartment was hidden in the old oak. The problem was, there was no obvious way to open it. No keyhole or raised edge that one could pull out.

She thought for a minute and then did what she'd seen done in bad old detective films and gave each corner of the compartment a firm prod, more in hope than expectation.

"Come on, come on," she muttered. "I've got this far. Don't hold out on me now."

On her third attempt, she was rewarded with a loud clunk. The compartment sprang away from the shelf and slid smoothly toward her. Exalted but also a little fearful of what she was about to discover—all this cloak-and-dagger stuff seemed a little extreme—Suzie extracted a flat tin box and carried it to her grandfather's desk. Damn, the box was locked, but she wasn't about to let that defeat her. She searched the desk drawers, vaguely remembering seeing some keys that she couldn't find corresponding locks for. She located them, selected the smallest one on the bunch, and tried it. Bingo, she was in!

Seated behind her grandfather's desk, Suzie extracted a thick sheaf of papers covered with her grandfather's familiar handwriting. The papers were dated in the early sixties, were not addressed to anyone, and contained no sort of heading or anything by way of introduction. Suzie frowned. They appeared to be some sort of journal. She took a deep breath and paused, waiting for the tremor in her hands to settle before she commenced reading.

By September 1944, we all thought this terrible war was coming to an end. Hitler was in retreat, his High Command in tatters, his army poorly equipped and badly demoralised. But the same could be said of both sides. I'd lost sight of the ideological young man I had been in 1939, keen to join up and take my share of the glory. We would give the Hun a bloody nose—again—and it would all be over by Christmas. Everyone believed that, fools that we were.

I still can't believe the cruelty, the sheer scale of the inhumanity and discrimination, the unnecessary loss of life that took place even before the war had properly gotten underway. It ought to have told us something, but I suppose we weren't listening. The ignorance and fear displayed by ill-prepared young officers with hastily acquired, theoretical knowledge of warfare that bore little resemblance to the reality still rankles today. Their arrogant refusal to apply to their vastly more experienced NCOs for advice before giving badly thought out and often conflicting orders caused many of my comrades to lose their lives unnecessarily.

Living through such experiences changes a man. How could it be otherwise? Ideology gave way to cynicism, compassion was a word we could no longer spell, England a land we barely remembered. Most of us were no longer even sure what we were supposed to be fighting for, or why it mattered so much anyway.

Understanding something of the German psyche by now, and even more about Hitler's staunch refusal to admit defeat, it came as no surprise to many of us when German High Command attempted to reverse the tide of war by striking through the Ardennes and crossing the River Meuse to retake the port of Antwerp. The idea was to isolate the British Army from our American allies, obtain a separate peace on the Western Front, and subsequently confront the advance of the Russian Army in the east. It was an ill thought out, badly planned, and very desperate last-ditch attempt to turn the tide of the war.

So it was that on the 16th December 1944, on a cold, fog-bound morning the Battle of the Ardennes, or as history has subsequently labelled it, The Battle of the Bulge, began. The US 10th Armoured Division bore the brunt of the fighting, but us British played an important part in the battle, too, Field Marshal Montgomery being in overall command of the 21st Army Group.

I was with the 6th Airborne Division. Due to atrocious weather conditions, we were unable to parachute in as planned and on the 22nd December were instead rushed by boat and truck to the Ardennes. We took up defensive positions between Dinant and Marche-en-Famenne, at the tip of the German offensive.

On the 24th December, the 3rd Royal Tank Regiment, supported by US tanks and the RAF, crossed the River Meuse and stopped an armoured column of the 2. Panzer. It was the first encounter between British and German troops in this particular battle, and we prevailed. The German Army was never to cross the River Meuse, and their tactical objective was no longer Antwerp and its port but Bastogne.

Christmas brought no respite, and on all fronts the fighting was conducted with the same relentless fury. On the 3rd January 1945, in biting cold, snow, and ice we began on the general counterattack as decreed by Allied High Command. My 6th Airborne Division, supported by tanks of the Fife and Forfar Yeomanry and the 23rd Hussars, were the first to become involved in the counteroffensive. After ferocious fighting and sustaining heavy losses, we were eventually able to liberate the village of Bure.

The battle continued on its bloody way until finally, on the 28th January, the German Army was pushed back to its initial positions, beyond the Siegfried Line. Thus ended not only the Battle but also the *invasion and occupation of Allied regions.*

No one who served in that battle with ever forget the horrendous weather, rough terrain, and fierce fighting. Over 300 allied servicemen were left behind in the Commonwealth War Cemetery in Hotton, and they especially will never be forgotten by those of us that survived.

Whilst we were risking our lives to bring this terrible battle to a conclusion, we had little idea about a conflict of a very different type that was being played out in an area of about one hundred square miles of Southern Bavaria. It was an engagement in which intrigue, murder, conspiracy, and theft were commonplace.

The Nazis not only carried out a programme of brutal ethnic cleansing but also confiscated the wealth amassed by their victims and plundered national treasures from the countries they occupied. As the defeat of Germany became inevitable, so Garmisch in Bavaria became a central point for smuggled wealth. The bulk of Nazi treasure worth in excess of three billion dollars was moved from the German Reichenbach in Munich and Frankfurt to Garmisch. Much of it didn't complete its journey and mysteriously disappeared en route.

Garmisch quickly established itself as a centre for the black market, where anything was available, at a price. It was a melting pot of intrigue, racketeering, corruption by high-ranking Nazi officers, murder, double-dealing, and so much more. Amid the confusion of an army in retreat and the convergence of the allies into the region, keeping order was next to impossible. Large portions of gold, currency, diamonds, and other valuables disappeared and have never been accounted for by the authorities.

Because of my linguist ability—I was fluent in both French and German—I was seconded to the Intelligence Corps and despatched to Garmisch. My orders were to get close to the British troops still in the region and report back any information that came my way regarding the disappearance of looted treasure. It should be mentioned that this territory was largely occupied by the Americans, who had amazingly unearthed, amongst many other things, no less than 728 gold ingots.

I teamed up with another British Intelligence Officer named Peter James, and together we attempted to make some sense of the madness. Battle weary, we were strangely immune to cruelty by then and showed no particular reaction to the rumour that thirty-four civilians had been murdered by the Germans on Christmas Eve in Bande near Nassogne. We had discovered long ago that news of atrocities that would once have turned our blood cold and have us baying for revenge were now accepted with an air of almost casual inevitability. War does that to a man. If you let the horror get to you, then you're finished. Adopt a hard shell, do your job, keep your head down, don't think, don't question anything, and you just might survive.

Peter and I were hampered at every turn. Everyone seemed to have something to hide. Maintaining discipline was difficult but accounting for treasure which had never been itemised in the first place was next to impossible. Everyone was out for himself. Our task was hopeless.

I was getting nowhere, and Intelligence Corps ordered me back to my regiment. The night before I was due to leave, Peter and I got comprehensively drunk. I went outside to relieve myself and noticed several men hovering suspiciously at the edge of the muddy street, close to a deep stand of trees. I called Peter and, strangely sober now, we followed at a distance. They weren't in uniform, but we heard them speaking in German. They were deserters and, from the clipped, authoritative tone of their voices, fairly high-ranking ones. We learned later that fleeing German SS Colonels, many of whom found their way to Argentina and subsequently formed successful companies, did so by burying stolen gold in the vicinity of Garmisch and using it to buy their way into legitimate businesses.

That was precisely what Peter and I witnessed, although of course we didn't know it at the time. We waited until they left and commenced digging in the same spot. We unearthed bars of gold, diamonds, and other precious stones, the value of which we could only begin to guess at. We would, of course, turn our find in to the authorities.

"What authorities?" Peter asked me later that evening, as we discussed the matter in hushed voices in our shared room. "Whose treasure was it in the first place?"

The argument raged between us for most of the night. Peter was persuasive. This loot had been stolen from someone. But whom? Why should we not help ourselves to some of it? The Yanks were at it big time. So obviously were the Krauts and just about anyone else who could lay their hands on something worth having.

When I remained unconvinced, Peter tried a different tack. What about all the atrocities we'd witnessed over the past five years? The bungled orders given by frightened young officers, still little more than schoolboys themselves. The ill-judged advances toward almost certain death, the betrayals, the torture and brutality. What about all the men who had been our comrades and were now no more? What had they suffered and died for? When I suggested it was for the freedom of the world, he could tell I didn't really believe it myself anymore, and he wanted to know what we had risked our lives for anyway? There were no jobs waiting for us back home, no grateful masses willing to set us up for life. If we had learned nothing else during this conflict, then we should, at least, realize that it was every man for himself. If we didn't help ourselves, then who else would? Whoever we handed it over to would almost certainly appropriate at least some of it for himself. I should take a share now, and if when I'd had time to think more calmly about it, my conscience wouldn't allow me to keep it, then I should donate it anonymously to some deserving cause.

To my shame, he convinced me. I was to leave first thing in the morning and took as many diamonds as I could secrete about my person. I left the lion's share of treasure behind. Most of it was too bulky for one man to take without arousing suspicion, but Peter told me not to worry. He would make arrangements to have it removed, and when we were both back in England, we'd meet up and divide the rest of the spoils.

I got away with it. I had expected to be searched when I returned to my regiment. In a way, I almost hoped I would be, but it didn't happen. Everything was chaotic. We were to return home, and everyone was literally demob happy.

I never heard from Peter again. I wrote to the address he gave me but received no reply. I later discovered that it didn't even exist. I checked with the war office. He had not been lost in action, nor had he been arrested. What happened to him and the rest of the treasure remains a mystery, but he obviously never had any intention of sharing it with me. I didn't mind. I had more than enough for my needs, and it played on my conscience to such a degree that I couldn't bring myself to do anything with it.

Returning home was much as Peter had predicted it would be. A hero's welcome—yes. But then postwar depression. No jobs, little prospects. Still riddled with guilt, I volunteered to return to Germany and help the humanitarian operation. Émigrés were returning to the area, frantically seeking information about loved ones, and we did our best to document cases and bring people together. Occasionally we were successful. Seeing separated relatives who had survived on their wits for the long years of the war reunited with families they had all but given up on was reward enough for our efforts.

The stories I heard from Jews who emerged from the concentration camps as walking skeletons haunt me all these years on. As I listened to their accounts of Nazi evil based solely on religious intolerance, the extent of which I hadn't even guessed at, made me feel a little better about the crime I had committed.

It was whilst I was in Berlin in 1946 that I met and married my beloved Flora. She was an Army nurse who had also volunteered her services to help displaced people. I had never truly believed in love at first sight before then, but as our eyes met across a room full of grim, half-starved refugees, I knew that such a thing existed. Something changed within me as I observed the compassion in eyes full of unshed tears, and I knew I was looking at the woman I would eventually marry.

Flora and I returned to England in '47 and lived with her parents in Southampton whilst I tried to decide what I was going to do with myself. Flora's parents were kind people. They were religious but didn't try to thrust their faith down the throats of others. Flora and I attended Sunday service with them. After all the horrors I had experienced, I could no longer believe in or take comfort from their God and had a hard time reconciling this compassionate, all-caring entity of theirs with the savage reality of the conflict I'd lived through.

Restless, I spent the next three years searching for an occupation that would engage me and took time to examine my conscience. I was a part of an archaeological dig in Egypt, offered my services briefly as a mercenary, took increasingly stupid risks, and barely spared a thought for the anguish I was causing to my gentle Flora. I knew why I did it though. I was running from making a decision about those wretched diamonds, hidden in a safety deposit box.

In 1950, Flora wrote me that she was pregnant, and this brought me to my senses. By then all sorts of information was coming to light with regard to looted treasure, especially the escape of all those high-ranking Nazi officers to Argentina. No mention was made of the heinous crimes they'd committed and a bewildered world gradually understood they would never face a court of law. There were also rumours about the Americans. Those 728 bars of gold had all, inexplicably, disappeared. A full investigation by the US army failed to uncover them but significantly absolved US forces from all blame.

The hypocrisy left a nasty taste in my mouth but also made up my mind for me. I had responsibilities now that I was to become a father. I sold some of my diamonds, receiving less than they were worth because the only dealers I dared approach were as dishonest as me. Nevertheless, I realized enough to purchase Shalimar and settled down to the trade, which, I suppose, was always intended to be mine. I became a bookbinder. It provided an income for my fledgling family, flamed my compulsion for the written word, and was the start of the intriguing collection of books housed at Shalimar today.

My son was born in the spring of 1951. I was full of hopes for the future of what was to be my only child. When he came of age, I would explain about my loot, now carefully hidden in the compartment I had made for it in my library at Shalimar, try and make him understand how things were at the time, and let him decide what should be done about it.

My son Peter didn't grow into the kind of young man I hoped he would be. As was the case with most families in those days, we took him to church regularly and enrolled him in the local Sunday school. Unlike other children, he never attempted to wangle out of going. He mulled over everything he learned there in his slow, deliberate manner and appeared to accept it all as...well, as gospel. He was a loner, didn't make friends easily, possessed few social graces, and only ever showed animation over religious debate. Flora and I still hoped that as he reached adolescence so his interests, most particularly in the opposite sex, would outweigh his religious fervour.

This might have proved to be the case had he not, at the age of eighteen, met a new family at church. Their daughter Celia was a year older than Peter. The pair struck up a rapport and became inseparable. God will forgive me for saying that I disliked Celia on sight. Her religious zealousness made Peter's appear mild by comparison, and she possessed an alarming propensity to disapprove of anything that lacked religious connotations. Any lighthearted pastime such as attending the theatre or cinema was frowned upon. She disapproved of drinking and smoking, ate the plainest of plain food, wore shapeless, mostly secondhand clothes, and donated every penny she could spare to Christian causes. It was only when she spoke of such things that her face showed the slightest animation. The rest of the time, she wore a pinched expression, appearing to disapprove of everything she observed and quickly endowed the impressionable Peter with the same censorious attitude. Celia lacked humour, compassion, and any sense of proportion or forgiveness. She bore no truck with human frailty, and it was a sad day for Flora and I when the couple married.

I knew then that I couldn't entrust Peter with my guilty secret. Celia would have all the funds diverted to Christian charities in the blink of an eye. After all I'd seen of the corruption that existed during and after the war, I was no longer certain that this would be the right thing to do.

Suzie stopped reading, rubbed her tired eyes, and tried to make sense of it all. Her head fell forward into her hands. Of all the wild ideas that had been running through her brain, none of them had come close to the truth.

"Oh, Gramps, what have you landed me with?" she cried aloud.

There was still more to read, and Suzie couldn't leave it until she knew it all. She perused the remaining pages. There was a triumphant note in 1975 when Derek was born. Another such in 1980 to celebrate her own arrival. Her grandfather felt reassured to be blessed with two grandchildren.

The final page of her grandfather's account was written just after her marriage to Mark.

At last I know I can die in peace. My beloved Suzie has married an intelligent man with great strength of character who will bring her happiness. I don't for a moment doubt that. I shall make Shalimar over to them and realize a little more money from my stash of stones to invest for them. I suppose I should also set some aside for my disappointing grandson who is proving to be too much like his parents for my comfort.

I trust Suzie and Mark to know what to do and only hope they can find it in their hearts to forgive an old man for both his original sin and constant vacillation thereafter.

With tears streaming down her face, Suzie's fingers searched the corners of the tin and located several pouches. She poured the contents of one onto the desk. Uncut diamonds, she imagined. They weren't shiny like in her engagement ring, but rough, dull pieces of stone.

It was all too much to come to terms with. Her head was thumping, and she couldn't think about it now. She placed everything carefully back in the tin, including the letter Gramps had written to her, and concealed it in the alcove. She needed to think hard about this one.

And she needed to talk to Mark about it.

* * * *

Jim's report brought to light some interesting stuff.

"She's clean," he said. "Can't find anything on her that might interest you." Even so, he gave her a rundown on the woman's Bible-bashing family and the fact that she'd been brought up at Shalimar by her grandparents. "Word is she loves the place."

He paused, presumably expecting something from Annabel. "Go on," she said impatiently.

"They've been married ten years, and I couldn't find a whiff of an affair on her part, *but* she appears to have moved out of the marital home in Epsom."

"How recently?" Annabel asked sharply.

"Less than a month ago and she's now living full-time at Shalimar."

Annabel's ears pricked up. "Which implies that hubby hasn't been a good boy."

"She's friendly with the crowd at The Grange, and there's a local vet, Jack Simmons, who hangs round her when her husband's not there."

"Is there indeed."

"Alexander's at Shalimar most weekends but spends a lot of the working week travelling."

Annabel made copious notes, impressed in spite of herself as Jim told her about Mark Alexander's career. He sounded like a formidable opponent, but she was no slouch herself. And she had an edge because she wasn't too bothered about playing fair.

"What about their finances?"

"Not enough time to get much, but Shalimar is theirs outright and they only have a small mortgage on the Epsom pile."

No wonder John hadn't been able to buy them out of Shalimar.

"I hung around some of the crowd from his office. He has a very attractive female associate, and I just happened to sit at the next table in a bistro whilst she had a heart-to-heart with a girlfriend. Seems Mark Alexander is the office heartthrob, but he's not known for giving out. This Rebecca boasted about getting close. Apparently they spend a lot of time together in Brussels and find more to discuss over dinner than the state of the EU."

"Hum, is that so?"

"It's probably all talk. Haven't been able to find anything to back up her boasts, but if you give me more time—"

"No, that will do for now."

Annabel thanked him and hung up, deep in thought. She had enough to sow the seed of doubt in Suzie Alexander's mind, especially if she'd moved to Shalimar because of matrimonial strife. Nothing sounded the death knell for fragile relationships quicker than rumour and innuendo.

The question was, did she want to do that? If she broke their marriage up, then Shalimar would, presumably, have to go, and John would get what he wanted. But she'd still be firmly under his control.

What to do?

Chapter Fourteen

Still distracted by all she had learned, Suzie attended the normal Sunday lunch at The Grange nursing a hangover and with a whole raft of unanswered questions rattling about inside her aching head. Jack was more possessive than ever, seeming to think that because they'd had supper at the pub the night before and he hadn't taken advantage of her inebriated condition, he'd passed some sort of test. Only now did it occur to her that he was responsible for that condition, feeding her alcohol at a steady rate and drinking little himself. True, he hadn't forced it down her throat, but it was obvious that he'd been intent upon getting her drunk. He'd kissed her quite passionately when he dropped her home. She hadn't done anything to prevent him but hadn't participated either. She'd been drunk enough to be curious, hoping to feel a spark of some sort that would indicate she was getting over Mark.

Nothing. What was wrong with her? Jack was attractive, uncomplicated, single, and available. He clearly had his sights set on her, and she ought to be flattered. He'd wanted to come in but hadn't pushed it when she told him *no.* Her behaviour could have been construed as encouragement, what with the way that she hadn't stopped him from kissing her, but he accepted her decision not to let him over the threshold without trying to change her mind.

He sat too close to her during lunch, taking every opportunity to touch her. His expansive mood gradually gave way to truculence when she didn't pay him any particular attention. Sulking wasn't an attractive trait in a man. With a feeling of relief, she watched him drive off early when he was called out on an emergency.

Mark phoned whilst she was at The Grange.

"I've managed to get a flight back late this evening," he said. "But it doesn't get into Gatwick until gone eleven."

"I shall have been tucked up for hours by then."

"What an enticing prospect."

"Don't even think about it, Mark."

"Trying to control my thoughts now, are you?" The soft, throaty chuckle that echoed down the line melted her insides. "How are you doing with your grandfather's riddle?"

"I've solved it."

"Clever girl. I knew you'd get there. And," he prompted when she said nothing into the silence.

"I need to talk to you about it but not over the phone."

"That's great, but I won't be able to get to Shalimar until next weekend." She could hear the frustration in his voice. "I've closed the deal," he added with quiet modesty.

"That's wonderful, Mark, congratulations!"

Suzie shared his triumph vicariously, truly proud of her clever husband. For over a year now, he'd been attending to the legal niceties pursuant to selling an arthritis wonder drug that his company had developed. The production was the easy part. Selling it to the EU as a whole, trying to unravel the individual laws of the member states, and satisfying them all had been the major cause of his recent hectic travel programme. Bringing the contract home represented the pinnacle of his career.

"I've got information to share with you as well," he said. "I think I know who's behind the attacks on The Grange and Shalimar."

"How on earth—"

"Shush, I'll discuss it with you and Jane at the weekend."

Suzie disconnected, feeling isolated and alone despite the fact that she was surrounded by her friends. This was Mark's moment of triumph, and they ought to be celebrating it together.

The next morning Mark phoned again.

"After all the delays and setbacks," he told her, "everything to do with the contract is now moving forward at breakneck pace."

"Isn't that often the way?"

"Yeah, I guess. Anyway, there's a ceremonial signing of the contract by EU officials in London on Wednesday, attended by the usual press circus." It would be a defining moment for Mark, Suzie understood, even though he didn't say so. "I have a huge favour to ask of you," he said.

"Tell me."

"There's a gala dinner in the banqueting suite in the evening. It will be my moment of glory," he said in a self-deprecating tone. "Will you be there to share it with me?" When she hesitated, he pushed gently. "Please, Suzie, it would mean a lot to me."

"All right, Mark," she said, unable to deny him such a reasonable request when he'd worked so hard to reach this point. "I'll come."

"Thank you, darling, I'll send a car for you. Can you be ready to leave at five o'clock?"

"Yes, that shouldn't be a problem."

Suzie hung up, already wondering about the wisdom of her decision. The bottom line was that she simply wanted to be with him and bask in reflected glory. She was proud of him. When it occurred to her that she'd left all her suitable clothes in Epsom, she decided upon a shopping trip. She had no energy to venture into Basingstoke, but she'd noticed a small, exclusive-looking boutique in the village. She'd give that a go.

She entered the palatial banqueting suite in Mark's prestigious offices half an hour late and paused to scan the crowded room with her eyes. They focused on Mark's tall figure almost immediately. He wore his evening clothes with panache, his natural style defying the awkwardness apparent in many of the other men. Her heart flipped over, and she wanted him suddenly with an intensity that was frightening.

Presumably sensing her presence, Mark turned his head and a

slow smile lit up his features. He excused himself from the people he was talking to and came across to join her.

"Sorry to be late, Mark," she said, accepting his kiss. "The M3 was chockablock."

"Don't worry, everything is running late, and so your timing's perfect." He raked her body with his eyes. "You look stunning."

"Thanks. I had nothing with me to wear, so I hit the village boutique."

"They did you proud. I hope it cost me a fortune."

She laughed. "Oh, don't worry. It did."

She was wearing a simple white off-the-shoulder sheath that finished just above her knee. The colour enhanced the light tan she'd acquired working in the garden. Her legs were bare, her feet encased in high, strappy sandals. She had pinned her hair on the top of her head, and long tendrils curled about her shoulders. The diamond studs in her ears were a present from Mark many years before.

"You make every other woman in the room look overdressed," he said quietly, his gaze still resting on her face with an intensity that stole her breath. "Thanks for coming, darling."

"I wouldn't have missed it for the world."

"Ready?" He tucked her hand into the crook of his arm, grabbed two flutes of champagne from a passing waitress and steered her into the melee.

The first person to accost them was Anthony Walton, Mark's senior partner.

"Suzie." He kissed her cheek. "I hear Mark's been hiding you in the country." He looked her over, his eyes twinkling. "You look remarkably well, so I guess all that fresh air agrees with you."

"You don't look so bad yourself, Anthony."

"Ah, if only that were true." He smiled amiably, but Suzie wasn't fooled by his absent professor routine. His mind was at least as sharp as Mark's. "Now what do you have to say about this clever husband of yours?"

"Oh, I've always been a great admirer of Mark's talents."

Anthony chuckled. "Probably best not to go there. I should hate to come between husband and wife." He grasped her arm. "Come on, let me introduce you to some of the bigwigs. Watch out for the chap from France. He is the most dreadful letch."

He proceeded to steer her round the room, making introductions, dispensing banter and witty asides with all the easy charm of a man born to the task.

Suzie and Mark were placed at the table of honour. Suzie was seated between Anthony and some Euro MP who appeared dazzled by her. The food was excellent, the speeches short and witty, especially Mark's, although perhaps she was biased in that respect. When he sat down to prolonged applause, he winked at her, and a fine tremor worked its way through her body. Something would happen between them tonight, she knew that now for a certainty. Perhaps she'd known it on a visceral level when she accepted his invitation. There was just an inexplicable something intangible in the air. Whatever it was, it had been between them the entire evening, palpable, exciting. Mark sensed it as acutely as she did. She could tell that much from the searing intensity of his gaze whenever he glanced in her direction.

When the evening broke up, Mark made it clear that he didn't intend to linger.

"I'll call a car for us," he told her in an unusually gruff voice.

It arrived within a minute. The chauffeur opened the back door, and Suzie slid across the soft leather seat, making room for Mark.

"Am I telling the chauffeur to take you to Shalimar before dropping me at Epsom?"

Suzie turned to look directly at him. "That would be a very circuitous route for him," she said.

"Yes, but it's what he's paid to do."

She allowed her heart to rule her head. "Let's not put him to the trouble tonight."

Mark picked up her hand and turned it over, raised it to his lips and kissed the inside of her wrist. "Are you sure?"

She laughed. "Are you trying to talk me out of it?"

"Hardly, but I don't want you to regret it in the morning." He groaned. "God, that sounded corny, but I don't want to be accused of taking advantage again."

"About that, Mark. I'm sorry, I shouldn't have said it."

His teeth flashed white in the darkness. "Shalimar it is then, but no demarcation lines this time?"

It was her turn to smile. "No, but I don't want you reading anything into this. I want you with me tonight, but I don't want to discuss our future, my grandfather's legacy, the problems at The Grange, or Kate and Graham. I just want some time for us."

She could sense the satisfaction in his smile. "Don't worry, sweetheart. With what I've got planned for you, there won't be much time left for talking."

As the car moved away, he pulled her into his arms and kissed her with a gentle urgency that lent proof to his words. The pulsating passion invested in that kiss so accurately mirrored her own impatience that an electric charge whipped through her entire bloodstream. She felt his hands tugging at the zip to her dress.

"Mark, the chauffeur!"

"Shush." His lips grazed the top of her head. "He can't see anything. The glass in that privacy screen is opaque."

"But we can't, not in a car."

"No, but we can have a little fun, can't we?"

She felt cool air peppering her skin as her dress fell away and ceased to care about being seen. He kissed her again, his hands claimed her breasts, and she surrendered to his touch.

Mark dismissed the chauffeur when they arrived at Shalimar, asking to be collected again at seven in the morning. He helped Suzie out of the car, extracted the key from her hand, and opened the front door. Something made her glance at the bushes behind her parked car. They were swaying, and yet there was no breeze.

"What is it?" Mark asked.

"I thought I saw something."

Mark glanced in the same direction. "There's nothing there."

"No, I expect it was just an animal, or something."

"Where's Sparkle?" Mark asked as they stepped into the hall.

"He's spending the night at The Grange."

"Good. Come on." He took her hand and led her up the stairs so fast that she could barely keep pace with him.

He closed the door to Suzie's bedroom behind them, switched on one small lamp, shrugged out of his jacket, and threw it across a chair. Suzie reached up and unlaced his bow tie, something she'd always done for him in the past. Still without speaking, Mark held out his wrists. Suzie extracted his gold cuff links and threw them on the dressing table. She felt cool air on her back as Mark moved behind her and again unzipped her dress. It fell to the ground in a gentle swoosh of silk and pooled round her feet. He removed the clip from her hair, and she felt it cascade down her back. Suzie stepped out of her dress and turned to face him, clad now only in a lacy white strapless bra and tiny matching knickers. Mark groaned and beckoned her toward him. Without hesitation, she stepped into his arms and felt them enfold her.

Suzie didn't bother to close the curtains. There was no one out there to see them. Mark lowered his head, and she tilted her face toward him, impatient to be kissed. His tongue plundered her mouth in a gesture so familiar, so natural, that Suzie simply melted against him. Heat was building inside her at an alarming rate, and she wasn't prepared to wait. She broke away and unbuttoned his shirt so that she could spread her hands across his glorious chest. She sought out his nipples and ran her fingers round them in tight circles as she reached up and captured his lower lip between her teeth, nipping gently. She was surprised at Mark's pacifism. His erection pushed against her stomach, but he seemed content to let her play with him and set the pace. Which was all very well, but she didn't want to play anymore.

She needed release and she needed it now. She slid her arms around his neck and pushed herself from the floor so that she could wrap her legs around his waist. That was better. The bulge inside his trousers was now rubbing against her clit, exactly in the right place.

Mark removed one of his hands from her buttocks and unzipped his pants. Matching her urgency, he pushed her knickers aside and eased himself into her.

"You're killing me, Mrs. Alexander," he muttered, nibbling at her earlobe.

They groaned with simultaneous pleasure as he rammed himself home. Suzie threw her head back and screamed for him to plunge deeper. The deep well of passion simmering just out of her reach needed to be excavated soon, or she'd go out of her mind.

"Mark, I…oh God!"

The muscles of her vagina closed tight around his prick.

"It's all right, baby, just ride it."

He thrust upward again, and her body sunk down to meet him halfway. With a strangled cry, she climaxed, shuddering as exquisite sensations enveloped her entire body. Mark groaned and shot his load deep inside her. She felt him pulsating, and before her first climax had subsided, she was rocked by a second, even more intense. Sex with Mark had always been fulfilling, but this was beyond anything she'd ever known before.

"Sorry," she said when she found enough breath to speak. "I couldn't—"

He shushed her and kissed the end of her nose. "Glad to be of service, ma'am."

His flaccid penis still buried inside her, he carried her to the bed. He withdrew and removed the rest of his clothing, before doing the same for her. Then he joined her on the bed and pulled her into his arms.

"I'll try and practise some restraint this time," she told him, sounding contrite. "It was the sight of you in all your finery this evening that did it. You know how powerful men turn me on."

He leaned up on one elbow and looked at her with what she hoped was mock irritation. "Oh yes, and what other powerful men have you been sampling?"

The question was a fishing expedition, and she had no intention of relieving his curiosity. "The way all the women looked as though they wanted to devour you whole tonight makes me think you shouldn't ask questions unless you're prepared to have them turned back on you," she said instead.

He chuckled. "Anything you want to do to get your revenge is fine by me. I'm all yours."

He reached for her breasts and began caressing them. She squirmed as he deployed his tongue with ruthless expertise, bringing her to a peak of desire before transferring his attention to some other part of her anatomy. She could feel the extent of his own desire pressing into her thigh, but nothing she did this time would persuade him to hurry. In a dreamlike trance, she rode the pleasure, truly alive as she responded to his increasingly urgent demands. Her mind was mercifully blank, her entire focus on the progress of her husband's tongue. It seemed like an eternity before he deemed the time right. Suzie came twice before he even entered her and twice more once he did.

When it was finally over, she fell into an exhausted sleep in Mark's arms and didn't move for the entire night.

She sensed Mark stirring as the first fingers of light filtered through the still uncurtained windows.

"What time is it?" she asked sleepily.

"Six o'clock."

"Oh." She pushed back the covers. "I'll make you some breakfast."

His hand on her breast stayed her. "My appetite this morning doesn't run to food."

Mark left wearing the trousers of his dinner suit and a very crumpled dress shirt that had spent the night hung up on the floor. It didn't matter. He had a private bathroom attached to his office and kept a small wardrobe of clothes there in case of unscheduled trips abroad. By the time the rest of the staff arrived, he would have breakfasted in the directors' dining room, be impeccably attired and already hard at work, all thoughts of their night of passion chased from his mind by the complexities of whatever he was working on. Suzie turned over and hugged his pillow, wishing she could dismiss it as easily. His cologne lingered on the pillow, as did the odour of sex. They'd been head to toe at one point, her vagina resting on his pillow, which would account for that. She sighed, wondering what madness had caused her to complicate an already complicated relationship by allowing him to stop over. It had been a mistake, but she was unable to regret it. She'd needed what Mark had given her last night, even if her actions had been guided by animal instinct rather than wisdom.

Her eyelids drooped. She curled into a tight ball, still hugging his pillow, and slept for another hour.

Her last conscious thought before drifting off was to wonder what kept him motivated and how much longer he intended to keep working at such a manic pace.

* * * *

Somehow, Annabel managed to accommodate John's brutal demands without flinching. She'd hoped to see Patrick, but he'd cancelled at the last minute, and she'd heard a young girl's voice in the background as they spoke on the phone. Was he cheating on her? The mere prospect caused her entire body to quake, and she'd never felt less like dealing with John. Worse, as though sensing her discomfort, he stayed the entire night— something he'd never done before—and didn't let her sleep for much of it.

"Come on, baby, make daddy happy," he extolled at one point.

Annabel froze. She'd banished those words from her mind years ago, hoping to never hear them again. John had broken his own rules. Not only had he apologized for brutalising her several times recently, but he'd also taken to giving her gifts. The latest was a cheque, a personal bonus for services rendered for ten thousand pounds. Annabel banked it with barely a word of thanks.

She left the office early the following afternoon. John was engaged in meetings for the rest of the day, had a dinner to attend with his wife that night, and was unlikely to miss her. Without bothering to don her disguise or change cars, she headed straight for Patrick's cottage. He emerged in the company of a pretty young girl as she pulled up outside. Was that the girl she'd heard the night before when he rang her? Jealousy, an emotion she'd never before experienced, gnawed at her insides.

"Annabel," he said, glancing at her BMW in obvious confusion. "What are you doing here?"

"I thought I'd surprise you." She examined his face. He didn't seem particularly pleased to see her.

"You were lucky to catch me," he said. "I'm just on my way back to a job. Nice wheels," he added.

"Company car," she explained. "I thought we could spend the rest of the afternoon together."

The girl was watching the exchange, but at a word from Patrick, she climbed into one of his vans and drove away.

"No can do, sweetheart, you should have phoned. I've got work to do."

"Can't it wait?" She felt annoyed. Didn't he realize that she'd opted out of an important meeting just to see him?

"No, Annabel, it can't wait." There was a hard edge to his voice that she'd not heard in it before.

"Who was that?" She waved in the direction of the departing van.

"That's Cheryl. I've got enough work now to take on an assistant. She trained at Wisley."

"I see." But she didn't see at all. Nor did she care for the idea of her Patrick spending so much time with such pretty young thing. "Well, if she's working, can't you spend an hour or two with me?" She was pleading and could see that he didn't like it, but she was desperate. She'd planned to tell him that very soon now she would be able to leave her present company and set him up in business properly. Anticipating his surprise and delight kept her going through the sessions with John.

"Sorry, Annabel." He headed for the other van without even touching her. "How would you feel in I swanned into your fancy office without notice?" He climbed into the van and turned the ignition. "No point waiting for me either, I've got something else on tonight. Phone next time, all right. See yer."

He blew her a kiss and was gone.

Furious, jealous, and confused, she drove back to the penthouse, intent upon a long soak in the bath and an early night. She entered her living room and stopped dead in her tracks. John sat there, working his way through a large scotch.

"Where the hell have you been?"

"John." She tried to summon up some enthusiasm. "I thought you were busy tonight."

"Change of plan. I fancied a bit more of what you gave me yesterday. Haven't been able to think about anything else all day. Come on."

He stood and pulled off his clothes. Annabel closed her eyes, hoping that the earth would swallow her up. Since meeting Patrick, she was finding it harder and harder to treat John's demands like an out-of-body experience. Somehow, she got through it, and he didn't seem to notice that she was even less enthusiastic than usual. When he was eventually spent, he lit cigarettes for them both and told her that he wanted her back on the Brooker deal.

"I thought Reggie was handling it."

"That little twerp couldn't find his way up his own arse if you gave him a lighted candle. He's cocked it up already. I need you to sort it. Brooker likes you. He's been asking for you. You can do that and The Grange thing as well, can't you?"

"Of course." This was interesting. He was criticising his kids in front of her so must be feeling very sure of her loyalty. Big mistake! "Will Reggie still be on it?"

John laughed. "Nah, don't worry, I've sent him down to Portsmouth. That's something even he should be able to handle." John hauled his bulk into a sitting position and looked her squarely in the eye. "You know how important this Brooker this is, don't you?" She nodded. "That's right. It's our biggest deal to date. Play on the fact that Brooker likes you. Take him out to dinner and charm him. Bring him back here afterward, and if he shows an interest, spread your legs for him."

Annabel gasped. "No way, I can't—"

"Cut the crap, Annabel, and think of the bigger picture. Sex is an important weapon, and you exude sex appeal by the bucket load because you try so hard not to. Just screw him, if that's what he wants, and make sure you do it right. Give him a night he'll never forget and get his signature on that contract as soon as you can. Put that thing on while he's fucking you." John pointed towards the hidden video camera in the bedroom. John liked to record their sexual romps and view them with her afterward, which inevitably led to a repeat performance. "I wouldn't mind watching him in action. Be interesting to see what the little git enjoys." John offered her an evil smile and framed her face with his hand. "Don't look so thunderstruck. It's only sex. Just think of the rewards. Your bonus for a satisfactory performance," he said, chortling at his own wit, "will be enormous. Bit like I am now," he added, indicating his erection. "Think of the money, Annabel. That's always been your god, hasn't it?"

"All right," she said, through tightly pursed lips.

"And don't ever think to defy me again. Whatever I tell you to do, you do it without question."

Annabel merely shrugged.

"Just remember that I own every little bit of you." He grabbed her snatch and squeezed, seemingly angered by her lack of response. "Now come here and give daddy his reward."

As Annabel straddled his fat thighs, she thought of the exorbitant amount of money he paid her. Was it really sufficient compensation for the humiliation he enjoyed subjecting her to? Unless she walked out on him, she was trapped. And if she walked out, she wouldn't get paid, so she'd have done it all for nothing. Her situation was hopeless, so she did what she always did and emptied her mind even quicker than he managed to empty himself into her.

After he left, Annabel sat chain-smoking and quietly fuming. It was the last straw. She could take no more of John Greenberg, and her agile mind went into overdrive. There had to be a way out of this, and slowly a plan formed.

Oh, she'd entertain Brooker all right, but in a very different way to that which John had suggested. And she also knew now what she'd do about the Alexanders.

Chapter Fifteen

The sun streaming through the uncurtained windows woke Suzie with a start. She peered at the clock and was astonished to find that it was past nine o'clock. She'd been dead to the world for the three hours since Mark had left. Wide awake now, she stretched and waited for guilt to surface, but it didn't seem to want to know. Damn! Mark had abided by her rules and not discussed their future, but she could guess what he was thinking. She was a pushover, and it had been a doddle to win her back. In light of the hopelessly rumpled bed she now occupied, she couldn't entirely blame him for taking that view.

Her body ached gloriously in all the right places. She fingered her tender breasts, felt the muscles in her thighs tighten as she moved her legs, and grinned like a moron. How could something that felt so right possibly be wrong? Just the thought of all the things that Mark had done to her turned her on all over again, and she was now hopelessly confused about whether they could somehow have a future together.

Sparkle was being good this morning. She glanced at the clock again, surprised that another hour had disappeared. This wasn't like her at all. She'd never been one to laze about in bed. Suzie sat up and whistled to her dog. The poor chap must be desperate for a pee. She panicked when he didn't come running, until she remembered that he was still at The Grange.

Guiltily she threw back the covers, took a quick shower, reluctant to wash the lingering traces of Mark from her body but doing it anyway. She dashed down the stairs, feeling lighthearted and ready to greet a sunny day that perfectly matched her mood. Suzie fed the cats and picked up her keys. Conscious of time passing, she resisted the temptation to take the longer route to Jane's, via the garden that was now almost restored to its former glory and never failed to lift her spirits. Instead, she let herself out of the scullery door, pausing to give Honey a swift good morning kiss and tug gently at her floppy ears.

The path she took edged the side of the garden, shielded from curious eyes by the high hedge that flanked it. She arrived at The Grange, wandered in through the open kitchen door, and found Jane seated at the table, having a heart-to-heart with one of her new refugees.

"Oh sorry, Jane, didn't mean to interrupt. I'll just grab Sparkle and leave you to it. Sorry to have left him with you so long. I hope he's been good."

"Good morning to you," Jane said, examining her face and grinning. "There's no rush. We're all finished here." Jane dismissed the spotty, lost-looking teenager with instructions to find Gordon and give him a hand with the fencing in the lower paddock.

Sparkle barged into the kitchen and jumped ecstatically all over Suzie.

"Hello, darling." Suzie rubbed the sensitive spot behind his ears. "Have you had a good time?"

"Not as good as you by the looks of things," Jane remarked.

Suzie blushed—a ridiculous reaction given that she was a married woman in her thirties. "Yes, Jane, it all went very well. Mark's star is certainly in the ascendancy."

A knowing smile played about Jane's lips, but for once, she refrained from comment.

"What?" Suzie demanded.

"You look very well. Must have got a good night's sleep after Mark dropped you at home."

"Stop it!" Suzie's blush deepened.

"Thought so."

"Jane, I'm warning you. Don't go there."

"Wouldn't dream of it. Anyway, looks like you got there before me." Jane chuckled. "It shows in your eyes, darling. It looks like there's a fire burning behind them. He must be quite a stud."

"I'm going." If her cheeks burned any redder, they would self-combust. "Thanks for having Sparkle. Oh, and by the way, Mark says he knows who's behind all your problems. He's coming down at the weekend and will talk to us about it all then."

"That's really good of him." Jane's grin faded. "Someone cut the wire fence in the lower paddock last night, and the pigs got out."

"Oh no!"

"Yeah, well, we got them back but only after they upended half the wheelie bins down by the cottages. We're bracing ourselves for further complaints."

"Did you call the police?"

Jane pulled a face. "What's the point?"

"Well, if you can prove that the wire was cut, then you can't be held responsible."

"It wasn't cut exactly." She screwed up her features. "The posts were quite old, and someone pulled the staples out that held the wire in place. It could be put down to wear and tear."

"But you're sure it's not?"

"Absolutely certain. The fencing was old but in good order." She shrugged. "Anyway, Gordon and the new kid are putting it right."

"Good. Okay, I'll catch you later then."

Suzie said goodbye, and she and Sparkle made their way home, the latter galloping off in search of nonexistent rabbits.

In no hurry, Suzie sauntered behind him, intent upon loitering in the garden and drinking in the heady scent of the climbing roses. The scarlet peonies were in full bloom, too, waving their heavy heads bossily across the neat borders and scattering petals like huge drops of blood. Her favourite was the ancient honeysuckle. It had refused to concede its position to the rampaging weeds and rewarded Suzie for clearing them away by rioting along the fence, playing host to a myriad of worker-bees and butterflies. She spoke to that plant when she was in the garden, just as her grandfather had done before her, telling it all her troubles, confident that it would be discreet.

As soon as she opened the gate, Sparkle barged through ahead of her. Suzie savoured the moment. She felt totally at peace, both physically and mentally and had a hard time imagining living anywhere other than Shalimar. But Mark would never agree, and she would be forced to make her choice. The abrupt realisation spoiled the moment, and she no longer felt quite so content.

Sparkle's growls surprised her, and she glanced up to see what had caused them. Her breath caught in her throat, and she gasped, barely able to believe her eyes. The entire garden had been decimated. The roses had been hacked back almost to their roots, the heads of the peonies and just about every other flower in bloom snapped off, her beloved honeysuckle brutally assassinated. Worst of all, the flower heads had been arranged in the centre of the lawn to form a single word.

SLUT.

Hyperventilating, Suzie fell onto the bottom step to the terrace and dropped her head between her knees, thinking she might well be sick. How warped did a mind need to be to do something this vindictive? When the nausea passed, Suzie made a dash for the house, her mellow mood replaced with blind panic. Who the hell was doing this to her? And why?

"Calm down, Suzie," she told herself, drumming her fingers against the kitchen table. "Someone's still trying to frighten you. Stay focused and try to think."

No obvious answers came to her. Thoughts of that horrible Greenberg man briefly crossed her mind. She recalled his threats and how much they had frightened her, but surely he wouldn't stoop to such a level? Automatically, she considered ringing Mark but dismissed the idea. He'd be here at the weekend, and she'd tell him then. It was only two days away. Besides, after last night, if she turned to him again in a moment of very different need, she would never convince him that it was better to remain separated. She would just have to sort this out for herself.

Suzie grabbed the local phone directory. She couldn't bear to leave the garden like that and would need professional help to see what, if anything, could be salvaged. The first two landscape gardeners she tried, the ones with the big flashy ads, couldn't get to her for at least two weeks. She wasn't prepared to wait that long and tried a third. He had a local address but only a lineage ad. She got nothing but an answer phone from his landline and so tried the mobile number listed. A man answered on the second ring.

"Patrick Kelly, how can I help?"

Suzie, trying to keep her voice even, explained that she had an emergency. The lilting cadence of Patrick Kelly's soft Irish accent calmed her, and she was able to explain her problem without revealing the extent of her panic.

"Well now, that does sound like an emergency. I'll tell you what, why don't I try and rearrange a few things and call on you first thing this afternoon?"

"Oh could you, Mr. Kelly? That would be wonderful. Thank you so much."

Feeling better already, she gave him her address and cut the connection.

Good as his word, Patrick arrived at Shalimar at a little after one o'clock. By then Suzie had cleared away the flower heads and all traces of the hateful word they'd spelt out.

"Well, Mrs. Alexander," Patrick said, scratching his head in bewilderment. "I've seen some acts of vandalism in my time, but this one defies belief."

"Is it salvageable?" she asked, close to tears. She explained how her grandfather had lovingly built the garden up during his lifetime and how she'd just finished reclaiming it. A flash of compassion crossed his broad, open face. Verdant green eyes regarded her from beneath a thatch of curly red hair for a moment before he responded.

"Oh, I should think so," he said, crouching to examine the remains of the decimated rambling rose. "Some of it won't come back this year though. I hope you're prepared for that."

Encouraged by his calm reassurance, Suzie relaxed. "So what do we do now?"

"Well, it's almost a case of starting again. If we do that, we might as well give the soil a little bit of food whilst we're at it."

"My neighbour at The Grange has some extremely well-rotted horse manure. I'm sure she'd be delighted to sell to me."

"Well, that would certainly be a start. Leave me here to decide what's salvageable for a while. Tonight I'll draw out a sketch of the garden, decide what we should purchase to replace the damaged plants, and then I can let you have an estimate tomorrow. Is there anything in particular you would like to see in the garden?"

"Well, I've always thought that it lacked wisteria."

"Good choice. It would grow well against that wall. Do you want me to decide upon the rest, replicate things that can't be saved, that sort of thing?"

"Oh, yes please."

"Good." Patrick straightened himself up and then promptly bent down again as Sparkle put in a belated appearance. He scratched his ears. "Nice dog. Didn't he alert you to your intruders?"

"No. It happened last night when I was in London at a function, and Sparkle was staying with the neighbours."

"Pity. Someone must have known."

She shrugged. "I don't see how. I didn't tell anyone."

"Anyway, I'll call you tonight and let you have the figures."

"When would you be able to start?"

Patrick smiled at her. "It's obviously important to you, so if you accept my estimate, why don't I come round tomorrow and at least start raiding your friend's muck heap?"

Suzie offered him a dazzling smile. "Thank you so much, Mr. Kelly, I really appreciate it."

"No problem." He turned to leave. "Oh, and it's Patrick, okay? Every time someone addresses me as Mr. Kelly I look round expecting to see my father."

Suzie was badly shaken about the incident but tried to put it out of her mind by finding things to do. There was plenty to keep her busy, especially now that everything belonged to her. That made it even more personal. The phone rang mid-afternoon. At first she didn't recognize the voice at the other end.

"Calm down, Gordon," she said, anxious now she'd identified it. Gordon was never anything other than totally laid-back, and his panic was already communicating itself to her. "Take a deep breath and tell me what's wrong."

"It's Jane," he said. "She's been arrested."

* * * *

Annabel spent Thursday morning putting her next move against The Grange into action and the rest of the day working on the Brooker assignment. She phoned Trevor Brooker first thing, told him she was back on the case, and invited him to dinner in a smart restaurant in Basingstoke that evening to run through the figures. He accepted her invitation with alacrity.

She chose her outfit with care. Annabel knew how important it was to look the part and was crafty when it came to creating just the right impression. She owned a few basic designer pieces—skirts, jackets, and trousers in plain colours all acquired from secondhand designer boutiques. Her skill was in accessorising them to make each outfit look innovative. As far as she was aware, no one had yet guessed that all of her blouses and tops came either from High Street chains or charity shops. She gave the impression of being a woman in possession of a wardrobe that was both expensive and extensive. Nothing could be further from the truth. She had no intention of spending her hard-earned cash on something as transient and unimportant to her as clothing.

Satisfied with her appearance, Annabel set off in good time for her dinner. Brooker was the owner of a large, disused warehouse site on the Hamble River. Greenberg had pitched for the lucrative contract to convert the site into trendy, waterside bijou cottages. In this market, they would be snapped up in no time, and he intended to write into the contract a hefty share of the profits. Brooker had come close to agreeing that Greenberg was the right man for the job, thanks in large to Annabel's efforts, but the sticking point was the share percentage.

Annabel walked into the restaurant confident that she'd done her homework well. Only she knew about the butterflies performing Olympic-standard summersaults in her stomach. She was early, but Brooker was still there before her. He stood as she approached his window table and took her hand.

"Punctuality in a woman is a rare trait nowadays," he said, smiling at her.

"Time is too valuable a commodity to waste," she said, matching his smile as she lowered her rear into the chair he was holding for her.

They made small talk for the bulk of the meal, only touching upon Brooker's project occasionally. When coffee was placed before them, Annabel was about to manoeuvre the conversation round to the real purpose for this meeting, but Brooker preempted her.

"How long have you worked for John?" he asked.

"Two years."

"Well, I can only say that I've had many dealings with your boss over the years, and they have never been more professionally handled than since you've been there."

"Why, thank you, I—"

"That idiot son of his shouldn't be allowed anywhere near a major project," he said, disgust in his tone. "He's completely out of his depth."

"Yes, well—"

"He takes after his father."

Annabel elevated one brow, wondering where this was leading and what response she was supposed to make. Was her loyalty being tested? "But I thought you and John went back a long way," she said, opting for a neutral reply.

"We do, but that doesn't mean I entirely approve of his methods."

"I'm sorry, I don't understand. Why would you consider using us if you feel that way?"

Trevor answered Annabel's question with one of his own. "John sails pretty close to the wind, and some of his methods are…well, would underhand be too generous?" Before Annabel could construct a diplomatic response, Trevor spoke again. "Do you intend to stay with John?"

Annabel could hardly believe her luck. She hadn't had to turn the conversation in this direction. Trevor was doing it for her.

"No," she said, meeting his gaze. "In confidence I'm prepared to tell you that I've already made arrangements to set up on my own."

She half expected him to laugh at her audacity, but instead, he sat up and took notice. "Are you now? That's interesting."

"Yes." Annabel took a deep breath. Now was the time to say what was on her mind and get it out in the open. "I've rented offices in Basingstoke that are available immediately. I have a secretary lined up and two experienced associates keen to join me." Encouraged by his continued interest, she pulled her document case toward her and handed him a neatly prepared sheaf of papers. "I've taken the liberty of drafting an alternative proposal regarding your warehouse. I've used an architect that won't work for John, but I've heard great things about him, and he drew up these plans to my specification. You will see that he's made better use of the space but allowed for two less cottages." She looked up at Trevor, encouraged to see that she still had his full attention. "At the prices you want to charge, people expect more than glorified rabbit hutches nowadays. Quality not quantity is the name of the game."

Taking a deep breath, she ploughed on, talking about time scales, penalty clauses, contractors, suppliers, health and safety regulations, and, significantly, the percentage she would expect from the sale prices if she got the commission. It was well below the revised figure John had told her to put forward on his behalf.

Trevor looked at her for a long time. "Why are you doing this to John?" he eventually asked.

"I have very good personal reasons that I'm not prepared to discuss with anyone," she said, meeting his gaze head-on. "Even if it costs me this contract."

He didn't press her. "Why should I trust such an important project to a firm with no track record?" he asked instead.

"Because you know me and have already admitted that you have faith in me. Because I've surrounded myself with people too ethical to deal with John. Because you would be my first client and I would work tirelessly to bring the project in on time and within the set budget." She paused and settled her gaze on his face. "And because I'm hungry to prove something to myself."

"Perhaps we should go back to your place and discuss it?"

Her gaze didn't falter. "No, Trevor, I've no wish to do business with you on that level."

She thought she'd blown it, but to her astonishment, he grinned broadly. "Good, I'm glad to hear it. John intimated that you might be willing, but I wouldn't want to work with anyone that desperate." He laughed, indicating his middle-aged body with his hands. "I mean, I'm hardly Brad Pitt."

"Well—"

"It's all right. I don't expect you to answer that." He held out his hand across the table. "When can you start?"

Annabel felt faint and suddenly full of self-doubt. She'd done it! She'd actually pulled it off. But could she deliver?

"I intend to hand in my notice at close of play tomorrow. How about Monday morning?"

They shook hands on the deal. Annabel smiled to herself as she imagined John's face when he discovered what she'd done. He was going away for the weekend with his wife, so she would leave her resignation letter on his desk only when she was sure he was well on his way. That would leave her with the weekend to move out of the apartment and reestablish herself where he couldn't easily get to her.

Whoever said revenge was a dish best served cold clearly knew their stuff.

Chapter Sixteen

Suzie's slumped in a chair, her mind reeling. First the garden and now Jane. It couldn't be coincidence and was definitely one for Mark. If nothing else, he could get Jane out of police custody. She picked up the phone and dialled his private line. He answered on the first ring.

"Suzie, I was just thinking about—"

"Can you come down?" she blurted out.

Mark chuckled. "Well, I'm glad you enjoyed our night together but I can't just—"

"No, it's not that, I—"

"Are you all right, darling?" he asked, his tone wary. "You sound fraught."

"It's Jane."

"Oh, is that all?" His voice reverted to normal. "What's she done this time? Clouted a protester over the head with a pitchfork?"

"A bit more serious than that." Suzie gulped air into her lungs, still hardly able to believe what Gordon had just told her. "She's been arrested."

What! When?"

"Just now. Gordon rang me in a dreadful state. What can we do to help her?"

"Where have they taken her?"

"To Basingstoke."

"I see. And have they actually arrested her?"

"Gordon seems to think so."

"What's the charge?"

Suzie swallowed down renewed panic. "Child molestation."

"You're kidding me!"

"That was my reaction, too. A less likely child-basher it's hard to imagine, but Gordon said two police cars turned up and the officers had a search warrant. They turned the place upside down and took some papers from Jane's office. Then they arrested her."

"Okay, I'm on my way there." Mark's voice was reassuringly calm. "Get a message to the nick. Tell them I'm her legal representative and she's not to be questioned until I get there. Try not to worry. I'm sure we can sort it out."

"What can I do?" Suzie asked.

"Nothing. Just keep The Grange crowd calm, and Jane and I will see you shortly."

Suzie felt marginally better now that Mark had taken control. Gordon, Ellen, and Pansy materialised at Shalimar, apparently looking to her for guidance. They sat huddled together, going over and over what had happened, trying to make sense of it all.

"They wanted to talk to us individually, but I told them they couldn't without an independent adult present," Gordon said.

"Good for you," Suzie responded. "I'm sure you're right about that."

"I am. I haven't been in and out of care all these years without learning something about the system."

"They knew it, too," Pansy said, scowling. "They were just trying it on."

It was after two o'clock when they heard a car pull into the drive. All four of them rushed to the front door and let out a collective sigh of relief when they saw Jane in the passenger seat of Mark's Mercedes. They took turns to hug her as soon as she got out of the car. Suzie turned toward Mark with a smile of gratitude, and he responded with a reassuring wink. Back on the terrace, the inevitable bottle of wine was produced. Jane, trancelike, sat down and took a healthy swig of the full-bodied red. No one spoke, but all eyes remained fastened upon her, waiting for an explanation. Mark had removed his jacket and loosened his tie. Suzie thought he looked drained and tired.

"Thank you, Mark." Jane's voice sounded unnaturally loud on the quiet terrace.

"No problem," he said. "Ready to talk about it?"

"I would if I knew what was going on."

"Who's Jason Curtis?"

"That little wanker! Sorry," Gordon said, not sounding sorry at all. "Is that who this is all about?"

"Yes, I discovered him one evening outside Basingstoke station. It was the usual scenario," she said, waving the hand clutching her wine glass in the air. "A young frightened kid acting tough as he plied for business."

"Selling himself to other men?" Suzie asked, appalled.

"It's not that unusual," Jane said. "Anyway, I coaxed him into the station buffet and gave him a good meal. God knows when he'd last eaten because the amount he tucked away could have put even Gordon to shame." The brief reemergence of Jane's extrovert personality cheered them all.

"What was his story then?" Mark asked.

"Oh, nothing out of the ordinary. Father unknown, mother on the game with an expensive habit to support, no interest in her son. Jason had been in and out of care as often as he'd been in and out of trouble. I suggested he might like to come back to The Grange, but he said he'd had more than enough of care institutions and would rather make his own way."

"Not so surprising, given what life had thrown at him," Suzie remarked when Jane paused and Mark refilled her glass.

"Thanks. That's what I thought, but I figured it was worth trying to turn him round before it was too late for him. You know me," she added, flashing a brief grin. "I enjoy a challenge. I persuaded Jason that things were done differently at The Grange, and he agreed to give it a go. But I knew almost immediately that it wasn't going to work. He was lazy, wasn't prepared to pull his weight, and wouldn't obey the rules. I caught him smoking dope twice and told him that if it happened again he'd be out. The next time I caught him it was far worse. He had tablets that looked like ecstasy to me. God knows where he got them from, but that was it as far as I was concerned. He was a disruptive influence, decided he hated the countryside without really giving it a go, and was scared of animals." She shrugged. "It was never going to work. Sometimes you just have to accept that and let go."

"So what did you do?" Mark asked when Jane stopped speaking and appeared to turn in on herself.

"I found him a place in a hostel in London. He wanted to be in the city, so I took him up there myself. He stuck it a month and then disappeared. I hadn't heard anything about him again until today."

"Why do you think he's trying to drop you in it, Jane?" Gordon asked in a belligerent tone.

"I think I know the answer to that one." Mark glanced toward the garden and did an abrupt double take. "Suzie, what the hell happened here?"

"I'll tell you later. We've more important things to discuss now."

"It was vandalised on the night Suzie went up to town to meet you," Jane said.

Mark turned to face Suzie. "Why didn't you tell me?"

"You're busy. Anyway, what could you have done?"

"Suzie, whoever is doing this to you and Jane isn't playing games. Do you think I would have left you alone here if I'd known?" Suzie remained silent and refused to meet his eye. "You must have been horrified and very upset, especially after all your hard work." He placed his forefinger beneath her chin and tilted her face until she was forced to meet his eye. "I know how much the garden means to you," he said, his voice a soft, gentle caress meant only for her ears.

"I've found a gardener to sort it out for me."

"And what's to stop the saboteur striking again once he has?"

"We need to discuss Jane's problems, not mine."

"Well, I think I know who's behind both."

"Who?" they all asked together.

"Greenberg. He owns all the cottages behind you, Jane. Some of them have been tenanted by the same people for years, but three of them were recently relet. And guess what? All the complaints against you have come from the new tenants."

"Meaning?" Jane asked.

"Meaning that for some reason Greenberg wants you out of The Grange and will stoop to any means to achieve that end. We already know that he wants Shalimar, and it's obviously him, or someone working for him, that's been trying to frighten Suzie."

"But why would he want The Grange?" Jane wrinkled her brow. "It was on the market for ages before I bought it. It was so dilapidated that no one else was daft enough to take it on. The land is greenbelt, so he'd never get permission to build. Anyway, if he wants it so badly, why didn't he just come and ask if I'd be willing to sell?"

"That I don't know, but he must have his reasons. What I do know is that he's probably behind this ridiculous charade with the police today. From what they said to me, they don't think there's much likelihood of charges being pressed. There's no evidence, apart from the word of this one rather suspect character, and I guess they know by now that just about everyone else at The Grange will speak of you as the second Mother Teresa."

"They'd bloody well better!"

"But, Mark, why even attempt to have Jane arrested if there's no case to answer?" Gordon asked.

"That's the clever bit. The police are obliged to take such complaints seriously and investigate them thoroughly even if they think there's nothing in them. There was no serious talk of pressing charges today, but mud sticks. There was a reporter from the local rag hanging round outside the station when we left. He called to Jane by her name and asked if she had any comment to make. Now how do you think they found out about it?"

"Greenberg," they all said together.

"Exactly. The investigation will be dropped, but it'll still be reported in the paper and think what that will do to Jane's reputation locally. No one will believe that there's no smoke without fire, unless we can prove otherwise."

"How?"

"We find this Jason character and get him to tell us who put him up to it. My investigator is already working on it. In the meantime," Mark said, tightening his tie and picking up his jacket, "I'm going to pay a call on our friend Greenberg and spell out a few facts of life."

"Are you sure you should?" Suzie's hand on his arm stilled him.

He bent to kiss her. "Of course I should. It's bad enough what he's done to Jane, but you don't think I'm going to let him get away with wrecking your grandfather's garden and putting the fear of hell into you, do you? Don't worry, I'll be back soon."

"Suzie," Jane whispered as she watched Mark walk away. "If you let that man slip out of your clutches, then you're madder than your poor grandmother even was."

"Be quiet, Jane, or I'll drive you back to the police station myself."

"Just giving you a friendly word of advice. I'm never wrong about these things," she said smugly, indicating Pansy and Gordon walking hand in hand back to The Grange.

"A right little matchmaker you're turning out to be in your old age," Suzie said caustically as she refilled their glasses.

"Middle age, if you don't mind. And I'll take that as a compliment."

"It wasn't intended as one."

Jane grinned properly for the first time since getting back from the police station. "I know."

* * * *

The intercom on Annabel's phone buzzed. It was Greenberg.

"Get in here," he said brusquely when she answered.

Annabel covered the short distance to Greenberg's office, reminding herself that it was the last time he would ever summon her to do anything. As soon as he was safely out of the way tonight, her resignation letter, already drawn up, would be left right in the centre of his horrible desk. She walked into his inner sanctum. It was a room that she'd taken an instant dislike to, thinking that its ostentation perfectly suited its occupant. The furniture, designed to impress, lacked symmetry. The walls, lined with pictures of Greenberg with just about every dignitary he'd ever met, made him appear desperate and rather ridiculous.

"Yes," she said, taking the seat opposite his desk.

"Mark Alexander is here."

"Really?" She quirked a brow. John liked to be important and never saw people without an appointment. "What does he want?"

"He says it's about Shalimar."

"Oh well, that doesn't have anything to do with me. I don't even know why you want it."

"What happened about The Grange today?"

She told him about Jane being arrested.

"Is she still at the nick?"

"I have no idea. I thought it better to keep a low profile. We'll find out soon enough."

"A lot of fucking good that is!"

"You think he's here about that?"

"I've no idea, but I don't like seeing people blind."

Annabel shrugged. "Then don't see him."

Greenberg dealt her a withering glare and told his secretary to send Alexander in.

"Mr. Alexander," he said, standing and extending a hand. "This is my assistant, Annabel Burton."

Mark shook Annabel's hand. She maintained a professional smile, all the while wondering why it was never men who looked like him who tried to entice her into affairs.

"I knew I should have approached you direct about Shalimar," John said when they were all seated again.

"Your first mistake," Alexander said, "was to threaten my wife." Annabel sat a little straighter. What the hell was he talking about? "Your second was to intimidate Jane Grant." This time Annabel knew precisely where he was coming from. She glanced at the rigid determination in his expression and quailed, only now realizing that she'd taken on a formidable opponent. "Both of those actions were ill-conceived but nothing compared to the stunt you pulled today in putting the police onto Mrs. Grant."

"What are you talking about?" John glowered, but it didn't seem to affect his visitor.

"I know what you've been up to, Greenberg, but now you're going to set things straight. You will arrange for all complaints about noise disturbance against Mrs. Grant to be dropped. You'll also arrange for the trumped-up charges levelled against her today to be dismissed and for the complainant to issue a complete denial in the local paper."

Annabel and John exchanged a prolonged glance. "I still don't know what you're on about," John said, sounding halfhearted to Annabel's ears.

"I don't care what excuse he uses for his actions in the first place," Mark continued, ignoring the interruption, "but I'm sure you'll think of something convincing."

"Now look here, you can't just come in here making wild accusations when you have nothing to back them up with."

"Have I not?" Annabel admired how the man remained perfectly relaxed as he raised one ironic brow. "Care to put it to the test?"

"I've had enough of this! I don't care to be threatened in my own office."

"No, but you're quite willing to threaten defenceless women."

"You're out of your mind."

"Another thing, Greenberg, if one more act of intimidation takes place against my wife when she's at Shalimar, or if any of your goons dare to set foot on the property again, then —"

John and Annabel shared another brief glance. "What do you mean?"

"You know very well what I mean. I've got the measure of you, Greenberg. Leave it alone because I'm on your case now, and believe me, you don't want me as an enemy."

"I don't know anything about damage at Shalimar," John said. "I approached your wife and made an offer to purchase." He shrugged. "Okay, perhaps I got a bit carried away when she turned me down. I can be short-tempered sometimes, but I certainly haven't done anything to cause her harm, nor have I tried to damage the property."

Mark Alexander paused, clearly unsure whether or not to believe him. Annabel was similarly minded.

Chapter Seventeen

When Mark returned to Shalimar, Jane was still there with Suzie.

"How did it go?" they asked together.

"Well, it's interesting. Greenberg defended himself robustly when I accused him of meddling at Shalimar. I'm almost convinced he knows nothing about it."

"But you think he's behind the stuff that's happened at The Grange?" Jane asked.

"Absolutely convinced. He's not used to having his word challenged, so he's a lousy liar."

"Will it all stop now?"

Mark smiled at her. "Let's hope so."

"Thank you, Mark," she said with heartfelt sincerity.

Jane declined Suzie's offer that she remain for supper. She made a big deal out of eyeing Mark's back when he went back to the house for something and smacked her lips in appreciation.

"You could probably do without the competition," she whispered, smirking.

Suzie recalled her recent ordeal and resisted the temptation to throttle her.

Left alone with her husband, Suzie felt tense and overwrought. Her emotions were haywire after the day she'd had, and she wasn't ready to face him alone.

"I'll cook some supper," she said, not looking at him. "Why don't you take a shower?"

"Good idea," he said, kissing the back of her neck and disappearing up the stairs.

He came down again fifteen minutes later, freshly shaved, wearing cream chinos and a short-sleeved blue denim shirt. His feet were bare, and his hair fell in damp curls round his face. He smelt of soap and the distinctive cologne that set him apart.

"Something smells good." He walked up behind her and wrapped his arms round her waist. "I'm starving."

"It won't be long," she said, moving away from him on the pretext of checking the oven. "There's some Chablis in the fridge."

As they dined on roast vegetables, followed by grilled trout with sweet saffron rice and green salad, Suzie slowly relaxed. Mark made it easy by filling silences with a light flow of conversation that avoided the emotive issues that lay unresolved between them.

They cleared away together and returned to the terrace with the remains of the wine. It was only then that Mark asked about her grandfather's letter.

"Well done for solving the clues," he said. "Not sure I'd have managed it."

"Don't patronise me, Mark."

"I wasn't." He pinioned her face with a gaze of such smouldering luminescence that she was obliged to turn away first.

"I've no idea what to do, Mark. I need your help."

"I think you'd better let me read the letter then."

"Come on."

Suzie stood and led the way into the library. Mark looked on astounded as she stood on the library steps, cleared the books from the appropriate shelf and opened the hidden drawer. She removed the tin box, handed it to Mark, and climbed down again. Seated at the desk, Suzie unlocked the tin and handed Mark her grandfather's explanation.

Mark read quickly, without making any comment. Suzie watched him carefully and could see he was completely taken up in the account, just as she had been when she first read it. When he finished, Mark placed the papers carefully back in the tin and smiled at her.

"Enterprising chap, your grandfather. Always did think so."

"Mark, how can you make so light of it?"

"Darling, what's to get so upset about? Gramps was right. From all I've read about the aftermath of the war, everyone was at it. What's such a big deal about a few diamonds?"

"It's a bit more than that."

"Okay, plus the money he left you. Fifty thousand pounds, same as Derek, I assume?"

"Try adding another nought."

Mark let out a low whistle, a gesture of respect as much as surprise, Suzie suspected. "The crafty old fox!"

"And it's more than just a few diamonds." Suzie emptied the contents of just one pouch onto the desk. "There are three times as many as that."

Mark seemed at last to appreciate the enormity of the situation. "Yeah, I can see now why you're so bothered about it all."

"What are we going to do? All this wealth didn't seem to bring Gramps much happiness. It obviously played on his conscience too much for him to enjoy it."

"It brought him Shalimar," Mark reminded her.

"True." She was silent for a moment. "Oh, Mark, what are we going to do?"

"I don't know yet. We can't make that sort of decision on the back of the sort of day we've just lived through. We need to sleep on it." He took the empty glass out of her hand and whistled to Sparkle. "Come on, let's walk this beast and then, I think, an early night."

She panicked at his mention of bed. As soon as she knew he'd be staying over, the question of the sleeping arrangements had plagued her mind. "Mark, if you don't mind, tonight—"

"Okay," he said with a resigned shrug. "You don't need to spell it out. I'm banished to the spare room again."

"I'm sorry, Mark, I know I'm giving you mixed messages, and you have a right to know where you stand with me, especially after

Wednesday, which, by the way, shouldn't have happened."

"I disagree."

"It was just the euphoria of your success, and you looked so handsome, I was so proud of you and…oh I don't know but—"

"You just wanted to hitch your wagon to my star. Is that it?"

"Don't be silly! I'm confused, that's all, and don't know what to do yet. There's so much else going on that I don't seem to have time to work out what I want. Whenever I think I have, something else happens and throws it all out of kilter." She stopped walking and turned to look at him. "I'm not being fair to you, I know that. I also know what will happen if we share a bed tonight, and that will only confuse me more."

He placed his hands on her shoulders and smiled at her. It was a smile that could have melted stone and made short work of her determination to hold out against him. "I understand, sweetheart. Don't worry, you don't need to resort to locking the door or, God forbid, Granny's nightdress. I'll be the perfect gentleman."

Well, he didn't have to be that perfect, she thought as they wandered outside again with Sparkle. She was teetering with indecision again, and the smallest persuasion on his part would bring about another change of heart.

"But tomorrow we're got the whole day to ourselves, and perhaps then we can sit down quietly and make some decisions." He looked back at the shabby façade of Shalimar. "About a lot of things."

He took her hand and led her back to the house.

"Good night," he said, kissing her lightly and opening the door to her room for her. "Sleep well."

Much to her surprise, Suzie did sleep surprisingly well. Mark, good as his word, left her alone. They had just finished a leisurely breakfast on the terrace when Patrick arrived to start his labours. Mark chatted to him for a while, and then Patrick trundled off to The Grange with his wheelbarrow.

Suzie and Mark resumed their seats, neither of them knowing how to start the conversation they could no longer avoid. A knock at the door interrupted them before it even got under way. Suzie leapt up to answer it, grateful for the excuse to delay, and was confronted by a woman she'd never seen in her life before.

"Mrs. Alexander?"

"Yes."

"My name's Annabel Burton. I met your husband in Mr. Greenberg's office yesterday."

Suzie stiffened. "He said."

"Is he at home? I'd appreciate a quick word."

"You'd better come through."

"Who was it?" Mark asked, not looking up from the papers he was reading.

"Someone to see you," Suzie said.

Mark glanced up and frowned. "What can I do for you?" he asked with only the barest hint of civility.

"It's rather more a question of what I can do for you."

"Then you'd better sit down. I suppose Greenberg sent you."

"No, he has no idea I'm here."

In a voice devoid of all emotion, Annabel explained the part she had played in intimidating Jane. It included moving the three families into the cottages behind The Grange and priming them to make regular complaints. She also admitted that she'd been responsible for alerting the Revenue to Jane's situation as well as the Charity Commissioners and regularly employed people to make mischief.

"Why are you telling us all this?" Mark asked.

She shrugged. "I have my reasons."

"Won't it make your position at work untenable? It won't take your boss too long to figure out who blew the whistle on him."

"I resigned last night."

Suzie detected a thaw in Mark's frosty attitude. "Congratulations, but that hardly explains why you're now—"

"My reasons for what I'm doing are my own." She reached into a briefcase and withdrew a folder. “Here are copies of e-mails between Greenberg and myself in respect of Jason Curtis. He usually left all the arrangements to unhinge Mrs. Grant to me, didn’t want to get involved with the details. But when you wrote to the council and said you were representing her, he went berserk and suddenly wanted to be in on everything.”

“How did you persuade Curtis to make those ridiculous accusations?”

“It was luck that we got on to him. Mrs. Grant took him up to London by train when he decided he didn’t want to stay at The Grange. Someone who works for me happened to be on that same train, got the gist of what was happening, and followed Curtis to the hostel Mrs. Grant took him to.”

“You have some very peculiar employees.”

She offered him the hint of a smile. “You have no idea.”

“You’ll have to do better than that.”

“All right, the guy was following Mrs. Grant on my orders. Satisfied?”

“Not nearly, but the rest can wait. Carry on.”

“We got someone to link up with Jason after a week or two, took him out of the hostel, and put him in one of our flats. I had a feeling that he might be useful at some stage.”

Disgust poured off Suzie in waves. “Do you enjoy your work, Ms. Burton?” she asked.

“Please don’t judge my actions, Mrs. Alexander. You know nothing about me. I did what I had to do at the time but had no idea John intended to go so far. Now I’m giving you the ammunition you need to put matters right.”

Mark conceded the point with an abrupt nod. “Thank you.” He regarded her in silence for a moment, choosing his next words with care. “If you really want to make amends then—”

“Who said I did?”

“Then what are you doing here?” Leaving the question

unanswered, Mark continued. “If you want to help put matters right, why don’t you tell us why your ex-boss is so keen to get his hands on The Grange.”

“You don’t know?” Annabel sounded surprised.

“We don’t know.”

“John wants to build a golf course.”

“What!” Suzie and Mark exchanged an elongated look. It explained so much.

“The land on the east of The Grange was held by the same family for generations, and they refused all offers to sell. Recently the old man died, and his son is anxious to offload it because he’s in need of the cash. He wants an equal partnership with John once the scheme gets off the ground.”

“That won’t be enough land for a full course,” Mark said.

“No, but the land on the west is council owned, and John’s a very accomplished networker. He makes a point of cultivating people that could be useful to him.”

“All those pictures on his office wall,” Mark said.

“Exactly. He has several high-ranking officials at the council in his pocket. The guy is charge of the planning department owes him quite a bit of money, which is proving very useful for his ambitions. He also makes sure he’s seen to give generously to local charities.”

“What a charmer,” Suzie said, her lip curling with disgust.

“Quite. He plays golf regularly with a couple of the Tory councillors and has convinced them that if they give permission for the golf scheme to go ahead, they can score a lot of brownie points by offering membership to locals at discounted rates and opening the course for public use.”

“In other words, the council would be seen to be making an elitist sport available to all and taking a fat backhander from your boss in the process.”

“Exactly.”

“Clever. But you have a problem because The Grange falls slap bang in the middle of the proposed course?"

"Yes, John sees it as an ideal club house."

"It's all starting to make sense now," Mark said, settling more comfortably in his chair and rubbing his chin as he assessed all he'd just heard. "The land only became available after Mrs. Grant brought The Grange, I assume?"

"Yes."

"So, why didn't he just approach her direct and see if she was willing to sell?"

"He couldn't risk showing his hand. The property had been on the market for ages before Mrs. Grant bought it, and if John then showed an interest, questions might be asked. He's well known locally, and suspicions would have been aroused. Besides, he did put out a few feelers, but everyone he spoke to assured him that Mrs. Grant considered herself settled for life."

"Okay, I can buy that, but why does Greenberg want Shalimar, too?"

"I had no idea that he did, until your visit yesterday," Annabel said, meeting his gaze and holding it. "It's just an ego thing, I think. He fancies living in style on the edge of his own golf course."

Mark snorted. "Yes, but even so, he must have—"

"Excuse me, Suzie," Patrick said, stepping onto the terrace, "but I—"

Annabel, who had been sitting with her back to the garden, whipped her head round so fast that she had to be in danger of giving herself whiplash. "Patrick!"

"Annabel?" The two stared at one another. "What are you doing here?"

"You two obviously know each other," Mark said. "Ms. Burton was just explaining her part in the tricks played on The Grange and Shalimar."

"You?" Patrick's friendly expression transmuted into contempt. "You did all this?" He waved his hand toward the decimated garden.

"No, Patrick, you don't understand, I—"

"Oh, I understand all right." He turned his back on her. "I need to get some supplies, Suzie. I'll be back shortly."

Without uttering another word, he strode away.

* * * *

For possibly the first time in her adult life, Annabel had done the decent thing. It had taken guts to face Mark Alexander's withering disdain as she admitted to the campaign her boss had compelled her to orchestrate against the residents of The Grange. No, not compelled. Annabel adjusted her mental deliberations, prepared to be honest at least with herself. When John asked her to put pressure on The Grange, she knew that she'd have to fight dirty but hadn't turned a hair. It was a dog-eat-dog world, and the welfare of the people she was attempting to destroy hadn't cost her so much as a wink of sleep.

Annabel hadn't undergone a character transplant or suddenly developed a conscience. Nothing that dramatic. She'd come clean with the Alexanders partly because she did feel just a twinge of guilt when that hunky lawyer descended upon John and spelled out the consequences of her actions. The feeling would have passed, but the opportunity to gain a modicum of revenge on John was too good to pass up. By quelling his plans for his beloved golf course, she could get back at him for all the indignities he'd inflicted on her during their relationship, businesswise but more especially from a personal standpoint.

It felt good to put matters right, there was no denying that. But then Patrick strolled onto the terrace, smelling of fresh air and horse manure, and seemed to think she was responsible for the destruction of the Alexanders' garden. Of all the damnable luck! Her one and only crisis of conscience had possibly cost her the only relationship she'd ever cared about.

She sat where she was, staring after Patrick even though his broad shoulders had long since disappeared from view, unable to move or even to cobble together any coherent thoughts. She felt bereft, totally and completely drained of all feeling.

"Are you all right?"

The Alexander woman was talking to her, and Annabel made a huge effort to pull herself together.

"Yes." She shook her head. "No, actually." She endeavoured to smile but suspected that it came across more as a grimace. "Perhaps a glass of water. It was a shock, seeing Patrick here."

Suzie Alexander poured her a glass of water from the jug on the table. "Here you go."

"Thanks."

"You know Patrick then?"

"Yes," Annabel said. "Well, I did, but he seems to think I trashed your garden, so I guess that's that."

Chapter Eighteen

For purely selfish reasons, Suzie wondered if she'd done the right thing in asking Mark to represent Jane. She had assumed he'd get Jane out of the nick and dash straight back to London, but it seemed he planned to hang about until Monday morning. She could hardly complain when he'd only come down to help her friend out of a tight spot, but living under the same roof as him was proving to be one hell of a strain.

They did need to thrash out their personal relationship once and for all. It was a situation complicated by the acquisition of Shalimar and her grandfather's ill-gotten gains. Annabel's visit on Saturday morning and her extraordinary revelations had put paid to that, but at least it gave them something they could talk about.

"I have to go and tell Jane at once," she said.

"Let's take a moment to think about it before we get her hopes up," Mark suggested.

"Why? We know what he was doing and have all the proof we need."

"Yes, we do, but bringing copies of private e-mails between two individuals into the public domain is a risky business."

"I suppose," she conceded, not surprised that Mark's legal brain was already looking for pitfalls. "But surely that won't be necessary? If we tell him we know what he's up to and threaten to take our proof to the police, he'll have to back down. After all, Annabel said he cares about his reputation because he built his business on it."

"Never make threats unless you're prepared to carry them through."

"Well, we could carry through if we have to. The e-mails would be enough to get Jane off the hook with the police, but if the kid who made the allegations publicly refutes them, then she'll be in the clear and we won't have to use them."

"I think I rattled Greenberg enough to make his think twice about his bloody golf course," Mark said, stretching his arms above his head and yawning.

"So why can't we tell Jane and use the e-mails to get Greenberg off our backs once and for all." She paused. "Annabel was really upset when Patrick turned his back on her. She obviously cares for him, and I think she feels hard done by because she really didn't destroy the garden or know anything about it. That was all Greenberg."

Mark quirked a brow. "And you feel sorry for her?"

"Well, she did have the courage to own up to what she'd done? That must have taken guts."

"You can bet your life that she was motivated by self-interest rather than an overwhelming desire to help Jane."

"Why not just say that you don't like her?"

Mark smiled. "It's not a case of liking or disliking the woman. It's more a trust issue. However," Mark continued, waving a hand to prevent her from interrupting him, "I think we owe her something for coming clean. Greenberg will soon work out who leaked those e-mails if it comes to the point where we have to tell him about them."

"Oh, we'd drop her in it, you mean." Suzie frowned. "Does that matter? She said she'd resigned."

"Yes, but still." He reached for her hand and whistled to Sparkle. "Come on then. You're right. I'm being overcautious, and Jane needs to know."

They strolled down the lane toward The Grange, Mark still holding her hand. Suzie didn't feel the need to snatch it away and wondered if that was progress. Jane greeted them in her usual verbose manner.

"You're just in time," she said. "I was about to pour a lunchtime tipple."

She did just that. Mark waited until they were seated round the kitchen table before he told her what they'd learned.

"The conniving lowlife!" Jane jumped up, looking ready to commit murder.

"Say what you're thinking, Jane," Suzie said, hugging her.

"So is it all over?" Jane sat heavily onto a kitchen stool and ran a hand through her hair.

"Sure, the prosecution never stood a prayer, but now it's well and truly dead in the water. But we need to do something to make sure the mud doesn't stick."

"Miracles take a little longer," Suzie quipped, anxious to lighten the mood.

"Oh, I'm already convinced that Mark's a miracle worker." Jane paused for a beat. "How about you, Suzie?"

"Trust needs to be earned," she muttered.

The rest of Saturday disappeared in a blur of celebration. Jane got comprehensively drunk that afternoon. It was the first and only time that Suzie had seen her incapable. It took the combined efforts of Ellen and Pansy to put her to bed.

Since lunch at The Grange the next day looked unlikely to happen, Suzie offered to feed the masses at Shalimar. Only Jack was absent. He was spending a week's holiday with his family, no one knew where. Suzie was grateful. The animosity between him and Mark increased every time they met.

Monday morning and Mark hadn't made any mention about returning to London. Suzie couldn't believe it. What with one thing and another, they still hadn't tackled the unresolved issues between them, but she hadn't thought that would prevent him from returning to his precious work.

"I have to pay another visit to Mr. Greenberg," he said when she tackled him on the issue.

"Then I'm coming with you."

"There's no need."

"Perhaps not but I'm the one he patronised and threatened, and I want to see him squirm."

Mark laughed. "Okay, I guess I can't argue with that."

"Not if you know what's good for you," she said, smiling sweetly.

Greenberg kept them waiting for almost an hour.

"Something I can do for you?" he asked curtly, when they were finally shown into his office.

"It's rather more what I can do for you." Greenberg hadn't bothered to stand up, and Mark towered over him. As intimidating tactics went, Suzie thought it was pretty effective.

"Cut the crap, Alexander. Say whatever you've come to say and get out. I'm a busy man."

"Then we won't keep you long. All you have to do is ensure that the charges against my client are unconditionally withdrawn and that the same reporter who miraculously appeared at the nick when she was taken in is granted an interview with Jason Curtis."

He glowered at Mark. "What are you talking about?"

"About your picking up Jason Curtis, housing him in your flat in Barking, getting him to file these trumped-up charges, and making sure the local rag was there to have a field day with their speculation."

Greenberg waved a pudgy hand. "Don't know what you're on about."

"Then I'll make it easy for you. Do it my way, keep your name out of it, and save what's left of your reputation, or I'll go to the press myself, tell them of the dirty tricks campaign that you've been conducting against my client and my wife."

"You do that and I'll sue you every which way for slander."

Greenberg's smirk was loaded with so much malice that Suzie felt ill. He clearly wasn't going to let this go without a fight, just as Mark had predicted.

"Slander?" Mark finally seated himself beside Suzie, looking completely unconcerned. "Not if I can back up my allegations."

"Then I don't have anything to worry about." Greenberg drilled them both with a look. "How do I know that? Because there's nothing for you to find."

"We're wasting our time here, Suzie," Mark said, standing up again. "I wanted to give this guy a chance to save his neck, but he's clearly not interested."

They headed towards the door.

"Just a minute."

Greenberg's voice halted them. Mark winked at Suzie before they turned to face him again, confirming her suspicion that he'd known this would happen. Greenberg was clearly overcome with curiosity and needed to know what Mark knew about his machinations.

"Yes?" Mark said, still standing just inside the office door.

"Why I would waste my time with such a ridiculous campaign?"

Greenberg was standing now as well. Although he was several inches taller than Mark and a whole lot wider, Suzie sensed that Mark was the one in control. He dominated the room with an aura of tensile power, and she'd never been more proud of him. The combination of machismo and superior intellect that she'd always loved about him had never been more potent and was a definite turn-on.

Instead of answering Greenberg's question, Mark simply raised his arms and made a passable golf swing action. Suzie had to bite back and laugh when she observed Greenberg's reaction. His jaw almost hit his chest, and he collapsed into his swivel chair, causing the springs to squeak a loud protest. Mark went in for the kill.

"I want my client's name completely cleared, Greenberg, no half measures. And just so you know, she has no intention of leaving The Grange. Any further attempts at intimidation and I'll know who started them." Mark's words were spoken quietly and were infinitely more threatening because of that. "Believe me, you don't want me as your enemy. Furthermore, Shalimar is not for sale, and if you try to frighten my wife again, then I will reveal to the press everything I know about your underhand tactics." Mark offered him a mock salute. "That should finish you off in the Rotary Club."

Greenberg was hyperventilating. "How…how did you know?"

"About your efforts at Shalimar?"

"No, that wasn't me. I haven't done anything there. I meant about the golf."

"Let's just say that I have my sources. Do we have a deal?"

Greenberg managed a sullen nod.

"Sorry, I didn't quite catch that."

"Yes. Now get out."

"With pleasure," he said, opening the door and ushering Suzie out ahead of him.

Everything happened very fast after that. Curtis withdrew the charges and gave the reporter his interview, saying he had been confused when he spoke to the police about another matter and inadvertently mixed it with his time at The Grange. He was on a drugs withdrawal programme and his spasmodic memory was addled. He couldn't think now why he'd made the allegations. Jane Grant did her very best to help kids who'd fallen on hard times. There should be more people like her about, and he was sorry for the trouble he'd unwittingly caused.

Jane, encouraged by Mark, spoke to the paper as well about what she was trying to achieve at The Grange. Gordon and Pansy gave eloquent descriptions of their lives before Jane rescued them, both admitting to criminal tendencies brought about by desperation. They talked about Jane's ability to get them to look dispassionately at their own actions, to take responsibility for them, and to think of the damage they did to others. They were full of praise for her quiet authority, and both felt they were now balanced, law-abiding individuals with something to offer society.

Mark left Shalimar on Tuesday evening.

"I really do have to be at the office," he said to Suzie.

"Of course you do. I didn't expect you to stay so long." Or to sleep in the spare room without protesting. "Thanks for what you did for Jane."

"You won't have to worry about Shalimar whilst I'm not here. Greenberg won't cause you any more trouble."

"No, he won't."

Suzie couldn't shake off the feeling that he hadn't done any of the things at Shalimar anyway. He looked genuine when he denied all knowledge of them. But who else could it have been? That two people would resort to such tactics on adjoining properties was too far-fetched to be credible. Besides, if she voiced her suspicions, Mark would probably never leave.

"Suzie," he said, grabbing her shoulders and standing very close. "I shall be back next weekend. Please don't arrange lunch for the masses. We really do need some time alone to sort ourselves out. I have something to say to you that I think you might want to hear."

* * * *

Annabel didn't recall driving back to the apartment but by the time she reached it she'd also come to a decision. She'd resigned from Greenberg's operation, had done the right thing by the Alexanders. Now she was going to bare her soul and do everything within her power to save her relationship with Patrick. It was worth saving, and he deserved the truth. If it disgusted him, then so be it, but at least she would have fought for him.

She loaded her personal possessions into her car. She didn't carry emotional baggage, so it didn't take long. Once she was finished, she left the key in the centre of the coffee table, aware that the apartment was the first place John would head for after he read her resignation letter. He'd probably expect her to try and hang on to it, which showed just how little he knew her.

Annabel had rented a miniscule flat in Basingstoke, close to her new office. She drove there now and unloaded her car. She showered, changed into casual clothes, and brushed her hair. Then she was back in the car again, not allowing herself to think about anything as she headed toward Patrick's cottage.

His van was parked outside, and she pulled up alongside it. The cottage door opened before she was halfway out of the car.

"What do you want?" He had an open bottle of beer in his hand, and his expression bordered on dislike.

"We need to talk." He made no attempt to move out of the doorway. Not an encouraging start. "I think it's time I did a little explaining."

Something about the determination in her tone must have struck a chord because he finally stepped aside. "This should be good," he said caustically.

Annabel entered his miniscule lounge and seated herself on the sofa. Patrick fetched her a glass of white wine and sat in the chair opposite her, as far away from her physical presence as the limited confines of the room permitted.

"Shoot," he said, his eyes examining the beamed ceiling with apparent fascination.

Annabel's heart plummeted. He couldn't even stand to look at her. She scrabbled in her bag for her cigarettes and lit one. Then she took a large swig of wine, crossed and uncrossed her legs, at a loss to know where to start now she was actually here. The things she'd kept hidden for so long were too shameful to be put into words, and she wondered what masochistic tendencies had made her come. He was a decent man, and what decent man could fail to hate her—to blame her—after what she had to say? But Annabel had never lacked courage. She wouldn't back down now, not if there was still the smallest chance of keeping the only man she'd ever loved. She took a deep breath and launched into her explanation.

"I've never told you much about my childhood, Patrick, and what I have revealed has been carefully edited highlights." He gave no indication that he'd even heard her. "Oh, my father was an accountant with his own business in Southampton, that bit was true enough. But my mother…well, my mother was always an enigma. My earliest memories are of a beautiful but vague individual drifting aimlessly about the house, never seeming to live in the same world as the rest of us. It was only as I got older that I learned I'd been the cause of her problems. She wanted a large family, but her first two pregnancies ended in miscarriages. Her third was an entopic pregnancy that almost cost her life. She was advised not to try for children again but didn't listen, and the result you see sitting before you today. I was born healthy, but she suffered internal bleeding. The hospital made an error. She was starved of oxygen and suffered mild brain damage."

"Good grief!"

Annabel, lost in her own version of hell, was barely aware that Patrick had spoken. "I remember my mother having good days when she recognized me and took an interest in things around her, but they were few and far between. The rest of the time my father held us together. The hospital trust eventually paid compensation for their error, and it was enough to employ a housekeeper. My father took over when he got home every night. He never, as far as I can recall, went to the pub or had any sort of social life. He was either working or at home with us. He was both father and mother to me, and I adored him. Nothing concerned with me was too much trouble for him. However drained and exhausted he was, however little joy life held for him, he always took an interest in me and encouraged me to go for what I wanted."

Annabel paused. It had been quite easy so far, but how did she explain the next part? "My father used to sit me on his knee when I was little and read to me. When I was older, I did the reading but the seating arrangement remained the same."

"Oh jeez, Annabel—"

"He rocked me back and forth on his lap. I didn't know what was happening, but my father would never do anything to hurt me." She glanced at Patrick's face, terrified by what she might see there, but his earlier disdain had been replaced with an expression of genuine compassion. "Dad jerked and threw his head back, seemingly distraught. I thought I'd done something to upset him, but he pulled himself together, smiled at me, and we carried on reading as though nothing had happened. That night, when I went to bed, there was a five pound note tucked under my bedside lamp. He said it was a present for being a good girl."

"Annabel, you really don't have to tell me all this."

"A couple of weeks later the same thing happened again," she said, unable to close the floodgates now that she'd finally opened them. "Patrick, he was my father, my idol, but he looked so melancholy that making him feel a little less bad had to be a good thing. Anyway, this time he left me ten pounds.

"I expect you can imagine how it progressed. The next time he unzipped and that was the first time that he used the words that still haunt me today, '*Make daddy feel good.*' And then he showed me how."

"Annabel." Patrick stood up, ducking to avoid clouting his head on the low beams, and ran a hand through his hair. "I don't know what to say."

"That's because you don't know the half of it yet," she said, lifting her head to meet his gaze square on.

Chapter Nineteen

Whoever said time was a great healer didn't have a clue what they were talking about. The truth had to be faced. Suzie loved her husband as much now as she did when she walked out on him over a month before. More perhaps because she knew now that Kate lured him into a trap and he resisted it. So if she loved him so much, why hadn't she run home again? The answer was glaringly obvious. There were other things beside infidelity that sounded the death knell for a marriage, and an empty existence that revolved exclusively round Mark was a prime example. She needed more. A career, a family, something to care passionately about whilst Mark was away changing the world.

"And what are the chances of that happening?" she demanded of Sparkle and Honey.

Her animals provided no answers, so she took out her frustrations on the cushions, attempting to thump them back into shape when they no longer had any life left in them. She hoped that wasn't an omen for her troubled marriage. Suzie abandoned her attempts to resuscitate her terminal cushions and flopped onto the settee that housed them instead. She simply had to ignore the physical draw she felt toward Mark and concentrate on the bigger picture. It was a bit obscene really. She was a grown woman but still harboured physical fantasies for the man she'd been married to for ten years. It wasn't supposed to work like that. None of her friends felt the same pulsating need to jump their husbands' bones. Mind you, they all had kids now and were too physically knackered to think much about sex.

The thought of children left Suzie wrestling with a different sort of pain that strengthened her resolve. She would not go back to Mark under the present circumstances. In the weeks since she'd left him he had been in England during the week for a total of six days. Six days! Okay, it had been a particularly busy time as he tied up his complex contract, and he would probably have a bit of a respite now, but it wouldn't last for long. Soon he'd be offered another major project to get his teeth into. When that happened, he'd get that ambitious gleam in his eye and rise to the intellectual challenge. He wouldn't be able to help himself. Before she knew it, the merry-go-round would be in full swing again and Mark would find more excuses to delay starting a family.

Anyway, he'd still want to live in Epsom, and Suzie wasn't prepared to go back to that empty existence. Something had changed inside her when she walked out on Mark. She loved it here in the country. She loved Shalimar even more. Somehow, she would convince Mark to sign his share of the property over to her. She'd keep the money Gramps invested for her. It would enough for her to live on and to start tarting up the house. She could get a job, too. That would help. As for the rest of Gramps's hoard, she still needed Mark's advice on that one and would find a way to dispose of it that would sit comfortably with her conscience.

Suzie moved a disapproving Dimple off of her knee and went in search of a bottle of wine, wondering why she didn't feel better now that she'd sorted out her position. As she attacked her second glass of wine, idly wondering if she could be bothered to eat, she was annoyed to find herself glancing at her watch. It was eight o'clock. Mark should be getting home about now, and the first thing he always did was phone her. She gave herself a mental shake. This wasn't an auspicious start. If she was serious—and she definitely was— then moping about waiting to hear his voice was a self-indulgence she must discipline herself to resist.

"Listen to your head, Suzie," she said aloud, "and put your heart back in cold storage. It's a devious distraction and no good to you whatsoever."

Suzie got up again and looked for something to take her mind off Mark. She hadn't found anything to fit the bill when a tap on the open French doors made her jump.

"Oh, Jack, hello. You gave me quite a start. I didn't hear your car. Come in. I thought you were on holiday." She was babbling because something about the set to his expression made her nervous. "How are your parents?"

"Hello, Suzie." His greeting was unusually subdued.

"Glass of wine?" Suzie didn't know why she'd offered. The last thing she wanted was for him to hang about and get the wrong idea.

"Thanks."

"You didn't say why you cut your holiday short." She turned to face him and handed him his drink. "Is everything okay?"

"My family is fine, thanks. How about yours?"

Suzie cast a considering look his way. Something was definitely bothering him.

"What is it, Jack? Is something wrong?"

"Why should anything be wrong?" He offered her a twisted smile that had nothing to back it up.

She frowned. "I don't know. You seem different. Anyway, all sorts of things have happened in your absence." She chatted away, attempting to cover her unease with a torrent of words. She told him all about Jane's arrest and how Mark had discovered that Greenberg was behind it all. "And just look at what he did to Gramps's garden." Suzie sighed. "It's hard to comprehend such maliciousness, isn't it."

"Is it?"

"Jack?" His noxious expression made Suzie uncomfortable.

"Sometimes people let you down so badly that the urge for revenge is overwhelming."

"Jack, you're not making any sense."

"Then let me spell it out to you, little miss innocent." He took the glass out of her hand and pulled her to her feet, gripping her wrist so hard that she cried out.

"Jack, please, you're hurting me!"

Sparkle, who had never taken to Jack, growled when he saw Suzie being manhandled. Jack aimed a vicious kick at him, forced him into the hall, and slammed the door on him. Suzie erupted in the face of such cruelty.

"Jack, what the hell?" Her anger spilled over. "How dare you treat Sparkle like that! You're a vet, for Christ's sake. Let me go and tell me what the matter is. Then I want you to leave."

"Oh, you want me to leave." He mimicked her voice. "Sorry to disappoint you, but I'll go when I'm good and ready and not a moment before." Still gripping her wrist, he stood back and ran his eyes over her body. She briefly considered giving him a taste of his own medicine and aiming a kick at his balls. As if reading her mind, he closed the distance between them. "You're quite a woman, Suzie. Shame you're such a cock tease as well."

"What are you talking about?" Suzie's anger was rapidly giving way to fear. There was something about him in this mood that made him appear dangerously unstable. She pushed the thought aside. Any display of fear would, she instinctively realized, be playing straight into his hands.

The phone rang. They both looked toward it.

"That will be Mark," she said, attempting to free her wrist and cross the room to answer it. He pulled her back toward him with a sharp, painful jerk, reached for the phone with his free hand, and pulled the cord out of the wall.

"I guess he'll have to call you back," he said, smirking. "It's such a shame, Suzie. We could have been good together, and it would have resolved all my problems."

"I still don't understand what you mean," she said, forcing a conciliatory note into her voice.

Her mobile rang. That too was on the sideboard, in her handbag.

"Persistent devil, isn't he?" Jack said, reaching for her bag this time. He upended it, found the phone, and flung it across the room. It smashed against the opposite wall. "Still, can't say I blame him, given what's on offer." Jack undressed her with his eyes and smiled, almost like his old self again. "What, no comment to make?"

"I don't know what you're talking about."

"What I'm talking about, you fickle bitch, is you and me. I've been pursuing you ever since you got here, and you were coming round nicely. That Saturday night in the pub when you got pissed, you let me kiss you, and you would have let me do a lot more, but I was stupid enough to act the gentleman. I thought that would impress you." He shrugged. "I won't make that mistake again. Never mind, we're alone now, and we can resolve our problems."

"What problems, Jack?" Her mind whirled as her fear intensified. What would Mark do if he couldn't get her on the landline or her mobile? He'd keep trying, presumably, but if they were both permanently engaged, or unavailable, would he smell a rat? Even if he did, it would take him an hour to get here. Still, with no other means of escape, she'd just have to keep him talking and hope for the best. "What do you mean?"

"You would have given me it all that night if I'd pushed you. But I didn't. And then, the next day, you didn't seem to want to know. Never mind, I was making progress, so it didn't matter. But then what happened. Fucking hubby swanned along, that's what. You little whore!" He slapped her face hard. It took her completely by surprise, and her head snapped sharply backward, jolting her neck. She screamed, now seriously frightened. "I watched your little performance. You were so desperate for a fuck that you couldn't even wait to get your clothes off."

Realisation dawned. Jack had been in the garden that night. They hadn't drawn the curtains and he'd seen them.

"It was you," she said slowly, blushing with a combination of embarrassment and anger. "You wrecked Gramps's garden. You broke into the scullery and did all those other things. Honey could have been hurt, you bastard!" She was damned if she'd stay here like a helpless prisoner and struggled against him again, anger and fear lending her additional strength. He slapped her again so hard that the blow knocked her to the floor.

She must have lost consciousness because when she came to she was sitting in an upright chair, her hands tied behind its back with the telephone cord.

"Now that you're back with us," Jack said, strolling about in front of her, glass of brandy in hand, "let's get down to business." He leaned over and kissed her on the lips. She bit him, and he lashed out at her face again.

"What is it that you want, Jack?"

"What I want, Suzie, is what's rightfully mine."

She shook her head. "I'm not with you."

"Don't come the innocent. You know who I am."

"Sorry, but as far as I'm concerned, you're just the local vet."

He snarled at her. "I want your grandfather's stash," he said.

Whatever she'd expected him to say, it certainly hadn't been that. He clearly knew something about her grandfather's history. The question was, how much. She recalled all the times she'd caught him snooping in the library, the extended visits to the lavatory, and knew he'd used that time to try and undercover something of value.

I don't know what you're talking about."

"Nice try, Suzie, but you're a hopeless liar." He strolled some more, seeming to enjoy himself. "It was a piece of luck, a job coming up in Malton just when it did. It was even more fortunate when you moved into Shalimar. I'd wasted weeks getting close to Jane and her pathetic setup, trying to work out how I could get into this house undetected, so your appearance was right on cue. All I had to do was get friendly with you, and the rest should have been easy. And right from the first time I saw you, I knew that getting close would be no hardship." He kicked out at a chair leg. "Why couldn't that fucking lawyer of yours have just stayed away? You'd have turned to me if he hadn't interfered."

With a lightning change of mood, Jack flashed his harmless smile of old. "Never mind, we'll just have to do this the hard way, that's all. Now come on Suzie, where is it? You'll tell me in the end, so you might as well make it easy for yourself."

* * * *

Annabel levelled her eyes on Patrick. "It was all right. I didn't mind. It was our secret. I won a place at the grammar and did well. But Dad seemed tormented. Looking back, I don't know why he didn't just get a girlfriend, or pay a hooker, or find some other way to satisfy the needs that my mother was no longer able to accommodate. But he didn't, perhaps because he loved her so much. He was obviously disgusted with what he was doing to me but couldn't seem to stop himself and so started drinking heavily as a result. One night, long after I'd gone to bed, he stayed in the lounge drinking. Something woke me up, and I realized it was the sound of him sobbing. Without thinking twice, I got up and went to see what was wrong. He told me to go straight back to bed, but I stayed where I was, stunned because he never shouted at me. Then he lifted his head, looked at me properly, and groaned. He beckoned me toward him and pulled me into his lap." Annabel paused to blow her nose. "I could smell whisky on his breath but still put my arms round his neck and tried to comfort him." She let out a ragged breath. "He kissed me then. Not the usual chaste peck but properly on the lips." Annabel stared straight ahead, lost in her own version of hell as she forced the words past her lips in jerky staccato bursts. "He raped me for the first time that night. I was fourteen. The next morning there was a fifty pound note on the bedside table."

"Jeez, Annabel, I—

"My mother confronted me the following morning. She was having one of her rare good days and must have noticed something different about me. She looked at me with something akin to dislike and told me it was my own fault for encouraging him."

Patrick had moved across to sit next to her. "Whyever didn't you tell me before?" he asked, his voice loaded with compassion.

"I've never told anyone. It's my guilty secret, and Mum was right anyway. It must have been my fault. I enjoyed it at first, remember."

"Rubbish. Rapists always make their victims feel they're to blame." He took her hand. "How did you endure it?"

"I learnt to detach my mind from what was happening to my body. It's quite easy to do, once you get the hang of it." She flashed a brief smile. "You'd be surprised."

"Why don't you tell me the rest? It's not the sort of thing you should keep bottled up."

"It carried on until the end of GCSEs. I knew it was wrong, but I also knew what pressures he was under, what a terrible hand life had dealt him. But my love and respect had turned to hatred, and I was determined that as soon as I'd done my exams I'd leave the house and make my own way. I saved every penny of the conscience money he gave me, got a part-time job and saved all my wages from that as well, and worked myself silly in order to get the best grades I possibly could. The day after I finished my last exam, when Dad was at work, I packed my stuff and left for good."

"Where did you go?"

"To London. It was the only place I could think of where I'd be truly anonymous. I got a place in a hostel and enrolled in a sixth form college. I still intended to do A-Levels and get a degree. Naturally, I also got myself a couple of jobs. You see, I'd learned something important from what had happened to me. I had to keep control of my own life, and the only way to do that was to have money. Money spelt freedom of choice, and I'd do whatever was necessary to be financially independent. I never intended to rely on a man ever again."

Tears were streaming down her face, choking her. Patrick pulled her into his arms and let her cry on his shoulder.

"I've never seen you cry before," he said when the flood finally abated.

She offered him a watery smile. "It's the first time I have since I was fourteen, when he raped me that first time. I decided then that nothing would ever make me cry again."

"Crying's good for you, and you've definitely got enough to cry about. Don't you feel better for it?"

"No."

He shot her a quizzical look. "Why not?"

"Because I haven't told you the worst bit yet. Those things that happened when I was little, I had no choice about them. But the things I've done since then—"

"Just tell me."

"I worked my way through A-levels and University. I didn't make friends because I wasn't into trusting people."

Patrick grunted. "That's hardly surprising."

"It was safer to be independent. I never dated because I couldn't stand the thought of anyone doing *that* to me again. And I hardly ate, thinking that if my body didn't develop, it would make me less attractive. I got my degree and went for a job in property, where the real money was. I stayed with my first firm for three years, but it was too big, I wasn't good at office politics, didn't really fit in. I saw John Greenberg's advert in a trade paper. I knew he wasn't especially ethical but was prepared to go along with that just so long as he rewarded me financially. That was all I cared about. But then—"

Annabel pulled away from Patrick, stared straight ahead, and told him of the other arrangement she made with her boss. He heard her out, and when her words trailed off, the room seemed unnaturally silent. She didn't dare to look at him because she didn't want to see the disgust in his expression. He stood and paced, his tall frame crowding the tiny room, clenching his fists and punching repeatedly at the beam above his head.

"Why did you stoop so low, Annabel? Whatever made you do it?"

"I've already told you. I was dead inside, so it didn't matter what happened to my body. If I could use it to make the money to be independent, then why not? John wanted to exploit me, but what he didn't know was that he was the one being exploited."

"And where did I fit into your neat little scheme of things?"

"I hadn't met you when it started. I never expected to meet a man I was attracted to. Certainly never expected to *want* to go to bed with one." She looked straight at him, flinching when she saw the bruised expression in his eyes. "But you changed all that. You aroused in me a passion and strength of feeling I didn't know I possessed. I knew, as soon as I met you that I wanted you in my life forever."

"But you carried on acting as this man's whore."

She recoiled at the cold, hard fury he wasn't seeking to suppress. "I had to."

"For the money, I suppose?"

"Yes. But I was no longer doing it just for me."

Patrick let out a caustic laugh. "You'll have to explain that one."

"You and I need money so that we can live somewhere nice, so that I can help you to expand your business and set up my own." She focused her gaze on his face, willing him to understand, but his distaste was evident, and she knew she'd lost him. "It could have been so perfect for us," she said quietly, picking up her bag and staggering to her feet. "Thanks for listening."

"Where are you going?" he asked.

"Does it matter?"

"Come back here." She turned, her hand on the door. He beckoned, and she slowly resumed her seat beside him. "Why did you imagine that we needed somewhere to live? What's wrong with here?"

"Here?" Annabel was astounded. "But, Patrick, it's just a tiny cottage."

"A very special tiny cottage that I can afford."

"But—"

"But it's not up to your exacting standard, is that it?" he asked sarcastically.

"No, I just thought...well, I suppose I didn't think. But it is very small for two people and—"

"And there isn't room for all your possessions?"

"I don't have many possessions."

"Annabel, if you want me, then we're going to have to get a few things straight. First off, I like this cottage, and I can pay the mortgage without any help. I don't want your money." He looked her straight in the eye. "I want you." She gasped, wondering if she'd heard him right. Even after everything she'd told him, he still wanted her. "But you're gonna have to live life my way, which means moving into this cottage. If my business expands, it will be though my own endeavours, not through any financial intervention on your part."

"But, Patrick, I—"

"And another thing, I don't like fancy restaurants with egotistical chefs who think they can get away with charging a fortune for little more than a few lettuce leaves. If you want to be with me, you're going to have to make do with a pie and a pint and a game of darts in the local pub."

Annabel, who had never played darts in her life, could think of nothing she'd rather do more. "Does this mean—" She trailed off, still hardly daring to hope.

"It depends what you intend to do about Greenberg."

She told him about her resignation and the reason why she'd been to see the Alexanders that morning. It appeared to please him. He reached for her and held her at arm's length.

"I fell for you the first time I saw you," he told her in a gentler voice.

"You never said."

"I thought it was hopeless. We led such different lives, but I couldn't bring myself to end it. I just kept thinking that perhaps one of us would change enough to make it work." He smiled. "Stranger things have happened. But when I saw you this morning and thought you'd been responsible for wrecking that garden, I was angry enough to commit murder."

"And now?" She offered him a soft, sultry laugh.

"And now I'm going to do three things. First of all I'm going to kiss you, then we're going to go upstairs and decide, amongst other things, where to put all your stuff, and then—"

"And then?"

"Well, obviously, then we're going to the pub for that game of darts."

Chapter Twenty

Suzie blinked at Jack, truly frightened now. "I really don't know what it is that you want," she said. "Something to do with my grandfather?"

"And mine."

"Our grandfathers knew each other?" she asked, suddenly afraid of what he might say next.

"Like you didn't know."

"I didn't, I promise you."

"My grandfather finished up in Canada after the war."

Oh God, Suzie really didn't want to hear this. "Did he?" She tried to sound casual, but her voice came out more of a nervous squeak.

"Yes, he met my grandmother there and married her, but it didn't last. He was rich and couldn't resist the lure of the gaming tables, to say nothing of a succession of younger and younger wives. My grandmother was cast off like an old shoe when he got tired of her," he said savagely. "My mother was the only child my grandfather ever produced, but he barely spared her the time of day. She moved to England, married, and I came along."

"What was your grandfather's name?" Suzie asked, already suspecting the answer to her own question.

"Peter James," he said, smirking. "Does that mean anything to you?"

Suzie shook her head. "Can't say that it does."

Jack merely smiled, clearly not believing her. "It didn't to me either, not until recently. Grandfather's name was always persona non grata in our house. But then Mum died a year ago, and I found something interesting amongst her things. A deathbed confession from her father, trying to make amends. Seems he was pally with your grandfather during the war, and he cheated mine out of a large sum of money."

"No!"

"I thought you knew nothing about it."

"I knew Gramps, and he wouldn't cheat anyone."

"Apparently he got a guilty conscience and never spent much of the money, so I'm here to collect. You don't need it, but I do, and anyway it's mine by rights. My mum grew up in squalor thanks to your thieving grandfather, and now it's payback time." He came up close and produced a knife, held to her throat, and nicked her skin. "Where is it?"

Suzie's limbs trembled. She could tell from the look in his eye that he really would kill her. She'd have to tell him.

"It's in the—"

Jack had closed and locked the French doors from the inside. They suddenly exploded open, and Jack looked toward them, his expression shocked. Before he had time to react, Mark was upon him. They struggled, but Mark was stronger and had the advantage of surprise on his side. Before the fight had even started, he knocked Jack to the floor with a savage right hook, and the knife clattered harmlessly away.

"Pick on someone your own size next time?" Mark said contemptuously.

Jack should have stayed down but instead staggered to his feet. Mark delivered a fierce upper cut to his jaw, laying him out cold. In seconds, he was beside Suzie, untying her hands.

"Are you all right, darling? What did he do to you? Did he hurt you badly?"

She smiled and then grimaced at the pain it caused her. "No, not really, but I've never been more pleased to see anyone in my entire life. What made you come?"

Mark carried her to the settee and made her comfortable. "I couldn't get you on the phone. When I tried again, I got unobtainable."

"Ah, I was hoping that might tell you something. I thought if I stalled him for long enough—"

"But it wasn't that."

Suzie frowned. It hurt. Her entire face hurt. "Then what?"

"I put an investigator onto Greenberg. I told you that." She nodded. "Well, I don't know what made me do it." He shrugged. "Jealousy perhaps because Simmons was all over you, or just plain old instinct. Anyway, the investigator got back to me tonight and told me about Jack's Canadian background."

"Yes, his grandfather was Gramps's co-conspirator. He just told me that and seems to think that Gramps cheated him."

Mark harrumphed. "Well, we both know that isn't true."

"Jack did it all," Suzie said, sighing. "All the damage here in the house and garden."

"I know, darling, but you're safe now." Mark paced in front of her. "Simmons was dismissed from his last post because money went missing. Did he tell you that?"

"No, he must have forgotten to mention it."

"I need to call the police and get him taken away."

Mark produced his mobile and did precisely that.

"I was going crazy when I couldn't get you."

"Why didn't you phone The Grange?"

"I did, but there were only a couple of youngsters there. All the others are in the pub, apparently."

Suzie rolled her eyes and immediately regretted it. "That figures."

"I thought that by the time I dragged them out of there I could get here myself, if I broke every speed record known to man." He smiled at her. "Well, I had a great incentive but thought I'd blown it when I got here. Sparkle heard the car and threw himself against the front door."

"He was going to kick him," Suzie said indignantly.

"Well, he seems all right," Mark said, watching the scruffy mutt sharing the sofa with Suzie.

"Yes, thank goodness."

"Anyway, I didn't have a key."

"So you did your James Bond act, crashing through the windows." Suzie cast a glance at the broken glass littering the carpet. "We ought to clear that up before the animals tread on it."

"I'll do it in a moment. You stay where you are."

"I could get used to being waited on."

"Christ, Suzie," he said, kneeling beside her and taking both her hands. "How can you joke at a time like this?"

"Defence mechanism," she told him. "I'm still shaking on the inside."

"I looked in through the library window and thought I was too late. All the books are pulled off the shelves, and the desk drawers have been rifled."

"He must have done that when I was unconscious."

Mark scowled. "He knocked you unconscious."

The police arrived at that moment. Judging from the look on Mark's face, that was a lucky break for Jack. It seemed to take forever to sort things out, but finally they carted Jack off and Suzie and Mark were finally alone.

"Come on," Mark said. "What you need is some painkillers and a good night's sleep."

Suzie was all out of arguments. She didn't think she'd be able to dispel the horrors of the night but managed to sleep soundly and didn't wake until the sun was high in the sky the following morning. She tried to sit up, but something was holding her back. It was Mark's arm. He was lying beside her, propped on one elbow, watching her.

"Hi, sleepyhead, feeling better?"

"I think so. What time is it?"

"After ten."

"What!" She eyed him suspiciously. "Have you been here all night?"

"You don't think I'd leave you alone after everything that's happened?" He winked at her. "Breakfast, madam?

"Yes, okay, I'll see to it."

"Oh no, you stay right where you are, Mrs. Alexander. Doctor's orders. It's breakfast in bed for you this morning."

He unfurled his tall frame and stepped from the bed, totally relaxed even though he wasn't wearing a stitch of clothing. He whistled to Sparkle as he pulled on a towelling robe and disappeared through the door. Fifteen minutes later, he was back with a laden tray.

"When did you become so domesticated?" Suzie asked, propping herself against the pillows that Mark piled behind her back.

"Oh, I have hidden talents you know nothing about."

"Obviously, and this is good." Suzie was astonished to find that she actually had an appetite and wolfed down the food. "Have you fed the cats, and Honey?" she asked, her mouth half-full.

He chuckled. "I wouldn't have had any peace if I didn't."

Drinking a third cup of tea, Suzie lay back and smiled at Mark. "I couldn't eat another thing. And I feel almost normal again." She peered across the room and caught a brief glimpse of her battered face in her grandmother's pier glass. "I look like I've gone ten rounds with Mike Tyson," she said, wincing.

Mark cupped her face gently with his hand. "The doctor says there's no permanent harm done but that you must rest."

"The doctor being you, I suppose." He nodded. "Thought so. I don't remember anyone coming to attend to me."

"You wouldn't let me call anyone."

"Because I didn't need them. It's just a few bruises, and what I need to sort them out is a good long soak in the bath. Then I'm getting dressed and coming downstairs. I want to know exactly what's been going on."

Mark sighed. "I don't suppose there's anything I can do to talk you out of that."

"Not a thing," she said, throwing back the covers.

Suzie appeared downstairs half an hour later. She noticed that Mark had replaced all of the books on the library shelves. The drawers in her grandfather's desk were back in place, and he had generally removed all signs of Simmons's presence. She paused on the threshold to the drawing room, scared of the memories it would revive. She looked straight ahead as she traversed the room, noticing in the periphery of her vision that Mark had already managed to have the French doors replaced. She sat on the settee and patted the seat beside her.

"I don't know what I would have done if you hadn't arrive when you did, Mark," she said, tears coursing down her face. "He would have really hurt me, I think. I didn't want to tell him about the diamonds, not because I think of them as mine, but because I felt he had no right to them either and I knew that, like his grandfather before him, he would fritter them away. Does that sound strange?"

"Not at all, darling," Mark said, covering her hand with his.

"What's going to happen to Simmons now?"

"He'll be charged with your kidnap and assault. He'll lose his job of course and will probably get a custodial sentence."

"What reason did he give for what he did to me?"

"He was banging on about your grandfather and saying you had something that belonged to him. No one's taking any notice. The police will want to talk to you sometime today though."

"All right, but do I tell them the truth? About Gramps and the diamonds, I mean."

"No, they'll only be confiscated as treasure trove. Either that or their value will be eaten up in legal fees whilst all the different factions argue over them. After all this time, rightful ownership would be impossible to establish, and they'll just finish up expanding the Crown coffers."

"Yes, you're probably right."

"Anyway, I doubt if they'll even ask you if you know anything about his ranting. Jane turned up when the police did. She told them he fancied you but I was back on the scene, he was jealous, and it had driven him over the edge. They believe her because she told them what she thought was the truth."

"You're not going to enlighten her either?"

"I don't think so. Not until we've decided what we're going to do."

Suzie took a deep breath. Now was as good a time as any to tell him how she felt, but before she could do so he spoke again.

"My sources tell me that Greenberg's plans for aggrandisement have been well and truly scuppered, thanks to Annabel."

"Good!" Suzie smiled. "It was brave of her to do what she did. I hope she doesn't suffer for it."

"Quite the reverse. She's starting up on her own and moving in with Patrick."

"Then I'm glad for her. From what you've told me, she has issues that need resolving."

"I doubt we know the half of it." Mark stroked her hair. "I also happen to know that investigations are being made into Greenberg's fraudulent use of his contacts on the council. More than one head will roll."

"As long as Greenberg's is amongst them."

"Oh, I'm sure it will be. And I doubt whether his wife will look too kindly upon his fall from social grace, either."

Suzie nodded emphatically. "Being ostracised by his peers will be the ultimate humiliation for a man like Greenberg." She glanced up at Mark, aware of his searing gaze resting on her profile, and blurted out what was in her head before she lost the courage. "Mark, I don't want to leave Shalimar."

"I didn't imagine that you would," he said calmly.

"Oh." She hadn't expected him to let her go so easily and tried not to show that she was miffed. "Well, in that case I'm sure you'll agree that my suggested solution is the best all round."

"Really?" He sounded distantly polite. "And what is your solution?"

"Well, as I want to live here, why don't you sign your half of the property over to me, and in return I'll relinquish all rights to Epsom."

"Suzie," he said, looking distinctly amused. "That's not any sort of solution at all."

"Stop being so superior," she said crossly. "It's a perfect solution."

"You haven't been listening to a word I've said to you these last few weeks, have you."

"Of course I have, I—"

"I've a better idea. Why don't we sell Epsom and both live here?"

"Here? But you'd hate commuting so far."

"True."

"So how—"

"I rather thought I'd work from here."

"Mark, either I'm concussed after all or you're talking complete drivel. Which is it?"

"It's really quite straightforward. I've resigned from Felpsons."

Suzie gaped at him. "You've what?"

"Last week. I have to work out my notice, hand the reins over to Rob, but in three months' time I'll be free as air."

She was too stunned to speak and merely stared at him. "I don't understand," she finally managed to stutter. "You love it there."

"Yes, but I love you more."

A rushing, surging thrill rocketed through her body. "But, Mark, I can't ask you to give it all up for me. It wouldn't be fair. Anyway, what would you do instead? You'd be bored rigid inside a month."

"Ah, but that's where you're wrong. I'm fed up with living out of a suitcase, never having a proper home life, never seeing you. So, I'm going to set up on my own as an independent expert in European Law." Mark chuckled. "It gave Anthony quite a shock when I told him. He thought it all came down to money and offered me a huge increase. Anything to keep his prized possession out of the hands of the competition is how he put it. It was only when I explained my intention to set up on my own that he relaxed because we both know that Felpsons will be one of my main customers. You don't mind if I take over your grandfather's study as my office, do you?" he asked, smiling as he placed a gentle kiss on the end of her bruised nose.

She levelled a gaze on his face, looking for flaws to the perfect solution he'd just suggested. Afraid that she'd think of one when her head cleared. "You're serious about this, aren't you?"

"Never more so. You made me think when you told me I'd never considered what you want for yourself and that you'd never feel comfortable all the time I was travelling. It made me realize how selfish I've been and how much I took you for granted. Well, if I'm here all the time, at least you won't have to worry about who I'm with."

She shook her head. "This is all too much to take in." She slipped her arms around his neck.

"Does this mean that you agree my scheme is better than yours and that you'll have me back?" he asked.

"I'll think about it."

"And whilst you're thinking, shall we decide what to do about the diamonds?"

"If only we could." She frowned. "It's all so complicated."

"Only if you allow it to be."

"What do you mean?"

"Well, I don't think either of us would be comfortable keeping the stones. Am I right?" Suzie nodded. "Okay then, who do we give them to?" Not waiting for an answer he ploughed on. "There are so many deserving causes. There's also the matter of your parents and their expectations to consider."

Suzie suddenly realized what Mark had in mind. "Their Sierra Leone water project?"

"Exactly."

"Mark, you are sometimes the most thoughtful man in the world."

"I just want you to be happy and have a clear conscience. I know how your parents have been banging on about doing the right thing. Well, now you can. They needn't know about your grandfather's past. We'll just let them think that they're getting the proceeds from the sale of Epsom."

"I think that's a brilliant scheme." She paused to reflect. "In spite of everything, they are good people."

"All I know is how badly they've neglected you over the years in favour of starving orphans."

"But I wasn't really neglected. I had Granny and Gramps, and I preferred their company anyway. Then I had you, too. Okay, they might be a tad short of parental sympathy, but they do so much good elsewhere."

"Don't be fooled by that. Most people who give generously of their time and resources do it as much for what they get out of it themselves as for their beneficiaries."

"I suppose you're right," she said wearily. "I've never really thought about it like that before."

"Anyway, any ideas for the rest of the stones?"

"No, will there be more?"

"Oh yes." He smiled at her. "How about something a little closer to home?"

"I can see you've got it all worked out. You look jolly pleased with yourself, so you'd better tell me what you've got in mind."

He lifted her up and sat her on his lap. "What about putting up the money to renovate The Grange and then setting about getting it proper charitable status?"

Suzie gasped. "Yes, of course, that would be wonderful!" She stopped abruptly and frowned. "But would Jane accept our help? She's very independent, you know."

"I think, when the dust has died down, we'll have to tell her about our dilemma. If we insist that we're not going to keep the money ourselves and that if she doesn't take it we'll end up giving it to …oh, I don't know, gay rights, or some such deserving cause, she'll soon see sense."

Suzie giggled. "Sometimes you're too clever for your own good."

"Anyway, there would be a lot of paperwork involved in getting the Charity off the ground. Thought it might be something that you'd enjoy."

"Mark, you're a genius. I'd love it!" She paused, lost in thought. "But do you think I could do it? It's bound to be complicated."

"Stop putting yourself down. You'd have it sorted in no time. And then there's Shalimar itself, of course. We'd need to do some renovations."

"Oh, I've got loads of ideas about that," she said, effervescent in her excitement. "I'd want to modernise, new kitchen and bathroom. We could knock through to the small bedroom next to ours and make an en suite and a dressing room. I don't want to change the character of the house though."

"Of course not." Mark said, smiling. "But what about the top floor? We'd need to pull that worm-eaten staircase out for a start."

"Yes, we could knock it into one big space."

"How about making it into a nursery?"

Suzie was quiet for a long time, uncertain at first that she'd heard him properly.

"Suzie?" he prompted gently.

"You mean it, don't you?"

"Yes, darling, I mean it. It's time to start a family."

Suzie was too choked up to speak, her mind on her suspicions. She'd discontinued with her diaphragm when she moved to Shalimar, thinking she would have no use for it. When she and Mark had unexpectedly been forced to spend the night together three weeks ago, the thought hadn't crossed her mind. But now she was a week late. It was only a week, but she was never late. She placed a hand on her flat stomach and smiled. She wouldn't tell him yet. Not until she was sure.

"Yes, Mark," she said. "It's more than time."

The sound of wheels on gravel interrupted their kiss.

"That'll be the police wanting to talk to you."

An hour later, they were alone again.

"Tired, darling?"

"No, I'm fine."

"You don't fancy a lie down?"

"Now that's an entirely different question."

Mark swept her into his arms and carried her up the stairs. "I think I would like a daughter to start with," he mused. "One who looks just like you."

THE END

HTTP://WWW.WENDYSOLIMAN.COM

ABOUT THE AUTHOR

Wendy Soliman grew up on the Isle of Wight in Southern England and started writing stories at an early age. She now divides her time between Andorra and West Florida. She lives with her husband and a rescued dog of indeterminate pedigree. When not writing she enjoys reading other people's books, taking long walks with her dog, drinking good wine and generally making the most out of life.

Also by Wendy Soliman

BookStrand Mainstream: *A Class Apart*
BookStrand Mainstream: *Silver Lining*

Available at
BOOKSTRAND.COM

CPSIA information can be obtained at www.ICGtesting.com
Printed in the USA
BVOW020825140312

285172BV00002B/3/P

9 781619 265578